THE PARDON OF SAINT ANNE

William Palmer is the author of four novels, *The Good Republic*, *Leporello*, *The Contract* and *The Pardon of Saint Anne*, and a collection of stories, *Four Last Things*. He lives in the West Midlands.

BY WILLIAM PALMER

The Good Republic
Leporello
The Contract
Four Last Things
The Pardon of Saint Anne

William Palmer

THE PARDON OF SAINT ANNE

Published by Vintage 1997

2 4 6 8 10 9 7 5 3 1

First published in Great Britain by
Jonathan Cape Ltd, 1997

Vintage
Random House, 20 Vauxhall Bridge Road,
London SW1V 2SA

Random House Australia (Pty) Limited
20 Alfred Street, Milsons Point, Sydney
New South Wales 2061, Australia

Random House New Zealand Limited
18 Poland Road, Glenfield,
Auckland 10, New Zealand

Random House South Africa (Pty) Limited
Endulini, 5A Jubilee Road, Parktown 2193,
South Africa

Random House UK Limited Reg. No. 954009

A CIP catalogue record for this book
is available from the British Library

ISBN 0 09 959701 2

The Random House Group Limited supports The Forest Stewardship Council® (FSC®), the leading international forest-certification organisation. Our books carrying the FSC label are printed on FSC®-certified paper. FSC is the only forest-certification scheme supported by the leading environmental organisations, including Greenpeace. Our paper procurement policy can be found at www.randomhouse.co.uk/environment

Printed and bound in Great Britain by Clays Ltd, St Ives PLC

BOOK I

THE AGE OF GOLD

1

I didn't know at the age of twelve or thereabouts what Lieutenant Marivaux wanted as he sat at my mother's table in the apartment above the shop. His legs were thrust straight out, his boots gleaming, his sharply creased breeches elegantly rucked up by finger and thumb. He had an oval face, a small, very red mouth, a brown, thin moustache, slightly sly brown eyes, and hair, full, brown, cut short but curling a little at the ends and parted just to the left of the crown. This is how memory constructs him in that very clean, rather shadowy room. I'm sure I've added a bottle of wine to the table. It was more likely to have been a coffee pot. But here he is – the French officer. My mother stands on the other side of the table, her hand on the back of a dining chair. I have just come in. He does not get up. My mother quickly introduces us. I make the deep bow that boys gave to their elders then. I am a little out of breath.

'Ah – you've been running,' said Lieutenant Marivaux. His German was good. 'I wish I was you. I can't run. Why, I can hardly walk. See.' He got up and limped on the carpet, towards my mother and then back again, swinging himself into the chair once more. 'Twisted my ankle.' For some reason my mother giggled. When I looked at her she smiled gaily, then straightened her face. I was astonished. I had never seen her look so young and happy.

'What I was going to do today was go round the town and spa and take photographs with my new camera here,' the Frenchman went on. His fingers tapped on the black, leather-covered box on the table. My mother went into the tiny kitchen.

'But then, what I thought was this,' he said. 'Why couldn't you – Walther – why couldn't you take my camera and get my pictures for me. You can be my eyes.' He picked up the box-camera and held it out to me. 'Take it. And when I come back again I'll bring the developed pictures and we can look at them. What do you say?'

Adults are always asking children to do the strangest things. After two minutes of instruction – I was impatient – I hurried off with the camera, my mother shouting after me to pick up my brother Peter from Aunt Hassel at four o'clock.

I remember distinctly, though probably wrongly, the order in which I took those first pictures. A French private soldier on the opposite bank of the river, striding out of the frame, leaving only his left boot in view, raised in step, while behind him a woman leans from an upper window shaking out a cloth. A large cream-coloured Mercedes car with a little wire-faced terrier like a miniature lion looking through the oblong back window, the number plate incised in perfect focus. The Lutheran church badly caught, as an insistent great grey corner of masonry, the foreshortened spire evaporating into mist. The weighing machine outside the Wald Café, empty; and again, with a thin woman standing on it and feeding it a coin. Flat-on views of our neighbours' houses. The butcher's window, Herr Müller staring out between a shaved pig and a side of beef. Peter in Aunt Hassel's garden. Myself, beheaded, taken by Peter. Two more frames, utterly fuzzed and undecipherable; and the last shot, a double exposure of Lieutenant Marivaux himself emerging from the closed gates of a woodyard which have somehow become mysteriously fused with my mother's side door . . .

The spa itself was best taken – I knew even then – from above; from the Bismarckpromenade, a wide path cut into the hillside, overhung by oak and holly, and much used by the spa-goers, and French officers and their mistresses. As you looked down, over a hedge cut so immaculately square that it resembled a green parapet, out of the tops of the lower woods rose the chalky dome of the grey and ochre pumphouse, the Kurhaus. The trees, thinning, showed the white colonnade that carried and hid the pipes to the great Kursaal, in whose entrance hall the spa waters were dispensed from tall gold-plated taps into small yellow conical glasses. The Kursaal held an improbable number of huge rooms: two restaurants, two theatres, lecture halls, a concert room, a library and reading room; a whole chain of interconnected sitting rooms and lounges on the ground floor whose high windows looked onto the Kursaal gardens and across the two wide paths that, divided by bushes and flowerbeds, ran beside the curving river bank.

From up on the promenade the roofs of the bandstands resembled two brightly striped children's tops. Tiny visitors walked on the paths; past the statue of toy-soldier-sized Bismarck, and this way and that on the Kaiserbrücke that crossed the green river. On the other bank were the round blue glass windows flanking the doors of the Russian church, the long, bland windows of the newest restaurant, the baroque line of turreted hotels, the wire railway ascending on that higher side of the valley to the grey view tower at the very top of the opposite rise.

The small town where we lived lay to the west, around a sudden twist in the river and so largely out of sight of the south-facing promenade, its first little houses to be seen where the gas-works and its pale green, iron-corseted gasometer marked the end of the gardens.

My mother's apartment was above a haberdasher's shop in a side street off the main Coblenzstrasse. We had moved there in 1919, mother, myself, and my younger brother, Peter, when it was certain that my father was dead. With the coming of the French and their terrible reputation, mother thought it safer to be out of the city.

Poor mother had nothing left of my father but a few photographic portraits, their wedding pictures, a collection of his expert, purely conventional watercolour landscapes, books which she did not read, and some little financial assistance from his family – for the sake of his children. A foreigner herself, with no money of her own, honest and naïve in her dealings with others, she had little training to deal with the dangerous business of being alive in the twentieth century in this particular place.

'If you don't behave the black devils will come and take you and eat your heart out . . .' A warning to children. It came when the French deployed colonial troops from Senegal and other colonies. This was a great insult and terrible were the rumours of these enormous ebony cannibals and rapists. Even, or especially, in the towns and villages that never saw one.

The French were hated most of all in the cities. Barbarians who pushed women and old men off the pavements, who must be saluted and be allowed to stride to the front of any queue. Their agents sacked the country, drawing away cartloads of looted goods, and trains full of machinery. Drunken soldiers robbed banks and rich men's houses, beating and murdering the mildly rebellious and outraging their womenfolk. So we heard. But they had been here a long time now, and when I became aware of them, the contingent stationed across the river hardly seemed to me the ravagers and ravishers of legend. The four junior officers, packed into a motor car, would cross over the lower bridge and park behind the Kursaal and walk and talk and initiate affairs with the wives and daughters of visitors to the spa; and hope no doubt that either the visitors would have to return home, or they themselves would be rotated to another command before the affair must be terminated messily, in rows, tears, or jealous accusations. The officers were, as if out of a cheap novel or movie, handsome. They had money. They were the victors. And, after all, they gave the town something to talk about during the winter and added to that store of ill-will without which no small community can flourish.

Now one of them had given me a camera.

Lieutenant Marivaux dealt the photographs onto the table on his second visit. We laughed at some of them, and I felt hot and foolish for not operating the wonderful toy well enough. But Marivaux said, 'You have a flair for it, Walther.'

Alas, he had left the camera behind this time, but he gave

us boys enough money for tea at the Kursaal and a boat ride on the river. At least two hours, my mother said . . .

On his third visit, and with the camera, he drove us all out for a picnic in the forest behind the northern hill.

There I photographed Mama and the French officer standing a little apart; sitting, leaning towards each other, their shoulders approaching intimacy but just avoiding it. My eye over the view-finder, the couple and Peter upside-down, I took delight this early in my career in ordering them into new positions and juxtapositions with the scenery and the props of picnic basket, doffed coats, and someone's bearded, grave-eyed dog, looking like an elder statesman, strayed from another picnic. When we had done, Marivaux opened the back of the camera and took out the little steel spool with the finished film wrapped round it. I asked him what happened to it now. If, he explained, we were in the city, he would take it to a studio or a pharmacist and have it developed; here it was left to the attentions of a brother officer whose hobby was photography. Oh, might I see? He looked puzzled – it wasn't very interesting, but why not? He would take me to the lieutenant next weekend.

I can't remember this other man in the same way at all. Only as a pair of hands. He had rooms outside the garrison in a large farmhouse. A corner of his bedroom was curtained off like a magician's cabinet, so small that we two could hardly get inside together. I squeezed in. A red bulb gave off a blood-coloured non-light and a peculiar faint stale smell, like burned blood. More pungent and intoxicating were the odours of the chemicals he poured into his trays.

Like all amateurs he chattered too much about effects and composition. His German was poor and Marivaux, from where he sat in the one armchair, had to call out interpretations and suggested meanings, stumbling and swearing in French over technical terms he could not translate. I strained to catch hints of technique, the names of chemicals and items of equipment. These were the true poetry of the craft. And truly magical was the moment when I saw emerge in the developing tray in that bloody light the images of Marivaux, Mama, birch trees; each slowly bringing itself like a ghost through time and space to lie in this oblong metal tray in a stranger's room.

Throughout the summer, almost half the number of times he visited us, Marivaux forgot to bring the camera. I was impatient, but forced myself to be twice as polite to him in my enquiries as to where it was, to enforce in his mind the association between boy and camera. Then, one day in late August, my mother sent us out before the hour Marivaux was expected, over my protests that I wanted to see him. When we came back, ten minutes before our time, his car was parked outside the street door. Mama was sitting at the table. Her face was pale, her eyes downcast. Lieutenant Marivaux leaned on the window sill, looking pensively at nothing in particular on the carpet, an odd, sheepish smile on his little red mouth. When we entered the room he brightened at once.

'Well boys – it's goodbye,' he said.

'Lieutenant Marivaux has received another posting,' said Mama in a whisper. 'We will not be seeing him again.'

'Come, come – I'll turn up. As soon as I can get leave. Well . . .' He looked at his watch. 'I really must be going. I only stayed so long to see you two lads. I have something for you both downstairs in the car.'

Mama stood. We shook hands gravely with the Frenchman. 'Frau Klinger –' He bowed deeply to Mama. 'Wiederseh'n,' he said, and then in English, 'Come you two.'

We followed him down the narrow stairs, sorry to see him go, but in the heartless expectancy of boys about to be given gifts. For Peter a popgun with a scarlet butt and a shiny dark-blue barrel; he clutched the gun to his chest, and ran back into the house without a word. Marivaux rooted around on the back seat and came out with the camera. 'For you Walther,' he said. 'I won't forget it again then, shall I? There's a film in. Here's a spare. You'll have to go to the city for others.'

He got in the car, smiled at me, stared straight ahead and accelerated away.

2

'Your little eye, I see it . . .' was what the old man shouted at me, as I raised the camera. He stepped back into the pot house, revealing the white and blue porcelain beer pump behind him, a poster on the wall above announcing a Nazi rally in Coblenz.

Being a foreigner, my mother had no vote. She had tried to tell me about the war between her British Empire and our dissolved one. She spoke in English to me, in German to Peter, because he would hear no other tongue. Her grasp on politics was weak, on life firm. I will come to that later. If she had been in England she would have been a Monarchist, a Nationalist, though she tried to explain that those terms did not have the same meaning there. She was no socialist certainly and the name National Socialists was a puzzle to her. Their anti-Semitism she could not understand. Why are they so down on people? she would ask. In her dealings with my father's family and his estate, she used a Jewish firm in Coblenz that my father had nominated in his will. Periodically we were charmed by a visit from Herr Rothstein, the senior partner, who made a habit of visiting annually all his customers, great or, in mother's case, small. He brought flowers. I took his photograph on the street outside with Mama leaning on his arm. He was a bald-headed gentleman in his mid-fifties, with a thin moustache and a pearl-grey suit and black shoes that winked in the sun. Future events were not to be foreseen in their smiles. The bright light slanted down, the only shadows pale grey under the awning of the shop below our apartment.

In those days of my adolescence, clever Dr Schacht had conquered the inflation, the occupiers were withdrawing, there was a boom in Germany; nobody wanted trouble.

Perhaps this sense of a self-satisfied lull was present in my pictures. I must have taken the picture of every man, woman, child, cat and dog going about their quiet business in that small place. But not one of these photographs was lastingly satisfactory. I began to realise that, however conscientious I was in framing my pictures, they were all disappointing. Not one of them came close to the sharp black and white that I had seen appearing in the Frenchman's tray. I assumed that the grey though dramatic pictures in the newspaper were taken with a camera similar to mine. What I could not get near was their mastery of speed; the slightest movement before my little box camera – motor cars, a cycle race, a running fight – all resulted in a blur. I had never enough film to experiment. Nor advice: the lieutenant photographer had left with Marivaux. I had to wait for revelation until I met Valenti.

3

Imagine a tall, well-built young man of twenty-four or five, his face a tanned amiable pear shape with a cleft in the chin emphasising the fruitiness, black curly hair parted in the middle, one camera slung round his neck, another to his eye as he stands in front of a fashionably dressed middle-aged couple on the path nearest the river in the Kursaal gardens, the sun shining on their faces and casting his long shadow towards them. 'Your portraits, sir, madam? For Posterity?' A barnstorming street photographer, too big to knock down, too relentlessly cocky to insult, he erupted into our quiet spa in the autumn of 1930.

Valenti was my university; my master, in the old sense of a painter taking into his studio a pupil. I was lucky to have him. Of course my mother wanted me to have a good standard education, a process which my younger brother underwent too thoroughly, and to her shame. I was, at that time at least, studious and clever at school. It lay halfway to Coblenz and was severe and precise in its grounding in the classics and mathematics. This is the best education an artist can hope for – one that does not recognise, does not even suspect him. And I knew, as soon as I saw this stranger's preposterous, magnificent posturings in the Kursaal gardens, precisely what schooling I needed.

On Saturdays and Sundays, I watched fascinated, from a distance, as he importuned the visitors, presenting silver-edged visiting cards with a whirling flourish, cajoling the old into stiff formal arrangements, the young to wrap amorously round each other. I pursued the sight of his white linen jacket and black trousers flicking between the rhododendron and azalea bushes.

On one of those weekends I stood in front of him as he bowled down the wide pathway, a smile already formed on his face, running his hand across his black curls. Did I raise my camera to snap him? All I would have registered was the rush of white and black reduced to the usual grey wash. He strode past, playfully shadow-boxing at my head as if I were a rival. How disappointing then to rush to the gardens the next Saturday morning, after a frustrating, waiting week at school, and to search for him and not find him, the whole place, despite the bright sun, suddenly dull, and all the carefully ambling tourists and patients seeming relieved, as if a storm had passed over leaving a calm blue sky and a resumed, blessed, boring stillness.

With what sense of loss I made my way to the Kursaal for a consolatory glass of lemonade. When I entered the hall I heard laughter from a side lounge. Four women were merrily squeezing up together on a sofa; their menfolk standing behind, exchanging jokes, were being commanded into position to have their picture taken by my friend from the gardens. A final joke; the laughter petered out into happy smiles; their bodies stiffened. The flash gun went off. They relaxed at once, exploding again into happy laughter. As the stranger straightened up I read the badge on his lapel; 'Official Spa Photographer – Michael Valenti.'

During a gap in his official business I summoned up the courage to introduce myself. I began to pester him with endless questions about his equipment, his methods, my own work, my urgent thirst for knowledge, for secrets, for craft – above all, for the gift of seeing.

He must have taken a liking to me to put up with this nonsense. And I did my tiresome utmost to be of assistance to him. Of course I idolised him from the start. And how many people can resist flattery? Especially when it is sincere. I ran errands. I touted for him in the gardens and restaurants, giving out his business cards and extolling his prowess. More personally (and only briefly a mystery to me), I delivered notes to widows and maidens and married women: first in the Kursaal itself, then across the river to the lobbies of the hotels, and sometimes to secluded villas taken for the summer . . . After all, the French garrison had closed down and moved off now, so that the handsome stranger had his pick. In return he instructed me in art and life.

He had an amazing array of cameras. My own miserable leather-edged box dropped immediately into the status of an irritating, antiquated, derisory object when compared with his ICA reflex, the small fast Ermanox, the beautiful Leica. He told me, in the many leisure periods that he contrived away from his official duties, that he had been a press photographer in Berlin. He had photographed fires, murder victims, accidents, suicides, weddings, funerals, goalkeepers, golfers, royalty, winning horses, statesmen, movie stars.

Why had he left this wonderful world?

'A slight error of judgement,' was all he would say, laughing. He had worked for private detectives on divorce cases – 'Dirty work – they need the truth' – and as a society photographer – 'Dirtier . . . they want only falsehood.'

There was nothing of the artist in him, so he was all the more an artist for that. He taught me about light and its tricks and pitfalls. How one might manipulate brilliance and darkness and all the fugitive shades between. How the subject is made of two elements, light in all its contradictory aspects, and time in a single, singular duration. How you do not have to wait to seek out images; they press in a tumult upon you begging attention, and how the gift is to be able to extract the one significant image from this inexhaustible horde. Your machine will do that for you when you know it, he said. In life or pictures.

While I was greatly Valenti's junior, I was not condescended to in the slightest on account of my age. If he lit up a cigarette in that little room of his in the Kaiserhof, the small, grubby hotel in the town where no spa-guests ever stayed, I must have one too. If a bottle of wine was open – which it usually was – I must drink with him.

Valenti showed me the other side of our community. It was no such nonsense as 'now for the first time the truth can be told,' or, 'the lid is lifted on . . .' but rather that he turned the town and its inhabitants into a theatre, with himself as producer, lifting away walls with an almost silent hiss, swishing back curtains with a velvety flourish to show beauty and terror, a pantomime with real people made grotesque by the sudden light shining on them.

So, here is Herr Müller, butcher and church-officer, approaching Valenti heartily in the café, leading him to one side, his enormous hand cupping Valenti's elbow like a ball, for a confidential request. Is it possible that you know, old chap, where one might obtain any of those pictures, you know, of men and women disporting themselves?

Tennis? Skating? Hockey? says Valenti innocently.

No, no, the butcher shakes the elbow roguishly but roughly – you don't argue with a man like Müller – 'In the more intimate of sports . . .'

My new friend told me – after hearing my halting, sighing talk about her – that the reason for the departure from the town of demure, Madonna-faced, sixteen-year-old schoolgirl Emma Giess, and her return a whole month later as a beautiful, grave-faced young woman, was not that she had been introduced to the noble world of German poetry and music, nor that her parents had removed her from the romantic but chaste affair with the handsome Clausen, her form-master, that I suspected and of which I was inordinately jealous – no, the true cause of her absence, Valenti breezily informed me, was to undergo an abortion at a private clinic in Bonn.

Frauen Zina and Zola Grobel, elderly sisters. The first tall, powerfully bodied, bespectacled, a terror to all. The second smaller, plumper, sweet-faced. They shared a house down by the river. They were not sisters at all, Valenti told me, but a lesbian arrangement of such long standing that everyone knew but pretended not to. And this pretence had lasted so long that it had become accepted that they were sisters and no contradiction was possible; anyone who had dared to state aloud the truth would have been regarded with horror and aversion. Thus any supposed offence was transferred to the discredit of the observer, not the observed.

Herr Sossel, the local Nazi boss, wore a wig and secretly owned shares in Jewish enterprises. With prosperity the town branch of the party had declined lately – but still Sossel performed heroically in leading his SA troop in their energetic activities in the meadow behind the Lutheran church. You could hear Sossel's hectoring and despairing commands rise from the field each Sunday morning, early before service – they were still rather timid of offending the Church. There was not any obvious target for them to attack in the village. They had, a year or so ago, when stronger in numbers, made themselves objectionable down in the Kursaal gardens, insulting visitors of Jewish or indeed any foreign appearance, but had been ejected by the local police-sergeant and banned from returning. The town considered that Nazi-ism was a state which local louts went through and from which they would recover when they grew to sense. A middle-aged man like Sossel indulging himself in these things was therefore slightly ridiculous. He and his friends did return, and in force. For now they were forced to play their games in earnest only in Coblenz, in fights with the Communists, when differing interpretations of millennial politics were decided with fists, knuckle-dusters, razors and clubs.

Three cases only from the many that Valenti had in stock. Two of love, and one of its opposite, its negation. And I see above that I have given equal comic weight to the aborted girl, the lesbians, and the Nazis. That of course is outrageous, but in those days, at seventeen years old, the whole adult world was to me a grotesque comedy which I viewed with a mixture of self-righteousness and avid desire.

4

It was Valenti who arranged the loss of my virginity.

As sentimental and infatuated as any other boy, I had enjoyed walks and embraces in the woods above the town with any number of the local Emmas and Gertrudes; I don't know if they had the same rather indistinct and romantic reveries that I half-painfully, half-joyfully entertained about them as I lay late in my bed on Sunday mornings during that summer; in any case, sex had not really entered into our meetings.

One Saturday afternoon, not finding Valenti as usual at the Kursaal, I went to his rooms at the Kaiserhof. He had lent me his Leica and I hurried to him with the first film that I'd taken. Frau Klinsmann, the owner's wife, looked at me with her hard hotel-keeper's eyes. She knew my mother and reckoned that I had fallen into bad company.

I knocked on Valenti's door. I heard a muffled shout that I took as permission to enter. He came from the bedroom, buttoning his trousers, white shirt flapping about his thick torso. 'Ah, Walther – it's only Walther,' he announced over his shoulder. In the bed, bare-shouldered, holding the sheet over her breasts, was a young woman. She smiled at me. 'Hallo, Walther,' she called. I looked away, then smiled back at her. This was Mitzi, Valenti said. A friend. Wasn't she splendid? Such a beauty. He spoke as if she were absent. She called again, asking if she could get up. He shut the door on her. 'Get dressed,' he shouted. 'Had to tell that old cow Klinsmann that she was my sister. She didn't believe me. Put Mitzi in a room on the other floor. Charging her the earth.'

Mitzi came out after a few moments. She asked Valenti to do her up at the back. I looked away again. Then we all went out. On the street Mitzi slipped an arm through my mine, the other across Valenti's and we walked interlinked to lunch at the Kursaal. Mitzi was very pretty. I see her now as all in white silks, her face pale, lips red, her auburn hair floating back in a beautiful cloud.

As we sat down in the restaurant a waiter I knew came over. Valenti ordered, flourishing his hands and speaking loudly. I saw the manager of the restaurant frowning at us from the doorway. Valenti lowered his voice. Grinning, he explained to me that his engagement with the Kursaal was at an end. The usual thing. He would be going south with Mitzi, to try his fortune out of Germany. Vienna, perhaps, or even Italy. When was he leaving? I asked, as calmly as I could. I was shocked. By next weekend, he said. He was still owed some money from this damn place. I would be sorry to see him go, I said. And I was truly sorry. I looked round the restaurant and knew it was damned. He had shown me how to use my eyes. He had made me restless, which is how the young should be.

'You will be coming back?'

'It's not likely.' He laughed and reached over and shook my shoulder in a friendly grip. 'But till then let's have a good time, eh?'

My mother took the news of Valenti's departure with quiet joy. He had called at our apartment only once and she had thought him dirty and not a gentleman. When I protested that he was an artist, she said, no, an artist was a gentleman. I knew she meant like my father.

Even in the past five years, since the disappearance of the Frenchman, she had seemed to draw into herself, to become more circumspect and conservative. She had us two boys to look after and that must have been difficult. I think now that she suffered from the backbiting and gossip of the other women in the town and as a reaction had grown over-prudent and protective of us. It is astonishing how rapidly people can change as they grow older, how the heart is shut up in deference to the imagined wishes of others.

I determined to make as much as I could of my friends in their last week. I drew out the savings I had made from my allowance so that I could play some sort of part. We went to Coblenz and visited a cabaret. I sat enthralled as two clever comedians, one large and overbearing, one small and feigning stupidity, satirised the Nazis and made their obsessions ludicrous. Within two hours I was very drunk. I remember walking, rolling almost, down the steep streets from the top of the city. And nothing else, until waking on a damp, thin carpet in a cheap hotel room while Valenti and Mitzi snored, curled about each other under the covers of a single bed. We arrived back in town, bedraggled and happy as gypsies. My mother cried when I got home. My brother looked at me with hatred. He had joined the Hitler Youth that year and thought Valenti's sort responsible for the decline of Germany.

We paraded through the gardens and the town, again arm in arm, and I gloried in what I imagined were the whispers at our dangerously bohemian ménage. Valenti took photographs of me and Mitzi; I took them of Valenti and Mitzi; an orgy of images I was laying up as treasure against their going.

The next morning I went round to their hotel. Looking back now, I think Valenti had genuinely taken to me; and perhaps my little money had come in handy that last week. He was up. Mitzi was still in bed. He was packing a suitcase that had straps like a bloodhound's ears and one large label with a sunset and the word MAROC in brilliant red, the last two letters OC made maroon by a stain. I moved round the room, talking endlessly as usual. 'Go through and talk to Mitzi, Walther,' he said. 'You're in my way.'

I sat on the edge of the bed. She asked for a cigarette. As she hoisted herself into a half-sitting position the cover slipped, revealing one of her breasts, the rosy-tipped full nipple and its darker, faintly dimpled aureole. She took no notice. I took astonished interest.

She chattered gaily. Valenti shouted from the other room that he had to pop out for a while. 'Back later.' I moved to join him, but Mitzi lay her hand on my arm.

'Don't go,' she said softly.

I heard the outer door shut.

'You know you can if you like,' she said. 'Michael won't mind.'

I was still in bed with Mitzi, the two of us naked, my inexperienced passion quickly done, but holding her and being held in a sweet embrace, when Valenti came back. He opened the door and called her name. I leapt from the bed and struggled into my clothes in a frenzy of horror that he should discover us. But, as Mitzi had said – Michael really didn't mind. He took his time coming into the room. When he did, I was standing, mock negligently, in shirt and trousers hardly done up, bare-footed at the window, pretending to look absorbed in the street below. 'Everything all right?' he said. 'Fine,' said Mitzi, and they both burst out laughing.

We lunched together that day and walked in the Kursaal gardens. It began to rain, and we walked up onto the promenade and looked down at the brown, swirling river. Not a word was spoken about the morning, but now we were a conspiracy of flesh and love. About four, Valenti gently dismissed me. They must go back and finish their packing. Couldn't I help? 'No, no – you've done quite enough for today, my lad, haven't you?' said Valenti rubbing his fist against my cheek.

Mitzi was his going away present to me. I came from her with stars bursting about my heart. I was churlish and bad tempered at home. My world had expanded and all the little images I had photographed and pinned to my wall shrank, looking what they were; a tiny world seen through a squint.

I hurried to the hotel early the next day. With all the naïvety of youth did I expect a re-run of yesterday's magic? My heart thumped. This was the day they had chosen to leave. Surely they would stay now?

I strode blithely into the lobby.

Frau Klinsmann barred my way to heaven, standing on the bottom step of the threadbare stair carpet, one hand gripping the banister knob. 'Where are your precious friends, eh?' she demanded.

They had decamped the previous evening. Somehow Valenti had spirited their baggage out of the premises and they had been reported by her spies boarding the train at the small station across the river, heading south for Mainz.

In his haste he had forgotten the Leica I had borrowed.

THE AGE OF SILVER

1

Two images on the way to the city:

The Brownshirts have assembled in the meadow and, in this picture, march through the town. Now they are no longer a dozen village idiots, but forty or fifty men; led by the standard bearer with a two-metre flagpole like a gigantic phallus inserted in a leather cup at his crotch; then group leader Sossel, grim-faced with the responsibilities of office, followed by farmers and farm boys; Clausen, the schoolteacher, a foot taller than anyone else, showing his handsome head, his platinum blond wavy hair; shopkeepers, including jolly Müller, the butcher; my brother Peter, leading the uniformed children in the rear, beating slowly and monotonously on the military drum balanced on his hip. All of their shades of brown, the flag black and white and red, the sky blue; and the crowd lining the pavements to watch them go by, its suits, dresses, shirts, waving handkerchiefs, open pink mouths cheering now instead of laughing . . . All in my new, sharp black and white.

The outskirts of the city. I stand at the open window in the corridor of the train, towards the front, where the sulphurous smell of the engine mixes with the summer air and is drawn in, like the waft from the door of an oven. I balance the camera as well as I can, my body compensating for the sway of the carriage. The buildings on the horizon very slowly shift and wheel like a constellation; the low walls, huts, all the near clutter of the line race past. A man in the middle distance stands by one of the makeshift shanties in the park, his shirt off, torso sunburned, hands on hips as he watches the express slow on the curve, enabling me to take him, and as a bonus, another man raising the canvas flap that serves as a door, emerging, a bayonet in his hand, like an assassin. And a hundred other people, men, women, children, the usual dogs, half hidden by the trees, the shanties, all to be revealed later . . .

2

The portrait of Grandmama. She was seventy years old when I moved to Berlin in 1932, and still recognisable from the painting of her that hung in the hallway. In this painting, an unmarried girl of seventeen or so, she sits in a low chair beside a table on which a spray of yellow mimosa and two red carnations loll from a tall Chinese blue and white vase. Her face is white, the mouth drawn in a confident carmine bow, the eyes grey-green, the lids rather vixenishly drawn to points over her high fine cheekbones. Her hands hold a posy of white and blue violets. The brown, ruffed silk dress is high-necked, her bosom modest, virginal, with off-white pearl buttons all down the right side until they meet and over-ride her full skirted lap.

By the side of her portrait was that of my grandfather; square-faced, in the middle-age pink of life. Behind his image a line is drawn in the golden section, below the line wooden panelling; above, functional cream wallpaper, on which is drawn another framed portrait of another man – his grandfather? a friend of the painter? – half obscured by his left shoulder.

I looked closely at this to see if there was another, and yet another endlessly recessive portrait included in this, but the artist had given up early on in his pursuit.

In both of their faces I searched for my father's face and located him in my grandmother's mouth and eyebrows, and in my grandfather's mouth; looks flit inconsequentially and bloody-mindedly across the generations – it is almost impossible, until we grow old, to recognise our parents in ourselves – then they return with a vengeance. It is as if the artists of the genes and chromosomes had re-mixed the colours, muddying them maliciously.

Other pictures – of my grandparents in middle age.

Here in my grandfather's desk, in the middle drawer sub-divided into square and rectangular sections, were the records of their foreign tours. Guide books. Maps. Letters. Postcards, used, stamped and travelled, or pristine and still wrapped in tissue paper, showing palaces, saints, mountains, valleys, farmhouses, the Lido at Venice. A whole series, in a cardboard folder, showed plump women in flimsy draperies, each card with the name of a Greek goddess on the back.

The letters home to my great-grandmother were written by my grandmother in a clear even hand in blue ink on plain oatmeal-coloured notepaper, or on the variously sized and tinted letterheads of hotels. Coming one every other day, they were accounts of sights seen, excursions undertaken, weather conditions, meals, fellow guests, local customs and dull eccentricities; all ordered in the same fashion as in a guide book; intended for reading aloud to the family at home. My grandfather's literary efforts were confined to large scrawled comments after my grandmother's signature – 'I will bring you some chocolate.' 'Weather most cold.' 'Young Franz is much sought after by the young ladies.' 'Karl sends his dearest regards.'

But what interested me most was a wooden box pushed to the back of one of the compartments in the desk. This contained glass slides, each ten by ten centimetres square, with a positive image in black and white, edged with a dark brown taped border.

I held the slides to the light.

Some were labelled. 'The House of Mr and Mrs Browning – the English Poets – in Florence.' 'A Peasant Wedding.' 'The Family in a Storm' – in three horse-drawn buggies the family rides, unrecognisable in furs and overcoats and with black umbrellas twisted to shield them from the driving snow. Another, untitled, shows my grandmother, taken from a distance, alone on an observation platform that juts out over a river gorge. She wears a thick coat over a bell-like skirt and a funny sort of hat like a biretta, and at the edge of the iron railings looks as if she is a cardinal about to step into icy space. And here are my grandparents, in what must have been warm sunshine, descending a path from the Hospice Bernina in the Engardine in Switzerland. Grandmother wears – this is black and white of course – a long white dress, pleated at the bosom, descending almost to her feet which are clad in black, perhaps dark brown, leather boots. Over the two of them she holds a parasol. My grandfather, trim-figured still, but with the suspicion of a pot forming at the inverted bottom V of his waistcoat, wears a fawn-coloured suit with rolled trouser bottoms. His pumps are so fine and of such supple white leather that it looks as if he walks barefoot. My uncle Karl steps in front; a fine young gentleman in an almost exact replica of his father's suit, a slight startled smile on his face as he looks directly at the unknown photographer. Bringing up the rear by more than a few yards, lagging behind, is my own father, the younger son. Not much more than my age, I reckon, working backwards, while peering at the slide. Twenty years old. Perhaps his rather dreamy, preoccupied look, his reluctance to catch up with the party is because he has already met the young woman who he was to marry. For certainly this was the last time he went on holiday with his parents, and it was on this Swiss tour that he met my mother, fell in love, and married a year later.

She was the object of the only, and then only slightly agitated passage in one of the letters home – a comment that 'young Franz has met and is seeing a deal too much of a young Englishwoman, some sort of servant to an English family on holiday'. In other family letters, after they were married, I found her referred to slightingly as 'The English Housemaid'.

3

My portrait of Grandmama?

Since I had arrived, I had not seen her stir from this one downstairs room. She went to bed after I had retired. If I was out and came in late she would be in her chair. Only at dawn would that dark, heavily furnished room be empty and then seem to be waiting for her. Its pictures, albums of photographs and hideous pot-bellied enamel-encrusted vases seemed to hold all the life that had left her own aged body spare. Like many old people she preferred to live in the dark; the curtains were always drawn, the tiniest shaft of light being abhorred. It was indeed as if she lived inside a camera. I think that sometimes, in the poor light of the one purple-shaded lamp, she liked to half mistake me for my father as a young man. I would enter, circle the room, sit down, begin to read perhaps, and look up to see her eyes fixed on me with adoration and sorrow. How could I not be spoiled?

After a few days, I asked if I might photograph her. She said that the idea was ridiculous, but I persisted.

I was allowed no daylight; the lamp she read by must not be moved. So she sits there in my photographs, her eyes peculiarly liquid, lit from the side, the mouth set in a trap, its young elasticity gone, the skin suspended in taut vertical lines, her hair drawn back in a silver bush, the thin nose lined with a perfectly straight edge of silver. No – she does not wish to see the result. What good would it be to her? She only did it to please me . . . But she is flattered, I know, by the young man who kneels in front of her, looking down into the lens.

She was glad that I had come, she said. I had rejuvenated her. The house was dying; she was tired of the servants' company. I could see why. She had a maid, Marthe, referred to as 'the girl', though, I think, older than her. As a small boy I had suspected the maid of living on spiders and mice in a cupboard – she had that sort of face. Most of the house was unused. I made my nest in a small bedroom with a gable window, high above the encircling firs in the garden.

After the first week she asked me what I intended to do? I must not be unemployed – though six million others were. Why hadn't I enrolled at the university? I must go to the university and do something useful.

I resisted.

What then did I want to be?

A photographer.

No, no – that was simply a hobby. She laughed. Or did I mean one of those absurd little men who stand in front of wedding parties and explode?

No, I did not mean that. It was possible, I told her, to be an artist with the camera. If nothing else was available, I said, I would become a press photographer. Valenti had impressed me with tales of police morgues and football grounds. To my grandmother such a person was not much above a mechanic. Photographs were an intrusion into her conservative newspaper. My request struck her as idiotic but she could refuse me nothing. She would ask Karl; he could help. He knew everyone.

4

Uncle Karl was sitting in Grandmother's room when I came in one morning. His back was to me. He was sipping at a cup and talking about politics.

My grandmother smiled, and said, 'Here is Walther.'

'My dear boy, my dear boy.' He rose from his chair and hurried over to embrace me.

He was then about fifty I suppose. Older than his brother, my father; yet I could see no way that my father, had he survived the war, could have come to this sort of middle age. There was no resemblance between the Karl of the early photographs and this short, plump man with already grey hair, carefully waved and pomaded, the moustache waxed.

After the customary, polite questions about my mother and brother, he said. 'I was just telling your grandmother the latest news. Things are very grave, Walther.' He shook his head sorrowfully.

But there was hope – there was always hope in Karl's world. Schleicher the strong general was poised to strike, he said confidingly to my grandmother. That was the last we would see of the little corporal. Hitler's paramilitary wing, led by

Röhm, would join with the army, and Germany would be safe. If not there would be a civil war. He had no doubt that the forces of the old Germany would win out in the struggle. It was one, not the most unlikely, of many different scenarios heard and rehearsed every day.

'Hitler will never be Chancellor,' he said firmly.

'Thank goodness for that mercy at least,' said my grandmother. 'I have never seen him, but from his portrait in the newspaper he looks most common. Anyway – to the matter in hand, much more important – what are we going to do with this young man?'

He had heard that I was interested in journalism.

Photography only, I said rather rudely.

Well, yes, he said, blinking. It so happened that he had an interest, a financial interest, in one of the popular magazines. He could not give me a job. He would ask the editor . . .

Meanwhile, let him show me the city.

'Not all of the city,' said my grandmother, turning down her mouth.

5

'I shall call for you, dear boy,' he had said, and he did, late the next afternoon. Repeating her words, 'Not all of the city', he conducted me in high spirits along to a cab parked in the road outside her house.

It was a quiet day for Berlin. We passed along a street littered with abandoned newspapers. The next had a body in its roadway, male, with no sign of distress or blood but quite dead, fully dressed; further up the street was one abandoned golf shoe, two-tone, brown and white, rather soiled.

'Communists,' Karl said. 'They make such a mess. Nothing to do with us, thank God.'

At the next junction, one of those large Berlin policemen halted us, his hand raised. He looked inside the car and saluted my uncle. Why? Because Karl was a gentleman. He wore the correct clothes. Karl was of that class in society that employs policemen. The Schupo waved us on, his broad back reassuring.

Then we were in the city of the tourist postcards, the city of plate-glass windows and posters for theatres and cycle races; the city of fine restaurants and great stores and their riches.

We wheeled round the clock in the Potsdamer Platz. I looked out and a cloud of pigeons, their wings slowly slicing the air, rose up into the clear blue autumn sky.

Most of this has gone in the bombing: the lines of opulent shop windows, full of books and furs and mannekins and chocolates and Chinese vases; the huge department stores; the restaurant across the way from where the car drew up that sold bread from heaven that I can smell from here. Karl led me to an archway between two stores. On top of the arch was a stone relief of two mirror-imaged stone maidens, their draperies falling away, exposing breasts. 'The household goddesses,' he said and smirked at me and then licked the lower grey spikes of his moustache with the tip of his tongue. Not in appreciation, but with an expression of tasting something unpleasant, expected to be pleasant. Bad oyster. Sour wine.

He opened one of the glass-panelled double doors. On each a large upper panel was engraved with a tumbling cornucopia of fruit that was being looted by cherubs; their little arses shone through by the electric candles in the lobby chandelier beyond. Ever since we had left my grandmother's house, Karl had seemed to be a different person from my Uncle Karl. In the lift, caged in a rococo riot of acorns and oak leaves, he hummed a tune and smiled at me, then looked away, stiffened a little, then smiled again, and stretched himself somehow in his suit, relaxing, like a dog accustomed to obeying, and then remembering that for the moment he is resting, he is free, then looking around again, triumphant and happy for confirmation.

We got out on the third floor and went along a corridor with several doors, all of brown panelled oak, widely spaced with name plates on them.

'You can't know how good it is to see you again, Walther,' Karl said as he inserted his key in the last but one door. 'It's been so very long. Why, you were no more than a small boy the last time you came to the city. Come in.'

In the hallway stood an extraordinary hat and coat stand in the shape of a madly contorted, antler-branched tree trunk – 'Ah – if you wouldn't mind . . .' He pointed at my shoes. There was a neat row of slippers in the hall. When I'd put on a pair he led me into a long narrow living room. The walls were white, hung with small Japanese coloured woodcuts in what struck me even then as rather kitschy bamboo frames. The carpet was fawn and thick like the fur of a pampered animal. The suite of chairs and dining table was the same odd mixture as the hall stand, the arms and legs fashioned from curved and twisted wood that looked at first sight natural and perhaps was – and selected for the way it curved with tendrils and tongues, and fangs and claws protruding at every angle.

'There is this . . . and the bedroom' – a brief glimpse as he held the door open – an ochre and green papered room, the enormous, dishevelled bed with a double set of great crimson pillows . . . 'the kitchen . . .' stainless steel and tiles . . . 'the spare room', a white-washed cell, a crucifix above the bed, a small bookcase, a tall cupboard . . . 'you are welcome to stay at any time . . . given due notice. A drink?'

How much of this am I inventing after the event? Quite enough – not all. Enough to show Karl as an aesthete of a very conscious kind. Not the sort of man who is an artist, but a man of taste. I am unkind to him. I sold work to his sort later; always men – women are hardly ever collectors in the sense that Karl was – those who wish to surround themselves with the obviously beautiful. I can't blame them. What else did I want? Collectors like my uncle only altered their immediate environment – I wished to alter the world. My uncle had better taste perhaps.

So we had a drink and he asked politely after my mother and brother without any interest beyond politeness. He had another drink and I declined one – I never liked the stuff much in those days. Well – what did I wish to do? To see? He suggested we dine early and then go to his friend, Count Zemdorf. Though Zemdorf was probably out of town. The theatre? Yes. Then a cabaret? Had I no evening clothes? He hadn't thought. Well – no doubt he could find me something. He went into the bedroom and shut the door. I heard him opening and shutting wardrobe doors and drawers and then he opened the door again and said, you may be able to find something from these, and I saw that he had laid out several suits on the bed, a neat row of them, like bodies, and at the end of them a stacked collection of shirts and collars and neckties.

'I couldn't possibly . . .' I must say that the prospect of wearing another's clothes didn't appeal to me.

Please – they were not his. Quite obviously not. Karl's smile was half pleading, half humorously dismissive of my small complaints. The clothes were all quite new, he assured me: if I did not like them he could find me something else . . .

And they were new – and as far as I could see never worn, or worn only once. They belonged to friends who had stayed occasionally, he explained. I could change back before I went home to my grandmother's, if I wished. That might be desirable . . .

I asked him to leave me and I changed into a selection of the clothes. It was of that order of excitement – in dressing up for a lover, or someone you want to deceive. 'Yes, yes,' he said, smiling broadly, dancing a little draper's minuet in front of me as he admired the transformation. 'Much better. How handsome you look.'

It was still possible to conceal oneself in an apartment such as my uncle's – to live among objects of virtue and of art; to pretend that the old world continued, that all would be resolved one way or another by the people who mattered. To have faith that the right people would prevail, and that some sense of civilisation be retained – he laid out the prospectus of delights. There was wine and Scotch, there were people who gave the most splendid dinners, and plays to see and art shows and theatres and . . . and for me, he supposed, looking slyly at me, the interests of any young man . . .

I presumed he meant women. I needed to start an affair soon, I said. I had been in the city nearly three weeks and the streets were full of beautiful girls. 'Oh – there are always plenty of those,' he said, in a slightly offended way. 'If you are so inclined.'

I see now that he didn't show me the side of life in which he was interested. I think he wouldn't have shown it to me anyway. He was a man who believed in family honour; our blood kinship would have permitted no other relationship. He would have been horrified at any such suggestion. So I was, regretfully but definitely, not admitted to that world in which he bought suits for young men. I learned from rumour and insinuation of his chums among the Brownshirts. I was very innocent for that city, at that time.

In my new, or second-hand, second-body evening suit, feeling faintly ridiculous, I walked out in the streets with him.

'There is a revolution going forward in this country,' Karl said as we walked past a cheerful brass band accompanying a group of SA men with flags and collecting tins. The tall muscular young men with smiling faces worked the street, and we stopped to watch – 'They have a most terrible, vulgar energy, don't you think?' he said. 'I dread to think what would happen if they were let loose without our correction.' He stuffed money into the held-out tin. He turned away, still talking, 'But then, revolutions are for the young; their revenge on the old, Walther, and old men like me must put up with that.'

When I said, no, he wasn't old, I could never think of him as old, he smiled and said, 'You really think so. Well – I have some life left in me perhaps,' and happily linked his arm in mine.

So he was careful where he took me. To respectable friends, the theatres – certainly never to the Communist cabarets that I went to, on my own at first, and then with journalists I got to know, or girl-friends. 'They should be whipped from town as trouble-makers,' was Karl's comment on the satirists. Instead, he took me to great houses and apartments that all the troubles of the depression seemed not to have touched. Fine wines, the voice of Tauber, or the piano of Cortot on the gramophone; good food; row after row of pale gold and ivory and lilac bound sets of Schiller and Goethe along the walls; the latest novels in their shocking, lightning-struck jackets on the tables; the beautiful, healthy, clear-eyed sons and daughters of these houses; all seemed a prosperous reproach to the Depression in the streets outside.

But even into these magically protected rooms the winter of 1932 came like a cold, long, dark fog after an energetic summer's day. There was an atmosphere of abandonment – of morals and conviction and hope. Abandonment in a literal sense too; houses were closed up, as their more prescient owners preferred to continue the long summer day elsewhere. The influential people Karl introduced me to turned out to have concerns of greater moment on their minds than how to help a young man from the provinces. One of Karl's friends said to me at a crowded dinner party that I was not the first nor, he supposed, the last of Karl's 'nephews' for whom he had been asked to find a job. This man was most amused when I assured him that Karl was indeed my uncle. In that case he would be pleased to help, he said, laughing. What could I do? I was a photographer. He laughed again – everyone in the country was a photographer. But bring my work along. He was the editor of – and he named a magazine I hadn't heard of. It was mostly pictures, he explained – people didn't like to read so much nowadays anyway. Nothing but bad news in words. I didn't tell him that bad news was my favourite subject.

6

I called on the owner of the magazine. I was horrified as only a young artist can be. Its pages were filled with pictures for sure: of adorable kittens; actresses lolling on sofas; snow scenes; the well-brushed children of the bourgeoisie; air-brushed, asexual Undines sheltering under waterfalls and mouing from leaf-dappled shadows . . . There was nothing that didn't insult the eye, and nothing that related to the sights I saw each day in the city, and then examined in the stripped-out, ikonised, flash-lit angry images of Communist and Nazi magazines. The disparity revealed between the two worlds, between the daring, brilliant ingenuity of the propagandists and this miserable soft-toned, fuzzy sentimentality, disgusted me.

Ashamed, I submitted work.

And had it accepted.

My grandmother didn't understand my outrage. She thought that perhaps now I would abandon this whole silly business, as she put it, and go to the university. Neither she nor Karl lived in the same city that I inhabited.

The Berlin they didn't know, or I thought they didn't know, was a medieval place of warring camps and contrasted banners. Here there was a block of flats under siege for days on end; there the siege was lifted and transferred to another street. A row of houses might be decorated with hammer and sickle flags; the ones round the next corner would be adorned with swastikas. Some young men's allegiances floated between the two camps. Those intelligent enough to cope with ideology and pamphlets and a distant view of paradise generally joined the Communists; those who preferred a more vigorous approach involving lots of shouting and marching up and down and a more visceral approach to politics usually joined the Nazis. Parts of the city were marked by madness or murder for a few spectacular hours, then the blood, or ideas, or vileness would be swept out of sight. Yet ordinary business went on and it still required a guide to find the riots and rallies reported in the press. People worked, bored and yawning, in their offices and factories and shops, ate, made love – and if you were not to hear the sudden crackle of gunfire or the wailing of a siren, or the sound of fleeing feet, it meant that you were in a concert hall or dance palace or night club – or in the plush, thick-walled houses of the western suburbs.

I'd come fired with a desire to record it all – in pictures. That seemed to be the only way. I didn't want my eye to record just the minutiae of my own life. I should have realised that in the end that is all we have, all we can carry. I had a half-apprehended vision of being the cold implacable eye that regards human folly. There was enough of that. I persuaded myself that I did not need to work at an ordinary job. The universities were stuffed with students, their only prospect unemployment. I didn't consider that I could learn anything from them. I was to be the Rimbaud of the filmroll; the laureate of the soup-kitchen and tent city glimpsed through the trees in the suburban woods. Of the lounging SA man on the street corner. Of the car roaring past, red banner streaming behind, laden with revolvers and certainty, a slogan shouted as it turned the corner. Of the returned, obscene gesture, the dropped cigarette, the gob of phlegm as life turned brown, grey, dead again. Of all the things I had seen from the train coming into Berlin, and on the streets the very first moment I came out of the main station. The wonder and intoxication and fear of it all were bubbling in me. I was young – I could live on air, the Moon, wherever I chose. But even I had to have somewhere to eat and sleep – and pursue my marvellous, alchemical craft.

7

It was lucky that Grandmother allowed me to draw money from my father's estate. A depression is good news for those with funds; especially with the terror of another inflation driving the government to destroy first two, then four, then six million jobs. You could buy cheaply then; I purchased a second-hand motorcycle from a surly young man in the Wedding district. His face was confused with heartbreak and loathing when I handed over the notes and wheeled away his darling. I learned to ride the motorcycle in the woods at the back of my aunt's house in only a few days. Valenti had told me how he had gone what the Americans call ambulance chasing. I roamed the streets looking for trouble.

It wasn't difficult to find.

Where to place my pictures of it?

I was most naïve. Perhaps deliberately so. The photographs I did manage to sell were handled by an agency and appeared indiscriminately – beyond my power of agreement or veto – in any of the factional magazines. The captions were written to suit their purposes; the pictures cropped for greater or lesser effect; only rarely did my original image stand proudly in a reasonably honest context. Mostly I did advertising and industrial work – I loved the cold gleaming neutrality of machinery, its calculated inhumanity, its ingenious, infinitesimally accurate shavings, its disposal of the unnecessary – and the freedom it gave one to explore outrageous angles and lighting, to employ montage and collage. Then there were nature studies for the pussy-cat and nymph magazine.

The one paper I – and every other photographer – wanted to get into was the *B.I.Z.*, the *Berliner Illustrierte Zeitung*. It was one of the Ullstein papers.

The press was divided politically between the nationalist Hugenberg empire and the Ullstein leftist journals and publishing house. Uncle Karl and his friends were on the Hugenberg side, but I knew several of the Ullstein men – one in particular.

Horstmann, his name. A ferociously intelligent, small, bouncy, charming man only a few years older than I but already almost completely bald. He had been pointed out to me as someone who bought illustrations for the press and I'd seen him again in a café on the Kurfürstendamm. As luck would have it his two companions got up and left. I took my coffee over. 'Herr Horstmann. Forgive me . . .' and I introduced myself as having just come to the city. Might I sit down? He shrugged his shoulders and his hand reached out for his newspaper – as a shield, I presume. I plunged straight in. I was a great admirer of the *B.I.Z.* I would like to work for it.

He stared at me, then laughed. 'What as, for God's sake?' he said. 'Have you any gifts?'

'I'm a photographer.' I had rehearsed this as a reply, disarming in its simplicity, I hoped.

'No doubt you are.' He put the paper down again. 'So are a lot of people nowadays. How old are you?'

'Almost twenty.'

'Name?'

'Walther Klinger.'

'Well, Walther, I admire your taste in wanting to join the *B.I.Z.* But you come too late. Do you realise that the staff of the Ullstein press, both here and abroad, consists of the most intellectually brilliant, witty, stylish, politically knowledgeable, highly educated and perspicacious bunch of men – and some women, of course – ever assembled in a shining galaxy of talent? And that we are all finished. Washed up. It's all over. Next week we'll be lucky to get jobs sweeping floors. Unless we're in jail . . .' Here he halted, smiled as if remembering his manners, then said, 'But if you must – and you look determined enough – send me some work. There may be a miracle. Who knows. I don't believe in them myself, but I am humble enough to let God contradict me. Must dash.'

He flicked his card across the table, rolled up his newspaper and as his bouncy walk carried him away, turned and gave me a cheery wave.

8

It didn't take long to see what Horstmann meant by things changing. The most brilliant occasion of the year was the annual Press Ball. By some sublime timing of divine, or diabolic, irony, the last ball ever to be permitted took place on the final weekend of January, 1933.

Karl had tickets. The Ullstein crew, he said, were all Communists but there were some amusing fellows and it was such a grand occasion. I should attend to see the last of the old regime. A new day was dawning.

I carry in my mind a picture taken at the ball. Where I saw it, I can't remember, and now it is buried somewhere in a newspaper library. It was luck that it appeared at all, but there were some lingering motions of independence and freedom from the press for a short while after the Nazis took power. The twitchings of a near-dead body . . .

The photograph is taken from the gallery above the – what do they call it in popular novels? – 'the glittering throng'.

The heads gleam in the darkness that surrounds them; hair pomaded and brilliantined for the men, beautifully dressed, waved and bobbed for the women; the faces seen from above, in that shelving angle that is the most flattering, that shows the best curve of eyebrow and eyelid and lips and nose. Mouths are open in jokes and compliments, in a silence sliced by the photograph out of the hubbub that fell and rose again from the tables. A few heads are tilted back, their faces looking straight up into the flash, like travellers caught on a road by lightning. These few are large-eyed, their faces seemingly fusing the sudden light and the inner anxiety that lay under the skin. The photograph shows a segment of the dance floor, the pale satinned rounded back of a woman dancing; it cannot recapture the music from the band. They played a tune, 'Mood Indigo', which was a lovely thing to dance to late at night with its soft, caressing chorale of clarinets – I see the three men take their clarinets off the spikes and stand and weave the bells of the instruments gently from side to side. And I have invented that too, I think, because the tune would have been played later than that date, or I remember it from another time and the woman I was dancing with and the smell of her hair. One of those Jewish-Negro tunes the Nazis banned later. It is not the devil who has all the best tunes, but the despised.

So, the picture showed, without music and conversation, six or seven tables in full and the edges of a dozen more. But not the one at which I sat with Karl, another Hugenberg man, and two Ullstein men.

I saw Horstmann coming towards us, nodding and joking to his friends. He stopped at our table.

'Welcome to the wake. Still want to work for us, Klinger?

Saw your photographs. Damn good. Can't do anything for you. Have you got a drink?' He was cheerfully drunk. 'A toast. To the New Age. The re-establishment of the Neanderthal.'

I looked at Karl. He raised his glass. 'I'll drink with you to part of that, Horstmann. I think you'll find our new masters aren't quite the monsters they appear as in your pages. Hitler will have his hands quite full enough without bothering you very much.'

'Ah, you think so?' said Horstmann in a musing sort of way, sitting down heavily at the empty place next to me. 'You may be right. He gives me the impression – the forcible impression – of a man who likes very much interfering with others.'

Karl smiled. 'The Civil Service has more than a few briefs to fully occupy the new Chancellor when he takes office. If, indeed, he does.'

'You think that the Wolf will be neutered – is that it?' said Horstmann.

'That's not the way I would express it,' said Karl rather huffily. 'You forget that there are capable men in the government who will hardly allow the more extreme elements of policy . . .'

'The hooligans are to be swathed in red tape?'

'I think you will see a good deal less of hooligans in the future – on both sides. Excuse me a moment – I see someone I must talk with.' Karl got up and went over to an elderly, elegantly dressed man who had just come in.

'And what are you going to do now, little Walther?' said Horstmann.

'I shall go on as I have been doing,' I said in a dignified way.

'Pursuing your art, eh? You may be all right. You're young.

You have no record. And pictures, unlike words, can be made to lie.'

'I would have thought it was quite the other way around.'

'Oh no – we have our words, thousands and thousands – millions of them – to count against us with our new masters. You're clean. You merely record with your camera. What the pictures tell us, that's a matter of interpretation. A picture of a policeman beating a rioter – that is either police brutality, or a gallant defence of the state against banditry and anarchy. Depends who's looking, don't you think?'

This was heresy. 'The picture comes as itself,' I said. 'It is the truth of the moment. It comes unencumbered by lies. If they are added, well, that is too bad – if the image is strong enough it will conquer all attempts to falsify it.' I felt hot and uncomfortable having to defend myself in this way.

'The Truth of the Moment. That's really very good. That should suit in these coming times. You should go far, Klinger.'

'Oh, Walther – there you are.' A girl rested her hand lightly on my shoulder. I'd met her in one of the grand houses I'd gone to with Karl. The daughter of an industrialist; she was slim, beautiful, dressed in a gown that was a thin shimmering other skin. 'Are you dancing?'

I would be delighted to. I was relieved. I rose and looked down at Horstmann's smiling face.

'And you – what will you do now?' I said in a cold way.

'Go underground,' he said in a deep, mockingly conspiratorial voice. 'Deep underground.'

The next morning Hitler became Chancellor of Germany.

The particular marriage of modernism and the medieval that

was Germany, that fatal lack of, and yearning for, the classical that has undermined and caved in the German soul – was about to have its heyday. I was that worst of all things, a neutral. I no doubt thought that I was a socialist, if only because socialists were intelligent and rightists were not. It was like sitting in a glass-bottomed boat in a shark-infested sea. The inevitability of the Nazis' rise was manifest in all our jokes and books and love affairs and anxious dreams. But most of all in our images.

Two more of that time:

I and two colleagues have just been going over an advertising layout, when someone comes in to say that there are SA men on the roof of the building opposite. Perhaps they are aiming to shoot up our building; a Communist magazine has offices lower down. We go to the window – what the hell, we are young, nothing can happen to us. On the roof across the way there is a line of seven or eight Brownshirts, but they are carrying satchels not arms. They lean over the carved stone parapet and proceed to pull out handfuls of paper and toss them so that each bundle bursts and scatters in the air, breaking into hundreds of black paper swastikas that drift and skim and fall to the street far below. I open the window and lean out. The chattering noise of an engine overhead, and an autogyro appears, a man standing precariously in the back seat, directing a movie camera down. Now the street and its wide pavements are starred with thousands of the black cut-out swastikas, thousands more are falling, their arms twisting over and over in the air, to join them, some settling on the awnings of shop fronts, in the doorways where people step tidily over them, avoiding the children trying to catch them in their fall, flirting with a couple of girls who pretend to swat them away, their mouths open in laughter.

A heron, attended by two white gulls, flying to its wooded island on the far side of the park lake. The bird outlandish with its broad wings, huge beak, the trees behind a blur, the icy edge of the lake a thick white glue. As I lower the camera, the pine trees on the rising ground across the lake fall back into softer focus; the bird descends with a lazy powerful droop of its wings into its secret kingdom, the gulls wheel and return, flying fast across my line of vision. A dull chock-chock sound as one of the two boys on the frozen rutted mud at the lake side throws a flat pebble so that it bounces and skids across the thick ice, and into and out of the square, brickwalled corner of the lake, sliding and slithering until it suddenly falls into the dark water. The girl beside me links her arm in mine and shivers.

9

Some of Karl's predictions came true, though not all, and not enough to save him. It wasn't difficult for even such a jovial man to make enemies.

The hooligans had their days and nights of interminable, triumphant processions and torchlight parades and beatings of any of their enemies unfortunate enough to be on the street. But after a very short while things became quiet and orderly.

There was an end to running battles and gunfights, to open gangsterism. The siege mentality moved first indoors, then inside the skull. The change was hugely welcomed – human beings like excitement, but they also crave shelter and warmth and a lack of disturbance for their dreams.

It was the Age of Silver. Silver and black. The tones I sought in my photographs were the colours taken for the uniform of the SS Black Guards. In a new age of uniforms theirs stood out as sinister, modernist, elegant, theatrical, efficient. They were still uncommon – a vision of the future. The immediate, visible victors were the Brownshirts – the lumpen SA. Where many of the SS were drawn from the middle class, the SA were overwhelmingly lower or working-class: adventurous, opportunistic, tough, living for the day. And it was their day. They had won this revolution. Some of them had grown to middle age waiting for this day to come. Strapping, thick-set, heavy-faced men, they stood astride street corners or barred the entrances to the Jewish shops as if they now owned the square metre of earth on which they stood. Each was a victim of *The Stab in the Back* that had lost the war, each had been robbed of his land and pride at Versailles, each ridiculed by the clever men of Weimar, each had lost the value of his money and savings in the great inflation – and behind all these terrible things, and, literally, behind his stout, straight back, in the shuttered and insult-daubed shop, stood the Jew. The hour of revenge had struck at last – and the hour of the young they had drilled and talked to endlessly of these things – their hour too had struck, their eyes wide in the torchlight, their mouths stretched in joyful song.

And ah, all those other uniforms. Suddenly there were hundreds of them, brown, blue, green, black, marked with emblems of rank and duty; all prepared and planned for in purposeful dreams that had now stepped from shadow into sunlight. All the years of planning, the nurturing of huge and petty ambitions, the infiltration of spies and informers into the police and ministries, the stealing and copying of files, the assembling of lists of enemies – all had been made ready in the long years of resentment and humiliation. Recruits in the police had passed on political records, neighbours' gossip about the slightest words of demurral or opposition had been noted down, names had been clipped meticulously from newspapers, files and index cards written and typed out – many of the first victims had no idea how they had been marked out for some remark casually uttered years before. Revenge was swift and joyful. I took a picture of a truck going lazily down a street. Those were smiles on the faces of the two guards at the back – just a glimpse inside of men sitting packed on the floor of the lorry, their hands on their heads.

Karl said that these things were unfortunate – why should I seek them out? He knew these SA men. They were rough, but good sorts. Order would prevail. If things got out of hand the police would step in. When the trade unions were closed down and a great sweep of unionists and socialists took place he insisted that I tell him about the work I had done for the workers' illustrated magazine. No, he would not ask names; he was not a police spy, dear boy, but he was worried for me. 'Socialists. Trades unionists. Bolsheviks. You don't see them now? They were riddled with informers. You must have no more to do with them. Nor try to help them. They're beyond your help.'

And so they were. They had disappeared. Karl ordered that

I stick to my grandmother's house. He would find out if there was anything known against me. Uncle Karl lived in a world where influence and friendship still meant much. For now he was able to help me.

'You do have a file,' he said a week later, standing, stern-faced, in Grandmother's living room.

'What do you mean a file?' she said sharply. 'They're no better than Bolsheviks themselves with their spying. A file – on Walther?'

'Mother,' he said patiently. 'We are living in difficult times. It is only a few contacts – Walther's name is recorded against them. It has been seen to. You do not like these people – some of them are my friends. We will hear no more from them.'

Money had passed hands. No – I was to say no more about it. But now was the time for all liberal foolishness to be put aside.

So, in 1933, I avoided Dachau or any of the other concentration camps that began to open that year, for the re-education, the straightening-out of the new regime's enemies. For, make no mistake, just like the designs for uniforms and the shadow offices and ministries and who should occupy them, these *other* places had also been planned; the sites chosen, the buildings designed for their new purpose long ago. Every detail of their tormenting regimes had been worked out, down to the calculated inadequacy of diets, the degrees of punishment, the insufficient length of bunk and thinness of blanket, the coarse uniforms, the badges for each grade of prisoner – all these had been urgently and fondly discussed and laid out with much hilarity in drinking sessions in cellars and bars.

Where other parties and movements had drawn up manifestos, economic plans, foreign policies, taxes, programmes for inflation, deflation – these men had bent their best endeavours to devising such ingenious inventions as a steel drum into which a university professor or distinguished artist, a diplomat or factory machinist might be inserted, bent double, and how that drum might then best be filled with smoke, or boiling water, or be lowered into a cesspit. As their enemies debated and refined already fine compromises and wrote down endlessly intertwined and balanced motions and constitutions, the victors had been content to plait whips from leather strips or steel wire to be put to a man's back.

This was their hour.

And the same hour too would go on striking, for the past was a tale of treachery and great deeds, the future a far shining promise, but the present, this wonderful present would last for ever, at the same time static and dynamic like an orgasm.

The many absentees caused by the new regime – the disappeared and the exiles – meant that there was at last more than enough work. The young gratefully flooded into the empty places. Work for me, especially with my family connections. I make no excuse. I was a young man; I was interested only in what I thought of as my Art. And it seemed, visiting the great photography fair, *Die Kamera*, that year, that it was going to be possible still to show avant-garde work among the new, amateurish sentimentalism and huge images of the State. The catalogue, for instance, was a typical product of the Bauhaus that the Nazis loathed. Perhaps pure art and vulgar propaganda were to be allowed to live together. The censorship, though immediately draconian and rigorously applied against the word, left the ambiguous image under much looser control. I registered with the new Photography Section of the Ministry of Propaganda, as was obligatory if you wished to work. I heard no more from them, except to receive every now and then a newsletter reprinting extensive speeches by Dr Goebbels.

How few rebelled. The great political parties that had argued and physically fought each other for decades vanished like mist under the new sun. Those who would have been focal points of political or moral protest were isolated, imprisoned, spied-upon, silenced. There was a great relief at silence. An almost holiday atmosphere. The most surprising people suddenly appeared with the party pin in the lapels of their neat lounge suits. Sometimes, having no prior knowledge that they shared any such beliefs, knowing their friends as one-time liberals, or even downright critics of the Nazis, they greeted each other with a slight shyness, even amusement; 'You too!' slapping each other on the back and guffawing, like students staring anxiously at the matriculation results posted in a school corridor, and turning to shout that they have passed, that they are part of the future . . .

All revolutions elevate those who have failed under previous regimes – that is part of the reason for their happening. Underneath the ideologies and nostrums, they are vehicles of vast resentment. No doubt there are a few disinterested revolutionaries. They don't last long in any new order. In the settling of scores. And there were few jobs for the old case-hardened revolutionary Brownshirts who had made this day. The book burning . . . The Jew raids . . . Life offered diminishing opportunities for such ecstasies. They couldn't be extended indefinitely in such a crude form. And for all his inside influence, Karl did not realise that, aside from the first revolution, a second was being prepared, that, as Spengler had written,

> 'We await today the philosopher who will tell us in what language history is written and how it is to be read.'

10

At the end of June, 1934, I walked in the afternoon on the south edge of the Tiergarten with Karl.

'What is happening?'

Car after car, then a stream of lorries passed going towards the centre of the city. Now two armoured cars. They halted punctiliously as a knot of people had gathered on the other side to cross. A policeman stepped into the road and held up his hand. We sought out a café and sat inside, by the window. The traffic went this way and that at speed, but no one seemed perturbed. Or they did not show it. Men and women were drinking coffee. Two women sat opposite each other at a table, their right arms crooked away from them like swans' necks, cigarettes held in their negligently beaked fingers. A man rustled his newspaper and barked like a seal. The waiter, young, tall, chi-chi, swayed between the tables. Karl's eyes followed him. Another car roared past. Then silence and chatter and the sounds of the street returned. Then we heard what had not been heard for some time now, the unmistakeable popping sound of small arms fire quite far off. As suddenly as it had begun, it stopped. 'Those trucks were all covered. They were not SS?' Karl asked suddenly and urgently. He needed to ask me – short-sighted, for reasons of vanity he would never wear his spectacles unless he was sure no one could see him. 'I don't know who they were,' I said. 'I think they were SS, some of them.'

'It couldn't be that,' he said, almost to himself. For the first time he looked nervous. 'I don't know how to ask you this. I am frightened.'

I looked at him astonished. In his grey suit and plum-coloured tie, his obvious prosperity, his ardent beliefs – how could anything frighten him on this bright sunny day?

'I must make a telephone call,' he said. He went to the booth in the corner of the café. When he returned he was pale. He sat and said nothing but, 'It is ridiculous. Ridiculous.'

For some reason his unease amused me. I knew all about his love of plots and conspiracies, but did not expect that this was anything but yet another raid on the enemies of the new state. If, that is, there were any left to raid on such a scale.

'These things . . .' I began.

'You don't understand, my boy,' he said in a whisper. 'This is what was expected, but not in any way I expected. I have just been told – I have been told that I am being searched for. That I am on a list. Because of my friendship with General Schleicher. I've never met Schleicher! It is unbelievable.' He looked round the café as if its windows and walls circumscribed the only safe place on earth. 'I have been told I cannot go home. Am I supposed to sit here, drinking coffee for eternity?'

I tried to calm him. I lit a cigarette for each of us. I would go to his flat, I assured him. He must remain here until I returned. No, no – there was too much danger.

'I'll just go up,' I said. 'If there's anything wrong, I'll ring Frau Rossbach's door – she's on holiday. If anyone asks me, I'm her nephew.' It was all like a spy story to me. I knew what these people could do, but I also regarded them as fundamentally stupid.

'Would you. I would not ask but . . . be careful.'

I squeezed his hand and got up, the brave young man. About to leave the café, I took a paper from the rack and went back to him. He started as I appeared at his shoulder. 'Read that. Try to look relaxed,' I said.

The streets were surprisingly normal. The traffic was still heavy with trucks and cars but they seemed to have slowed their urgency.

Perhaps that is the thing about extraordinary historical events: they seem almost ordinary to the immediate participants. I walked up through the summer city. People were shopping and talking. There was an edge to the air – there had been ever since the Hitler take-over. I entered the street where my uncle had his flat. Here again all seemed normal. I walked by his front entrance, glancing in. Nothing out of the ordinary. I turned at the corner, looking for spies and policemen. None. I walked back and swung into the hallway.

The lift was on the floor above. It came down with whispers and odd clanks. At his floor, I stood for a moment peering into the corridor through the lozenged grille, then pushed it back. I went to his door. I listened. No sound. I tried the key in the lock and then became truly frightened, for the door gave inwards without need of the key.

The slippers were still in a neat row, but the rugs had been twisted up by other heels. In the main room the bookcases had been emptied and books strewn across the floor. The drinks cupboard had been opened and looted except for a few bottles of mixers. Pretty oriental ornaments lay on the floor, broken by their fall, except for one little vase that had been ground to a glassy powder, only its neck remaining whole, a white-blue porcelain ring on the carpet. The desk had been opened and the papers gone through roughly; the carefully beribboned pouches of letters had been ripped apart. The inkstand had been emptied on the carpet in blotches of pale blue and blood red. The bedroom. His drawers and wardrobes were open, the clothes torn and laid about. The bed clothes had been dragged off, exposing the mattress, with one pale stain on its blue mottled surface. The word *Pervert* had been scrawled with a pencil on one white wall so that it was quite faint and interrupted by the pattern of the raised wallpaper. Saddest of all was the dispassion with which I viewed the destruction. It was with interest, only slightly mitigated by fear. This, I thought, is how the artist feels faced with new material.

I didn't try to tidy up. There was no possibility of Karl returning here. At least not while whatever present madness continued in the city. I could not imagine what enemies he could have in the new order. A coup by the Communists or anyone else on the left seemed impossible. I closed the bedroom door and went back into the living room. I stood there for a moment then heard a slight, apologetic sound behind me. A man stood in the hallway. He was large, with a bushy moustache, a powerful man who seemed to grow smaller as I looked at him.

'I heard someone in here. I was told to watch.'

'To watch? Who by?'

He was impressed by the abruptness of my questions. By my clean, well-dressed presence.

'By the gentlemen who were here before.'

'You are?'

'Herr Rossbach, sir.'

I hadn't seen him earlier. His wife I had seen occasionally, coming out of the next flat, greeting my uncle and me as we arrived, eyeing me with some sort of complaisant pleasure as another of Karl's young friends. I had thought of her as an intellectual, or at least a well-bred woman, properly tolerant of Karl's tastes. Perhaps a teacher or writer. To be met with this large peasant as her husband was a surprise.

'Who came, before me?'

'The police. The new police.'

'You haven't seen Herr Klinger since when?'

'I haven't seen him for a couple of days.'

'Say nothing. Do you know who I am?'

'Why no, sir.'

Then I grew tired of it. I went towards the door and he leapt aside and out into the hallway as if I was magnetically charged. This was the first time that I understood the impact of unequal force. Here was a great strong man who was plainly terrified. He understood that I possessed the power of the state behind me. I, foolishly, disabused him of the notion.

'I'm not from the friends who asked you to look out for Herr Klinger,' I said. 'I am a relative and friend. If everyone has acted like you today, God help us. The situation is changing. What will you say when Herr Klinger's friends come to call?'

His eyes popped and then seemed to fold back in his head. With some dignity, I must admit, he said simply, 'I obeyed the last men to call. If there are others I will obey them.'

I turned on my heel. I decided to take the stairs rather than wait for the lift. As I started down, he called after me. 'What do you expect? I am an ordinary man. What the hell do you want from us?'

When I got back to the café opposite the Tiergarten there was of course no Uncle Karl. I entered, looked at the table. Another man sat in his place, smoking a small cigar, the handle of a coffee cup hooked round his fat index finger. Karl had not moved tables. What was I supposed to do? I went home – to Grandmother's. With a feeling of shame that I had not fulfilled my part of some bargain. That I had lost Karl.

I pushed open the front door and wiped my feet on the mat. The 'girl', Marthe, appeared at once.

'Is that Walther?' came my grandmama's voice.

'Yes,' said Marthe, and disappeared again. I never located just where she lived, or existed, in that house.

'What on earth is going on, Walther?' said my grandmother. 'Your Uncle Karl is upstairs. He says that the government is trying to arrest him. It is quite ridiculous. Has everyone lost their senses?' She sat commandingly in her chair. The situation was not grave enough for her to get to her feet. 'Is there yet another change of government? Really, it is too bad. Your uncle came in like a rabbit. Go up and see him and tell him he must come down directly. If he is in some trouble, I wish to hear of it. It's all too absurd.' There was something heroic and ludicrous in her refusal to acknowledge events outside her world. 'Tell him', she said, 'there is dinner in half an hour. I expect him to be here.'

I went upstairs. On the second floor, the scent of a cigar guided me along the corridor.

In one of the rooms I had never entered before, Karl stood beside a disturbed single bed. He had evidently just got up. The curtains were drawn and the long summer evening light made his pale face yellow. 'You, Walther! Thanks be to God. I'm sorry I left the café. It didn't feel safe when you had gone.' He was marching up and down in an agitated fashion as he talked. He stopped and stared. 'Do you think I am a coward?'

I thought nothing of the kind, I assured him. There was some kind of general round-up going on in the city. But things seemed to be quietening down.

'My apartment. What of that?'

I told him the truth. Or most of it. That someone had been there. That the place had been searched. That they had made a bit of a mess of things. There was no one there now. No, it was not safe to go back.

'Is it the Communists?'

No. The streets were firmly in the command of the Nazis, I said. There was no sign of anyone else.

'It's what I feared. His side has struck against ours. My friend had just enough time on the telephone to tell me that arrests and executions are happening all over. This was our last chance for sanity. If it is the Hitler gang – well, you know what they are capable of!'

It would blow over, I said. It was only politics. Why on earth should they want him?

'Oh, you don't know, my boy. I don't want you to know. There were moves afoot. I was a fool to get involved. Perhaps though there will be a counter-blow.'

I asked if I could get him a drink. There was a bottle of brandy on the table by the bed.

'Yes. You're a good boy. Pour me one.'

From the look of the bottle and glass beside it he had already had more than one. I filled the glass and he sat down on the bed and gulped at it.

'Yes. There will be a counter-blow.' He looked up at me and for the first time smiled. 'Till then, courage.' He lifted the glass. 'We must simply sweat it out for a few days and see what happens. But why me? Why me?'

I am ashamed to say this, but like all the young, who are cruel until and unless civilised, I was secretly amused by his fear and intermittent attempts at courage. I was not afraid for myself. Poor Karl had removed my past from somebody's files. It had not occurred to him to look for his own name on those or other lists. But there were many lists – it was history that one set was consulted and acted upon before the others.

During that afternoon and night, as we learned later from the newspapers with their huge headlines and the grave and triumphant voices on the wireless, many hundreds were taken and shot to avert a second revolution. The opportunity was taken to settle old scores – some of an astonishing small nature, petty revenges, ending in beatings to death. In the SS barracks, the execution squads worked till exhausted, eliminating the last enemies of the new regime, until the walls before them were caked in blood and flesh.

For now, I told Karl that dinner was to be served and that my grandmother had insisted on his presence. Assuming a gravity far above my years I said that I thought he should come down, to forget what had happened.

'I should?'

'I think you should,' I said.

'You know – this was my room as a boy.'

There was a map of the world on one wall – the world before 1914: the British Empire in red; America in wheat-coloured yellow; sleeping, Chekhovian Russia in endless pale brown; Germany and the German-African colonies in pale green. In the bookcase were the westerns of Karl May, the scientific romances of H.G. Wells, school texts of Caesar's *Gallic Wars*, Cicero, arithmetic, algebra, physics, English, French, small ink-stained books of red and blue cloth. Two framed Japanese woodblocks, the colours slightly out of register, showed astonishingly blue seas and wooden wharfs and smiling women in costumes of curled parchment. Beside them, grey pictures of long-forgotten actors cut from magazines. And a photograph of my father and Karl as boys, knickerbockered and long-jacketed, fishing rods in hand, under a willow, the river slowed to silvery albumen behind them.

Marthe had set out the full dinner service. Grandmama sat at the head of the table. I slid into my seat and said that Uncle would be down in a moment. And he came. He had changed into a fresh white shirt and washed his face so that it glowed with false health and brandy.

'We shall hear no more talk of your trouble, Karl. For people in our position all these things are capable of resolution. If you wish, you may tell me tonight after Walther has gone to bed. We shall decide in the morning what is to be done.'

For the rest it was the usual, resolutely polite conversation. Grandmama spoke of her visit to Frau Klatschner whose husband was dying. She praised the devotion of Frau Klatschner to her husband, and that gentleman's fortitude in bearing pain and distress. Well, well, we must all come to that one day, she said serenely. She asked that Karl tell her what had been going on in the salons of this and that count or baron; who was to marry whom? They talked of a world that was gone, and by sheer force of personality and her steely questions and comments she made it live again. 'Now tell me the gossip,' she commanded. He started to tell her haltingly of the latest affair between Herr Goebbels and a young actress. 'Not those people,' she said sharply. 'The *real* people.'

Grandmama did not allow news of that sort to colour her view of how the world ought to be ordered. And Karl, good Karl, rose to the occasion and sketched gallantly, stumbling through, a whole Proustian world of aristocrats and artists going or coming from Switzerland or Denmark, of their daughters' engagements to this or that man – quite a good man, but not quite . . . There were many not quites. What of the Crown Prince? There was still talk of a re-installation of the monarchy, she understood. It depended on so many factors, Karl began to explain. 'In the present climate . . .' His voice tailed away. 'I don't want to know about the present climate,' said Grandmama. 'Describe the theatres. Is there anything one would wish to see?' I thought that at this point Karl would begin to cry. 'No,' he muttered. 'No. There is nothing of interest. Operettas.' 'Operettas – which?'

she demanded. She rang the bell by her side. 'Marthe, bring some more wine. When you have had another glass, Walther, you may go to bed.'

Amused, I obeyed. It was barely ten o'clock. The evening was still light outside. As I mounted the stairs there was silence from the room. Even when I halted on the landing and listened hard I heard nothing. People like my grandmother have a special sense of where anybody is in their house.

11

I sorted through my photographs. I thought of my girl. I had a lot of girls in those days. I began a letter to the latest. I read a little of Mann's *Buddenbrooks*. It bored me. I wondered what extraordinary things I was missing in the city. My camera sat on the dressing table reproaching me with its closed eye. But the wine and the brandy that I had shared with Karl made me at last get into bed. I wondered what they were speaking of downstairs. Even in the zoo that Berlin had become, I could not think, out here in the suburbs with the night grape-blue and silent outside the window, that anything could seriously threaten Karl or any of us. I fell asleep. That night I dreamed of my father. Perhaps it was the picture I had seen in Karl's boyhood room that sparked this dream.

Certainly here my father is – a boy whispering in Karl's ear, right hand concealing what he is saying. Karl is not a boy in the dream, but the grown middle-aged man. There is a rather malicious grin on my father's face as he takes his hand away from his mouth. Then a smell, of rain and cloth, of the grey felt-like cloth of my father's wartime uniform, the warm smell of beer and the more acidic, but not unpleasant, odour of tobacco. How could I have remembered him from the war? I would have been no more than two or three years old. So, was this an actual memory or a fabrication of my mother's and grandmother's tales? The dream moves with side-steps through time so that now I see him as in the photograph in Switzerland. He is coming down that long road that curves between banks of snow, but this time as he halts, or is stopped by the flick of the camera lens, the others in the party go on, Grandmother, Grandfather, Karl . . . They go on. My father steps forward – and the snowy ground becomes paving stones, a street, a carpeted room, the other side of a table, and there is a faint, charming, engaging smile of inquiry on his face, as if to say, 'I know you, don't I? Don't I? Please – what is your name?'

I woke early the next morning, about six, with the scent of Uncle Karl's cigar reaching along the corridor. I put on my dressing gown and went to his room, the sun palely radiant in the stained-glass window on the landing.

He sat in shirt sleeves on the edge of the bed. I had never seen him out of his suit before, and as if preserving the proprieties he stood, picked up his coat and put it on.

'It's all right, my boy. I'm still here. They haven't taken me away, you see. Even managed to sleep a little.'

He seemed to have recovered most of his nerve overnight.

'I have been thinking . . .' he said. It was all a terrible mess, no doubt, and some frightful mistake about himself. He had thought it all out last night. They had been through times like this before. He just had to lie low for a few days until proper authority was restored. Meanwhile – he hesitated to ask me, but there was really no one else he could trust. Would I take a letter into the city for him? There would be no danger to me – he would not ask me if there was.

Even if there were, I would do anything I could to help him, I said.

'Really? Really. You would? I knew you would.' Tears came to his eyes.

I was embarrassed.

'Come here,' he said.

For an awful moment I thought that he was going to embrace me. His hands had risen, as if he too thought of that, but he was content to rest one of them on my shoulder and to look into my eyes. He gripped me tightly and put his other hand to my face and stroked it briefly, his fingers trailing down my cheek cold and damp as little fishes.

'That's all,' he said.

He let go my shoulder and picked up an envelope from the bedside table.

I was to take his letter to Count S——. He had known him from school days. An honourable man with contacts on both sides of the party; he had the ear of Hindenburg and was related to Von Papen. That still meant something. If there was madness abroad, the Count's word would secure his safety until the mess was sorted out.

Count S—— was not at home. The voice on the telephone asked coldly who wanted him. I was ringing on behalf of Herr

Klinger, I said. They had had an appointment for this morning. Then I must contact the Count's staff at his office. 'The Bank,' whispered Karl behind me. The instrument went dead.

'Karl!' my grandmother's voice came from her room. The telephone was exiled to the hallway as she could not abide its presence. 'What are you doing? Your coffee. Is that Walther with you?'

'The Deutsche Bank,' he whispered to me. 'On the Behrenstrasse.'

'Really,' said my grandmother sharply.

'Go now,' he said. He opened the living room door and stepped inside. I heard his voice explaining that Walther had had to go out urgently.

'Urgently?' she said the word as if it were foreign and unwholesome.

I rode into the city on my motorbike. The bank was to the east of the quarter of government buildings along the Wilhelmstrasse. It was almost nine o'clock in the morning. The last workers were hurrying into the shops and offices. Though there were an abnormal number of police about, there was not a Brownshirt to be seen. I parked under the windows of Karl's flat. I walked the eastern way round to the bank. The newspaper billboards had great headlines announcing Röhm's death: *The Saving of the Reich from Revolution. Extraordinary Measures.* Still the clerks hurried from office to office bearing sheaves of post and documents; first shoppers lingered in front of windows, a girl smiled at me as we did that little dance of *I'm going this way, you go that* on the pavement.

The Bank. The side entrance to which my uncle had directed me.

A revolving door, its glass panes set in deeply polished mahogany. A tiled, round hall whose ceiling disappeared to the heavens. A dim, denatured light suffused the whole sarcophagus as if a wintry mist had just evaporated. Bluebeard's eight doors of temptation were ranged around. A porter in a tunic buttoned stiffly to his chin, the Cross of Honour and two other medals clinking discreetly on his chest, advanced towards me. He examined the first document, Karl's visiting card, with the Count's name written on the reverse. Without a word he led me across the floor. At the farthest point from the front entrance was a huge wooden desk, like a coffin. Behind it sat a second functionary. His uniform was of a better quality; he wore no medals but a party pin in his lapel. Above him were two huge portraits, the President, a distinguished vegetable with iron wool sprouting all over; and the Chancellor, outstaring Eternity.

'I have a letter which I must deliver to the Count in person,' I said.

Quite impossible. He pressed a bell push on his desk. I signed my name in the register to which his other hand pointed. A third functionary, a young, pleasant-looking man in a black suit appeared from the door immediately behind. The man at the desk gave him the card, holding out his hand for the letter. I returned this to my inside pocket.

The young man smiled and retired.

The man behind the desk brusquely motioned me to a leather bench against the wall. I sat and wondered what was going on outside? In the streets; in the headquarters and yards of the security police? I considered how quiet and hidden was this second revolution, how it did not touch at all these places of power and leverage and franked documents; this bank in whose offices vulgar money would be rarely if ever glimpsed. I felt safe here – my uncle was correct; nothing affects the basic institutions of power; they are like great rivers that make their own way through stone and sand. I was no revolutionary. I was an artist. My fingers itched to capture the man behind the desk, the porter, the odd light filtering down from the curved glass in the dome above.

The young man returned. He came across the floor, smiling. The Count would be pleased to see me. As I passed his desk, the functionary bowed his head to me. I was of some importance now, evidently.

He led me down a long corridor, lined with grave doors, each with a brass plaque announcing its purpose; Foreign Credit. Transfers. Commodity Values. Letters of Credit. Bills of Exchange. Like all public buildings it was made so by a rigorous avoidance of anything in the slightest personal. The warm-fleshed, red-celled inhabitants were parasites deriving a temporary living from handling papers, like leaf-ants carrying parchment from one place to another. We mounted a splendid staircase, we circumambulated – only such a latinate word will do for the feeling – a gallery high above the public floor of the bank. Counters and windows; the tellers' heads bent over the first transactions of the morning. The enormous doors to the world were still shut, the desks and armchairs for customers empty. The pattern on the huge floor would not be visible to people walking across it; from up here we, the privileged, saw it revealed as a great swirling mosaic of the symbols of the zodiac circling the imperial eagle. At its centre a woman picked up a galvanised iron bucket and mop and walked away.

More corridors; a marvellously clean and steady and neutral world. We stopped.

'The Count's office.' It was a surprisingly modest door for such a great man.

And a surprisingly young man. He rose gracefully from behind his desk and waved away my attendant.

'I had expected Herr Klinger,' he said.

'I'm his nephew.'

'Of course – I've seen you with him on more than one occasion.' For the first time he smiled and extended his hand. There were no Hitler salutes here – I presumed he was above such changes of fortune. He did not resume his seat until I sat down.

'But why doesn't Karl come himself?'

'There is some difficulty . . . I have a letter for you.' I handed the envelope over.

While he read I looked out of the window behind him. His office was on the corner of the building and I could see up the short connecting street to the Unter den Linden. The limes had been cut down to make way for triumphal processions and it looked wide and desolate. Cars and trucks passed every now and then and people hurried across the side street. Two men in police uniform stood and talked with their heads close together.

'I see . . .' The Count's voice was slow and easy. 'It is all most unfortunate. These upheavals are necessary, of course. But how they can involve such an innocent as poor Karl, it's difficult to see. But, it's obvious he is worried. I'm sure there's no cause. Mistakes are made in all these administrative matters. All the time mistakes are made. Now – if I am to help him – I see he is at his mother's house – your grandmother. A wonderful woman. My father knew her husband well.'

'His apartment was raided.'

'Indeed? You've read this letter?'

'Of course not.'

'Good. Wait here a moment.'

He left the office, motioning to me to remain seated. I looked around me. His doctorate certificate on the wall. A picture of him with a university cap, his arm round his friend's shoulders. A picture of the Count shaking hands with Herr von Papen, Vice-Chancellor. Always Vice-Chancellor . . . He came back in.

'Now have no fear. Everything is taken care of. Your uncle will be perfectly safe.'

I was to go back to my grandmother's and tell Karl to wait there; not to show himself for a few days while the Count straightened out matters.

I was delayed returning home. I visited a girlfriend who lived at the back of the Potsdamer station. On the wall above the bed were the photographs I had taken of her naked body. My uncle was safe; I was relieved of that and forgot him in the small soft bed with its big pillows. The world is very good to the young. The world of safety, of high corridors and solid desks and family ties and affections would move into smooth action and protect the old. I told the girl of dangers and my heroic part. She said she took no notice of those idiots. They would go away – there was only us two. A little later she moaned and squealed and looked with wide eyes and a flushed face into mine. She lay for a moment then moved me aside briskly and slid from the bed and ran lightly across the floor to her little bathroom. It was noon. I don't even remember her name.

A beautiful day. I walked with that step, dream-like, fully awake, the body lightened by love, the eyes keen, the world crisp and new. Soldiers and police and new uniforms strutted and stood at attention in doorways. One policeman eyed me suspiciously as I mounted my machine. I smiled broadly at him, raised my arm lazily and said loudly, 'Heil Hitler.' His scowl vanished, his arm shot up and he replied jovially, 'Heil Hitler.' He must have thought I was one of the victors too.

There is little more to tell. You know what is coming.

Here is the house. The gates I had closed were wide open, there were tracks of a car on the gravel. The front door too was open. I ran up the steps. I was met in the hall. Not by Marthe, the servant, but by my grandmother.

'Where have you been? There have been men here.'

I truly had never seen her with the daylight upon her. Even now my aesthetic sense registered her appearance before I took in the terrible reproaches she directed at me.

'Where have you been? Men have come. Brutes. Why were you not here?'

Her clothes, rich, expensive and heavy, looked faded and as if they stood on her insubstantial body like a wired costume. Her eyes stared from that handsome face whose precise balance was for the first time confused and distorted by emotion.

'I have never heard such language. *Shit. Pig.*'

The words were taken from her mouth in antiseptic packages, handled with a sort of horrified awe as if they were the actual objects they described.

'They beat him when he struggled not to get into their car. Until then he had gone quietly between them. That is when they used those words. Karl cried out to me . . .'

'Where have you been?' she demanded again. 'Come inside. We must do something now about this frightful affair.'

It was her turn to write letters. Surprisingly quickly and neatly on small yellow sheets of paper at the writing desk. This was for Herr——. This for the Police Authorities. This for Graf von——. I went with a letter to the court buildings in Alexanderplatz. They had no power to intervene with the political security force.

From a public box I rang the Count. I gave my name. He was in a meeting. I was sure of his treachery. Perhaps he was innocent. That afternoon and evening I delivered the other letters and lied to Grandmama that the authorities were urgently looking into the matter – but because of the uncertainty of the present situation it might be one or two days before Karl could be traced and whatever absurd mistake rectified.

She would go herself, she said. I was getting nowhere, that was plain. Respectable people could not just be taken from their homes. 'You will order me a cab in the morning,' she said. 'I will go to the Chancellory itself, if need be.' But her indomitability had been shaken; something she did not understand had entered the house and put the whole seventy-odd years of her life into doubt.

The car to the Chancellory was not needed. That night an official of the criminal police came to the house.

Uncle Karl had been found barely three miles away, in the woods below Charlottenburg. He had been shot. They were trying to ascertain the details. It seemed that he may have been abducted after . . . after his arrest by the political authorities. There would be an investigation. Unfortunately there had been many cases in the past twenty-four hours. My grandmother ordered coffee for the policeman, which he hardly drank. She was stone-faced and most polite to him, remarking how tired he looked. These, he agreed with her, were difficult times.

The body, she said, must be delivered back to this house.

'That, I'm afraid, will not be possible at the moment. The nature of the injuries. Perhaps you have someone who can contact me at my headquarters in the morning.'

It was not the Inspector's fault, she said gravely. Her grandson – she nodded to me – the Inspector looked at me with almost pathetic gratitude – would deal with the practicalities. If we would excuse her.

That night in bed I lay in guilt and shame. But death means little at that age. I had had a tiring day, after all, and began to sleep. I was wakened by a dreadful wailing cry from downstairs. Then silence. After a few, long minutes came the sound of Marthe scurrying down the stairs, and a little later, her steady steps back, going on to the top of the house.

THE AGE OF BRONZE

1

'With white blood the black arteries are connected to each city from Berlin; from cities to towns the veins spread . . .' On the map on the screen they obediently do so. With music swelling behind, the commentator goes on in that slightly hysterical way all public voices had then, 'To hasten our revolution German life must travel at high speeds. As in all else, the Führer shows the way forward.' Here is the Leader advancing on foot, surrounded by the usual courtiers striding behind him, or hastening in front and looking back with cheerful faces. The Leader is handed a spade by a shirtless, muscled and tanned torso. The great man digs the spade inexpertly into the ground. He is evidently unused to physical work. 'Too many pastries,' says a Berlin voice in the dark. There is snickering in the row behind. 'Who is that? Who is that?' cries a voice. 'Silence.' Out of time with the music, the Führer chops and turns the first sod of the first new road. He straightens and that curious, stiff-muscled smirk unsettles his mouth. He rubs his hands on his greatcoat and makes some silent remark and all his accompanying officials smile radiantly at him, and those at the back, unfortunate not to have heard the actual words, bend forward and have the words repeated to them, then they too break into smiles and nod. 'The Führer himself', the voice says breathlessly, 'has ordered a supercharged car capable of a hundred and twenty kilometres an hour.'

I was obeying this edict at least; travelling as fast as I could.

A distance west of some four hundred kilometres home – as the crow flies – but because our white autobahns are still only on film, nearer five hundred. It took me ten hours on my motorbike. I needed the journey to purify, to empty, my mind. I needed also to feel tired; to have achieved a journey by my own efforts; to cross half the country. It was the beginning of August. My hair flared gold in the sun. I would ride and ride and the pure air and warmth begin to heal my mind. Myself as the gallant lone traveller; 'To hasten our revolution . . .'

I had started at six that morning. My grandmother had insisted I go home. She had made a good recovery. On the surface at the least. She would not allow grief to show, even at the funeral for Karl. Only she and I were present; evidently none of his friends had thought it safe to attend.

The sealed coffin arrived at the gate to the graveyard as our hired car drew up. My grandmother wore a black veil. I had been astonished at the firmness of her step from the house to the car, and now again at her bolt-upright posture as she watched the four undertakers slide the coffin from the back of the hearse onto the bier. Two men on each side, they doffed their black top hats to the dead man, then took the handles of the bier and lifted. A cemetery official, in his uniform of short grey-blue coat buttoned to the neck, grey trousers, a soft, peaked cap, looked round one side of the arch, then ducked back. He must have given a signal, for the pastor in his long black gown came forward from under the archway. He gave a low bow to the coffin, then turned and led the way in. I offered Grandmama my arm; the fingers, hooked in her black glove, rested as lightly as a bird's claw. The bell in the lantern above the arch began to toll slowly. As we passed I saw the uniformed man in a tiny alcove working his arm up and down at the end of the bell rope. He gave me an idiotic smile.

The chapel seemed unnaturally cold on such a warm sunny day. Four men and one woman sang a Bach chorale in a dirge-like way. I heard Grandmother whisper something. I turned my head. She stared straight in front of her. 'There should have been more,' she whispered again. 'I asked for more.' The ceremony was short, dignified, infinitely depressing. The pastor's voice rang in the almost empty chamber. Our responses fluttered like leaves at his feet. The undertakers stood, hands clasped in front of them, silent at the rear.

At last we processed outside.

The Klinger family burial ground lay along one wall. The massive tombstones had been weathered and dilapidated in various degrees through the generations. The newest monument was to my grandfather; a massive double tablet surmounted by a stone angel pointing a finger heavenwards. Across the stone in Gothic letters was carved the message 'The Grave Is Our Last Hope'. One half of the stone was engraved with grandfather's dates; the other had been left blank. For my grandmother.

Poor Karl's freshly dug grave was to the right of this railed plot. The undertakers drew the bands under the coffin. They lowered it into the clay hole. The pastor read his words. His fingers reached into the silver bowl of sand that stood on a thin brass plinth at his side. Three times he spoke a sentence, and three times lowered his hand and threw in a little sand to sift with a fine scratching sound over the coffin lid. Then he had done and my grandmother's fingers fetched up as much sand as a pinch of salt and leaned perilously but steadily over the grave. It fell with no more sound than a handkerchief falling. She walked away, more unsteadily, looking from the back a little old woman.

In the house she sat stiffly in semi-darkness. That afternoon she received two of the elderly women who were her neighbours and contemporaries, those whom she had entertained in this house for many years. They were versions of my grandmother and when they were admitted to the living room I withdrew upstairs, leaving them to their icily polite interchanges of grief. There were no other callers.

Two days after the funeral I travelled into the city. The streets were still heavy with sentries and patrols. I half expected any minute to be halted and arrested. Most of those whose society I had sought a year ago had now left or simply disappeared. All wits and intellectuals were now most positively unwanted. Painters had nowhere to show; musicians' orchestra stalls were empty; writers could find no one foolish enough to print their work. For the ones who had got away – if they were lucky – there was America, or Paris, or England. Or enforced silence, a hiding place – either way, internal or external, a state of exile.

We lived from storm to storm. Paradoxically, out in the open air was the safest place to be, at least if you approximated fairly to the regime's new standard of human appearance. There was a lightening of hearts now that the bad blood had been let. I stopped my bike and got off to photograph some young Labour Service conscripts at work digging out new flowerbeds in the

Tiergarten. I never went anywhere without my camera, even at such a time.

Cold-hearted of me to begin again with my obsession so soon after Karl's death? Truth to tell, I would have photographed the funeral if I had been able to. And I was photographing a new city. The combination of summer and fear was intoxicating. The old Berlin we had been so proud of? The Berlin that had always the best jokes about Hitler, whose population never voted a majority for the Nazis, that had marvellous theatres, cabarets, night clubs, sex; the wonderful, bitter, biting spirit of those halting songs . . . ? None of it made any difference in the end, did it? I saw, in an American magazine before the war, a picture of a lean-jawed, tough-looking singer. On the side of his guitar was written 'This Machine Kills Fascists'. He was wrong. It didn't. His guns might do in the end – but there won't be any songs written about that. Fascists don't like guitars. They didn't like pictures of themselves. Not at least until they had come to power and could control the lens.

When I came to develop the pictures of those days I felt as if I was seeing the city for the first time. As if, indeed, it was no longer a city but a state of mind. Or lack of mind. Of appearances – and absences. There was an absence made up of absences. Zola wrote that we cannot claim to have seen anything until we have photographed it. The photograph sees, as a matter of physics, both less and more than the eye. If it is an art – and the question is open – it is one of abstraction, not absorption. It is an analytic tool, not a synthesising form. An art when most remote from other forms of art – from the commentary, the interpretation, the re-ordering of emotion by the artist's mediation. It succeeds most deeply when it denies art – it has long been my idea to leave an automatic camera, set at optimum exposure and infinity, at a street corner, simply to record at regular tiny intervals whatever passes or does not pass. The photograph succeeds when it denies art, when it rejects the whole subjective flow of experience that the painter and novelist and film-maker use. The photograph is a picture of what is for ever dead, of what is taken from time, out of time. It shows what we shall never see.

In the late Twenties, somewhere in England, in a country lane, two fleeing criminals were surprised by a local policeman. I see him walking in the night, solidly built, his stomach comfortably full of his evening meal, a bull's-eye lamp in one hand. At their trial the murderers said that they had first shot him in the belly, and then shot out his eyes because they had heard somewhere, in the way that is knowledge for the ignorant, that the retinas of a dead man retain the image of the last thing seen. The criminals believed that their faces were imprinted on the cones and jellies of the constable's eyes.

That little box looking into the Tiergarten was like the inside of a dead skull. It had a retina – but no nerves stretched away from it.

Halfway upon my journey, somewhere south of Hannover, just past Göttingen, where I refuelled, tired of the banners saying '*The Jews Are Our Misfortune*' strung across the entrances to villages – I stopped on a hillside road to eat the lunch that Marthe had prepared for me. Sausage, bread, a silver flask of coffee with cognac. Here was a valley of great beauty. A small snaking silver river. Blue-green trees and wide pastures dotted with cows. A farm on the opposite hillside. A large half-timbered house with barns set round, a chalk-white track leading down to the valley floor. A man came out into one of the toy-like yards. He wore a blue jerkin, brown trousers. He went into a barn. A dot of a dog nosed in his footsteps.

The sound of cheerful singing came from the road. I turned my head. Three girls, three boys, were marching along. Well built and sunburned, dressed in the uniforms of the Youth and the BDM, they walked with a swing to their step. The song was some folk air, not one of the terrible songs the Nazis had introduced. They were not militaristic, rather they bounced along, boy, boy; girl, girl; boy, girl – the last two holding hands. Their singing was so sweet that I recall it sentimentally. They went away down the road. The girls in the middle, I was pleased to see, looked back at me. They disappeared round the corner, their voices following.

The voices died. The man stayed in his barn. All was calm and beautiful. After a few moments more, I packed up the remnants of my meal and went back to my bike and set off again.

I had written to my mother several times in the past couple of years. The irony of that sentence is deliberate. Her letters came regularly each fortnight; anodyne, full of gossip about neighbours. My knowledge of the names she put down had faded since coming to the city. She wrote of how well Peter was doing at the university. She hoped that my grandmother was keeping well. No one picking up these letters a hundred years hence could have found in them a trace of the momentous events that had taken place in our country. They were short, dutiful letters to a beloved son, written in that flavourless, incidentless, sightless way that people have, that non-artists have, of describing the world. So I arrogantly thought. And I thought also, a neat philosophical point, that if people cannot describe the things in the world in anything like their true essence, then they cannot, must not be able to feel any of those things. It did not cross my mind that a work of art might be a screen rather than a window.

For me, then, the world consisted of my vision – or my camera's. And that world began truly only in 1839. On a boulevard in Paris. In Daguerre's first capture of a human being.

The few photographs before that day had shown only an empty world, of leafless trees and stone heads, of cities seemingly emptied by some catastrophe – the blank windows of apartment blocks, shops and hotel fronts, empty doorways and pavements; the buildings mounting to a sky stained by monstrous storms, full of great swagging clouds deeply scored with silver or scratched away to reveal black, starless space. Serene, celestial cities, the streets gleaming as if freshly washed after the Flood, waited for new creation. But life, proof of life, had to wait until that man halted by *that* fountain on *that* corner, and stayed, his right foot up on the stone lip, tying his shoe lace, keeping still long enough for his light to seep into the salts of the metal plate. For his image to form. Only then did a true record of life begin.

After that, I thought, we were all contemporaries.

The Germans are as given to philosophy as they are to song.

An open stretch of road; my bike roared forward.

The letter. Yes, the letter that had set me on my way. It was preceded by the short, heartless note I had written to tell my mother of Karl's death. It crossed with Mother's first atypical letter. She had heard on the radio of the terrible events afoot in the capital – was I in danger? I must return home at once. At least in the village – 'though there have been terrible happenings here' – her first hint of them – 'it must be safer than the capital.' I wrote her another, calming letter, saying that nothing untoward had happened to me – that there was no cause for any concern on my behalf. This again crossed with a letter from her to my grandmother about Karl's death.

My grandmother informed me of the letter. She did not offer to show it to me. She said, 'Your mother is a good woman, Walther. Your uncle did not know her at all well. I don't know if they even met. We have been kept apart – by distance . . . and circumstance. Family matters. She is provided for. But I think you should go to her. Nothing has happened – but you may still get into trouble here. It will be quieter in the country.'

I said I would not. Of course. How would she cope with me gone?

I had been worried about her. Only that morning as I had gone past her half open door she had called out, 'Karl?' and when I entered had blinked, appearing not to recognise me at first, and then said, 'Oh, Walther. It is you. How stupid of me, I thought . . .'

Now she looked coldly at me. 'I am not quite decrepit,' she said. 'There is the girl to look after me if I become so.'

And so we discussed it in that polite, useless way, because she knew, as I did, that I would go, that I had had enough of this house and its old presences and that I must strike away.

As if to hammer home that she knew my secret mind, she said also, 'And when you return you must have some purpose for doing so, Walther. You are a young man. This present situation will not last. You may stay here a while when you return, but then I think you must find something to do and somewhere to live. I will always welcome you here, you know that.'

It was decided. She had decided for my cowardice. In the evening I went into the city and sent a telegram to my mother saying that I would arrive the following evening. When I got back I went to the kitchen. Marthe sat beside the cooking range. I was surprised; I don't think I had ever seen her sitting down before. She listened as I explained that I was going away for a time. That she must take particular care of her mistress from now on. 'I shall always do that, Herr Klinger.' I had not heard her speak very often either; her harsh Saxon voice was reproving. It confirmed that I was the master of the house, that I was wrong to leave – and redoubled my guilt. I gave her my address. She shook her head. 'Everything will carry on,' she said. The mistress had already told her to prepare me a parcel of food for my journey.

That night I packed up my clothes in one of Karl's old suitcases.

In the morning I went into Grandmama. To my surprise the curtains were open, the room brightening with the early morning light. She was sitting in her chair, dressed perfectly as always. I suddenly realised what a mystery her life was to me. Its everyday habits and rituals. Reaching into a wooden box on her side table, she counted and held out a bundle of banknotes.

'Take it,' she said. 'I do wish you were not going on that contraption of yours. Write to me as soon as you can. Give your mother my greetings. Thank her for her kind letter. Pardon me to her for not replying sooner. I shall. Now – you had better be going, or you'll not arrive by nightfall.'

I shan't say I wept; her kind, stern face forbade such displays of emotion. But I bent and kissed the cold black opal of her ring and as I came out of the house, after the last farewell, tears did come to my eyes. Technically, a misting of the iris – my learning of humanity was slow and difficult always.

I came to the last great wooded hill on the other side of which lay the spa. Thick oak and beech branches overhung the winding road and I turned on my headlight. It shone like a giant's torch into the dark hollows where the trees clustered most thickly and beamed weakly forward on the road where they thinned and the light from the sky showed through. I roared upwards and then was at the top and descending towards the village, passing the spots where we had all picnicked so many years before. The blue of the narrow, deep river appeared below me and then the first houses. Two boys sitting on the stone edge of the Kaiser Bridge whistled and waved as I banked round the last corner and entered the main street. I waved back.

2

The spa was full that summer. I'd had the idea coming down that I would emulate Valenti and propose myself as the official photographer to the place and spend glorious long days taking pictures of the holidaymakers and visitors. But the Kurhaus was under new management.

At the entrance to the gardens yet another of those large notices read '*Jews Are Not Welcome Here*'. The red and black and white swastika flag was draped slack and brilliant from the portico. There were small silver-framed pictures of the Führer and his chief ministers on the sills inside the tall windows – and a large painting of the man himself on an easel in the foyer. Most of the male visitors were sporting the uniforms of the new State; men who had done well, their large, unrefined faces glowing with suntanned anticipation at doing even better, their wives and mistresses in long white dresses and pretty little hats. I found my camera avoiding them as I shot. With the crowds this was difficult. Time after time the edge of a grinning mug would materialise in my printing tray. It was not the place I had known.

The Kurhaus had been shut for a time last year. My mother told me why. Those people, as she always referred to the Nazis, had found out that Fischer, the owner, was Jewish. One day three trucks of Brownshirt louts had driven in from Coblenz. They smashed the windows of a shop up the street – Edelstein, the bootmaker's – he'd gone away with his family now. Then they drove on to the Kurhaus, going straight across the gardens and flowerbeds. They scared all the people out of the gardens, keeping back the ones they said were Jews. They chased women and small children away from the Women's Bath and made them run up through the town half undressed . . . 'The poor children crying, still in their bathing costumes, their mothers huddling them to their sides. It was pitiful to see. The men were driven off in the lorries. I don't know where.'

We spoke in English. She was always happier in her own tongue. With Peter away at the University in Bonn, her German, never very good, had slipped away even further. There was nothing, she said, to read in the paper now but incessant nonsense; you could get the *Daily Mail* in Coblenz – when there was nothing in it that they didn't want you to read. As for her neighbours – well, they were affable enough, but she had never been really close to any one of them. It was all so different since I'd left. She seemed to me like a tourist who had been detained on her way by an earthquake that went on and on.

Her delight at seeing me, her embraces when I walked upstairs to the apartment that first evening – these were soon tempered by my own feelings of guilt at knowing that I could never settle back here.

'Poor Karl. I can't say that I knew him at all well, but he and your father were the best of friends – which is rare for brothers –' she said this quite innocently, not meaning, I'm sure, to allude to the relations between my own brother and me. 'How awful. If a little place like this can be treated so . . . Well, I am simply glad you are safe now. God knows what your father would have made of it all,' she sighed.

I had outgrown the village once – I could not conceive of making any sort of life here. My mother knew this. And tried her best to prevent me from leaving. She cooked what she thought were my favourite dishes. I was too thin. Young Frieda, she said with a sly look, had grown into a fine young woman. It took me a moment or two to recollect Frieda. Ah, one of my sweethearts from long ago. A nice girl – as yet unmarried – she often asked after me . . .

Mother still received her allowance from the estate. Herr Rothstein had handled the business until this year. But now, it seemed, there were new laws. Rothstein had written her an apologetic letter saying that, alas, he was no longer allowed to deal on her behalf. Peter had objected to him even before that. They had had a fearful row about the matter and Peter had stormed from the house. She brought out from the sideboard the photograph album and showed me the pictures I'd taken as a boy. There was the lieutenant, Peter, my young mother. I looked at them with cold eyes. How bad they were – as pictures – but one or two, yes, they had something. I did have an eye even then, I said to myself. Do you remember this and this and this, she said, turning the pages.

After childhood there were the pictures I had taken down at the spa, in Valenti's day, and after he had gone; of Coblenz, of landscapes, studies of the great snow we had in '31, with the telegraph wires hanging down like great wool-covered tubes, the trees in spectacular black and white rhythmical beauty; Sander-like studies of those local tradesmen I had persuaded to stand in front of their shops for me. Here was the parade of the village storm troop with Peter strapped to his big drum. The streets of the town empty and gloomy at night. The village station empty in sunlight, the rail lines winding away, round the hill, into the future . . .

Much better photographs, I thought. I had learned my trade a little after all. Mother must have fetched them from the drawer in the bedroom I shared with Peter and stuck them in the album. There were no pictures taken after my departure.

It was all a part of the world that my mother had made in this apartment in this village in a foreign place. Lying awake at night in the old bedroom, I thought how this was safety to her; this album, these walls, her memories of husband and children – who were no longer children, but part of the whole, confusing, unsafe world outside.

The next evening, I took a walk around the town. It was light until after nine. I waited for dark and headed up to the promenade above the spa. The moon-shaped globes hanging from tall, curved cast-iron frames made pools of yellow light between the blue-black trees that bulged out over the path. In front of me, a pair of lovers, arms and bodies entwined, wandered slowly forward. I stopped, letting them go on until they merged into a single organism in the dark beyond the lamps. I looked down over the stone wall.

The white dome of the Kurhaus loomed out of the gardens. Just below the dome only a window high in the rear of the building was lit. Perhaps the one Valenti had used as his dark room. I had gone up there once, into the upper back floors. A world of narrow corridors and shabby rooms and offices, occupied by the maids and waiters and chefs and managers. The dressing rooms for the violinists and pianists and singers who appeared in the concert halls were, if anything, worse. Valenti had shown me one. Cracked linoleum on the floor, a dressing table that was hardly more than a ledge with an unemptied ashtray. An elegant tailed suit was laid over the back of an unclean sofa that leaked black horsehair. The suit, he told me, of young Moiseiwich, the pianist, who stepped from that room down the crowded concert hall and spun notes like diamonds and pearls into the night. That was the first time I realised the distinction between reality and illusion; between the cramped utterly other world of the artist and the show he puts on. That the show is artifice and technique and the summoning of spirit from despair – and that the audience must never realise this. To reveal the reality of how art and its magic are made would be to show that God is nothing but a shabby old man, a conjurer with gin on his breath, dressed in a long coat, its deep hidden pockets stuffed with his creations; the rabbit, the string of flags, the mirror that shows another face than your own.

When I came home Mother was waiting up for me. She had placed cigarettes and the half bottle of Moselle left from dinner on the cleared table. We sat and talked. She knew I didn't intend to stay. She talked of England. She had thought of going back there. There was a sister in Devon . . .

'Though I can't think what she can be like by now,' she said in a sort of wonder, holding her tiny glass of wine. 'I haven't seen anyone there since before the War.'

She told me of her early life before she had met my father. I think she hadn't done this before because she was determined to put it all behind her, to make a new life in this strange country with the man she loved. That she had nothing to go back to. Certainly it sounded little enough.

Her father was a shopkeeper who had gone bankrupt. Her mother, your other grandmother, she said, was a soft-voiced local girl who had had no education but read books all the time and kept the house and tended the shop whenever father was absent. One of his absences had grown into weeks and a letter had come saying he had run off with an Exeter woman. The shop, a ladies' dress shop, had rapidly failed. Her father had not paid any of his debts and they found themselves virtually penniless. Her mother had taken rooms for her and her sister. Previously they'd been lightly employed in the shop;

now they had to work. Fortunately, my mother had taken elocution lessons from some frightful woman in Exeter at her father's insistence. So, at twenty years old, in 1908, she had left home and taken a position as a lady's maid with a distant relative's widow. That was how these things were arranged in England. God help you, she said, if you knew no one at all well connected. And then, one thing had led to another; she had travelled with the widow – and met my father in Switzerland. 'He thought I was an heiress.' She laughed. They had travelled to England after their marriage. The dreadful war had come; her mother had died in the influenza epidemic in 1918, she had lost touch with her sister. She supposed there was hardly anyone left over there who would remember her.

'You've never thought of returning before now?' I asked.

'How could I – with Peter and you to look after.'

A few nights later Peter came home. 'Don't you recognise me – your own brother?' I said. For his homecoming I'd changed into the good suit that Karl had given me, and a white silk shirt and neck-tie. I extended my hand. Almost to my surprise he smiled broadly and shook hands vigorously.

Peter had filled out. The rather lumpy boy was now a well built young man. He resembled my father in the old pictures along the mantelshelf. Where was his student cap, I asked. He looked more like a worker in his brown breeches and black boots, his white shirt with the sleeves rolled up. The students, he explained, no longer dressed in the old Corps uniform. All of that was gone.

My mother had begged me not to argue politics with him. As we sat down to eat, she hovered over the table, fussing at both of us, now and then shooting me a frown as I asked Peter about life in Bonn. My voice must have held some mocking tone that she was sensitive to and recognised. Peter didn't.

What am I to say of my brother? He wasn't the boorish Brownshirt I'd expected. In many ways he was a quieter, softer person than I remembered in his adolescence. He was intelligent; he had passed into the university just before the barbarians had arrived. But now, as we talked, he rejoiced in the expulsions of Social Democrat students, the upheaval of the curriculum, the banning of books, the interruption of lectures by him and his fellows when the lecturer strayed from the party line, the complaints about professors whose views were suspect, their removal and replacement. There was a wholly new emphasis, he said, on work for the good of the Reich. All that was rotten and had contributed to the country's downfall was to be rooted out.

Later that night, we lay on the beds in our old room.

'Berlin must be wonderful,' he said. 'Were you there when the Government changed?'

'Yes.'

'The marches, all the marches – the excitement must have been tremendous. I saw the newsreels, but that's no substitute for the actual thing!'

'I saw the marches.'

'The Führer? You saw the Führer?'

'I photographed the Führer.'

'In person! Close to?' Peter sat up, his hands clasped in front of him, his eyes shining.

'No, only from a distance.'

'Have you got them – the photographs. Oh, do let me see!'

'They're in Berlin,' I said.

His face collapsed in disappointment.

'And the fighting last month? Did you see the fighting?'

'There wasn't any fighting,' I said.

Peter went quiet. Then he spoke.

'Uncle Karl was killed. There must have been some fighting.'

'Karl wasn't killed – he was murdered.'

'By the Reds?'

'Look, hasn't Mother explained this to you? Your uncle was shot by your friends.'

'My friends? What do you mean?'

'The Party. By the victors in their dispute.'

He slumped on to one elbow, supporting the side of his face on the palm of his hand. He looked like a boy again. Those we know and love have this odd way of drifting in and out of time. His mouth set in a petulant pout.

'He was one of those executed?'

'You could put it that way.'

He rolled on to his back and lay silent, his face twisted away, gazing at the wall.

After a while he began to say something about the last few months having been very difficult ones for the Party. It had all been explained to them at their lectures . . .

'Well, that's all right then, isn't it?' I said.

'Look, I'm sorry for Uncle Karl. But I hardly knew him. I can't be sorry if I hardly knew a man, can I?'

I told him it was late and time we went to bed. He pulled a blanket over him, still turned away from me. I put out the light, but didn't get undressed. I lay on the bed in my suit. I didn't know if he had fallen asleep, but after a couple of minutes I pulled the cigarettes from my pockets. The match scraped and flared, illuminating the room for a second. I inhaled deeply.

'Do you mind not doing that, Walther,' said his voice, clear and wakeful in the darkness. 'It's a filthy habit.'

3

In every window was a placard bearing the five-circle emblem of the Olympic Games. Other signs had been removed, so as not to annoy the tourists: the signs against Jews; the Party exhortations to Germany to Awake. These were in people's heads, but not now for public view.

I'd called into one of the biggest photo agencies in Berlin.

I knew him at once. He stood at the end of the long busy office. The man I'd come to see started to lay out the pictures I'd sent in and make some remark or other. I asked him to excuse me a moment and went between the desks and clattering typewriters to Valenti.

Had he changed? The Valentis of this world never change. Obviously, in the six years since I had last seen him I'd grown and changed. From a seventeen-year-old boy to a twenty-three-year-old man is a considerable, if shallow, voyage. For him; well, he had progressed in his building of the imposing edifice that was Valenti.

He wore a suit that seemed to have been cut from black sailcloth. The word 'cut' gives the impression of angularity. Valenti had never been in any respect angular, and he appeared in some bursting way bigger than his outfit. His face was tanned and florid. His once-wild hair had been suppressed into a waved, brilliantined mass combed back from his forehead. The desk behind which he stood was littered with prints marked with thick black lines, either cancelling them with a large X, or editing them for shape and composition. All was energy about him, the loud voice, the arms flung out, the violent blue eyes that finally settled on me as he came to a momentary halt.

'Yes?'

'Herr Valenti – you don't recognise me?'

'Recognise you? Course I don't bloody recognise you. Who are you? Somebody famous?'

He took me to lunch. Not to talk over old times. After a revolution there are no old times. Best forgotten. Nice to see you again.

At the table, he offered me a job on the agency's staff. I said I'd think it over. He raised his eyebrows. Independent bugger, eh? Whatever you like. But don't take too long. Afterwards, we strode down through the Tiergarten, much larger and more magnificent than the gardens where I had first met him. In his lapel was a party badge.

I asked him the question I'd been itching to all through our meal. 'When did you become a member of the party?'

'Meaning I shouldn't be? Of course I am, you young idiot. One of the spring violets. How the hell else do you get a decent job. Unlucky for you, eh? They've shut up the shop now.'

'Spring violets' was the term older members used contemptuously of those many thousands who flooded into the Party in the immediate aftermath of Hitler coming to power. After the Röhm purge the Party had declared a moratorium on new entrants; from then on membership was to be reserved for the élite.

'I wouldn't have thought . . .'

He stopped suddenly and stared at me.

'I do what's good for me, Walther. Not for anyone else. You must sail with the wind and hide in the storms.' He marched on.

'Yes, but do you believe in it – what they are doing?' I persisted, hurrying at his side.

'I do. And I believe in the sacred cause and body of Michael Valenti. I believe in my stomach. And in my mistress. Have you got a girl? Yes – the more the merrier. And, yes, I do believe. Whatever is, is. You'd better realise that.'

We had come to a gate.

'I'm going back to the office. Look, do you want that job or not? You need someone to keep you out of trouble.'

'Okay.'

His face split into the old, huge grin. He slapped my arm.

'Get your stuff and go and get some shots at Grünewald. The new stadium. Have them on my desk in the morning.'

The agency still had a reputation for some openness and daring; they even bought in American and European pictures from exiles, printing them under impeccably Aryan pseudonyms. In among the innumerable photographs of the Führer and other dignitaries there were advertisements with the old steely

Bauhaus-influenced diagonals and odd angles; fashion pictures that twisted the bodies of beautiful women into impossible arabesques of silk and flesh; nature studies that veered to abstraction – *Sunlight on Water*: a boy on a pier dangled his finger in the water of a lake making the circular ripples float ever outwards so that you knew that to the photographer, the ripples, the textures unfolding in the water, were more important than the boy and his uniform. Even in propaganda shots one sometimes felt the spirit of a like-minded comrade; shooting from below the massive torso of some stripped warrior, making his face a mask of moronic stone. But there was to be no bad news in our pictures.

So – no more studies of poor Silesian weavers or miners in their pitiful, overcrowded homes; the three pale children, the thin bony father, the mother with her face in shadow cutting the one loaf on the bare small table, the one onion lying already divided, the jug of water chipped in its mouth. Now there was another picture of another family; beefier, cleaner, the table an altar as the mother leans over, the man dandles the smallest child on his lap, and the two other children look on in adoration, all of their faces lit from below by the light falling on the radiantly white cloth, watching enraptured the magic angle of the mother's firm young arm as she enacts the caption of the picture, *Ironing The SA Uniform*; an altar piece, an Adoration. Then and Now! The wreck of the past! The joyful voyage forward!

And indeed it was for all of us – I include myself – a voyage into the future.

I was no rebel. There were no rebels. The death of Uncle Karl – I rationalised to myself – was because he had simply fallen foul of one of the innumerable cabals contesting for power. But things, everyone said, things were, for the first time in a long time, 'normal', 'pleasant' now. Order had been restored. If that meant the sacrifice of Law – well, who cared about that but lawyers? And what were the lawyers? Jews. The Jews in the city – their numbers swelled by those who had fled the small towns – well, their sufferings were largely bureaucratic. A matter of petty, demeaning restrictions, no worse than their ancestors had endured for centuries. After all, not for months had men been forced to stand on corners wearing demeaning and hateful placards. No longer were groups with beaten and swollen faces paraded through the streets between tall, grinning sentries. People stared from the pavement as these miserable processions passed. Some onlookers smiled warmly. I know. I took their pictures; not in protest, not as records of oppression, but for the fee in the papers I worked for. The papers that I had given up reading, unable to bear the captions put to my work. Oh, all the important Jews, the ones we admired, the artists and actors, the novelists and neuro-surgeons – they had gone away. The ones who were left kept to their own streets, eking out a living in their withered professions. At the time of the Olympics, some of them even came back from Holland and France, thinking that the worst was over.

I was lucky. We all counted ourselves lucky to be alive then, in that time. Peter had gone into his year's conscription in the Labour Service. My mother wrote to me from the village; life had got better. With those poor people gone, there had been no more disturbances. And my grandmother? She remained in a state of almost suspended animation out at Dalhelm. Her wits were not as sharp; this I took, with all the arrogance of the young, as the mercy of age blunting grief. I hadn't been to see her for months. Something musty and decaying had crept into the house and offended my keen nostrils.

All in all, looking back, I was a bit of a shit. But in the middle of a midden who notices his neighbour's smell, or his own?

The atmosphere in the office was hectic. The staff were young, energetic, their faces alive with their duties. This was the same wherever you went in those days in the Government service – and everything in the long or the short run was in the Government service. The workers were having it pretty hard with longer hours and a lowering of wages. But the unions had been shut down and the socialists locked up and not a word of complaint came through the press – so who knew, apart from those who suffered in a direct and forceful manner. A great project was afoot; a rebirth.

Unfortunately, unlike the earlier renaissance, instead of an upsurge in thought and expression, this birth resulted in a moon-calf – and the child grew stupider each day. There was a slow but ineluctable withering of the arts and thought. I had at first regarded many of the emigrants with some contempt, now I envied their freedom. *Amerika, du hast es besser.* But then, most of those who had got away were older than me; my generation had their formative years slowly suffocated. This, I admit, is hindsight; I too was caught up in the mad curious wave of optimism. As I said, there were jokes and doubts. But the jokes were always at the expense of the petty officials who abound in any state; never, oh, never at the expense of the Führer, of the police, of the overwhelming direction of the new philosophy.

Any excesses were due to 'the little Hitlers'; the bootlickers joked about and despised – if one chose one's friends carefully to share the jokes. None of it was down to the Leader. He had pulled the country up by its bootstraps, given it a direction and pride; he was not to blame for all the other idiocies. A brown god writ large in the million posters and panegyrics invoking his name. Prayed to at night – even I, after a day in the city, closed my eyes many nights and saw those images of the strong, retouched face staring into my internal darkness.

Doubts were suppressed by fear of the ubiquitous informers – and what lay behind them; the burgeoning apparatus of concentration camps and the terrible things whispered about what went on in them. But they were for others. We had plenty of work; not so much money, but enough. And I had my grandmother's allowance. I was a privileged young man.

You see what I was – as to where I was, well, since returning to the capital I'd lived four flights up at the top of a solid nineteenth-century apartment block on the edge of a decaying working-class district. Jews had crowded into some of the blocks. They gave me a sense of variety and life in a place that had grown drab; of necessary danger. That I could flee and they couldn't always slightly soured for me our meetings. The incomers were mostly solid bourgeois types, those who put them up and moved aside for them included some of the few musicians and artists who had decided to remain, or were too poor to leave, and who were still then allowed to pursue their crafts with some measure of freedom. They were always courteous and generous with their time and conversation when I met them in the restaurants and cafés to which they could still go. Perhaps they thought I was a spy. I was certainly not that. But perhaps I was in a way, deriving some solace of guilt from being near them, in being half in and half out of a dangerous world – in that I was culpable. An artist had his own laws, I thought – he was a free spirit. He could ignore the history unfolding around him. In his own body and mind he was king; as long as this citadel was preserved from the surrounding plague, he was safe. I was safe. I thought my neighbours were too. They had already developed a new way of breathing, like people in a fire, by holding their breath for a painful age and crawling under the smoke. When the time of the Games came, and all the terrible notices were removed, the yellow benches taken away from the Tiergarten, the city tented in flags and banners, they must have felt it safe at last to gulp in a few draughts of what seemed fresh air.

In our apartment block, my studio consisted of one long high room the walls of which I had whitewashed down the sides, and painted black around the window at one end, and the door at the other. Two roller blinds were fitted to the window; one white, which softened the sun into an even mellow light; the other blue, opaque, which shut off all light from outside. No carpet, the floorboards scrubbed clean. In the centre of the room a plate camera on a tripod faced away from the window to the black wall. Against the wall was a chair and a small table like that used by a conjurer, with a tulip-shaped wine glass and a white cup. A wire-jointed, life-size wooden marionette hung by the shoulders from a coat-stand. Along each wall ran a bench, on one side lined with my trays, lamp, bellows enlarger, above these a shelf with chemicals and printing paper; along the other wall the bench was littered with lenses, cameras of half a dozen sizes and ages, a drawing board, scalpel, rules, a set square; the last third was taken up by heaps of prints slewed across the surface. The shelf above this held boxes full of negatives.

The rest of the apartment?

A kitchen, full of poisonous chemicals.

A sitting room, rarely used, a place for lumber, and a dining table laid always with the same filthy cloth and the remains of last night's meal.

The bedroom. There was no lack of occupants to share this room.

If Berlin, or the parts of it that had excited me, had declined and gone underground, then its sexual life continued privately. Spied on by the block wardens who infested every street, women and men, boys and girls, continued, in whatever combination appealed to them, to love, or couple together.

And as for my girlfriends? If that is not too dismissive a term – perhaps we too, in what I can grandiosely term the artistic community, shared views of women not too far from the Nazis' troika of Children, Church and Kitchen. Though in our case it was Studio, Sex and Sense. The sense was not to get themselves pregnant. The studio was the place. The sex? I had one of those technical manuals they issued in the late Twenties – now of course unavailable. The memory of this book tells me something of myself. There were many plates. Some were in the form of technical information. The outline of a human, male body, cut off at the thighs. In the body all those rounded, bloody, vibrant organs, muscles and veins are replaced by a logical, hydraulic circuitry of chambers, valves and pipes, variously brown, red and blue, arranged like the boiler room of a brand-new steam yacht. The head is a telegraph office whose wires carry information from the accumulators and batteries, bells and coils of the brain down through the body to the receiving station of the testes and penis, their round soft shapes again occupied by these squared pipes and conduits and electrical wires. A few centimetres across the page from the profiled and cut-away eye in this male head is a drawing of a tiny, fairy-like female. She it is who is causing all the sparking and buzzing and signalling to the south . . .

And that is how I sometimes thought of it. The meltings, the flowers, the poetry, the photographs I took, the rows, the angry scenes, the meetings in cafés, the pangs of jealousy at seeing a lover with another man – all, all these were in the end subordinate to my view, as in the book, of sex as not much more than a pleasurable, energetic pastime.

It was Lotte who changed my mind.

4

Valenti and I sat in the beautiful big café on the corner of the Unter den Linden and Friedrichstrasse. I was surprised to be with him. I was no longer an intimate part of his life. He moved in brasher, rougher Party-dominated circles to which I wasn't invited. He hardly ever came out on assignment; editing, dealing and building his position in the agency seemed to be his true interests now. So, when I had said I was going out on the streets, it was a surprise to see him put on his jacket, clamp a cigar between his lips and say, 'I'll come with you, Klinger' (for he never called me by my Christian name in the office). That afternoon we photographed the huge trailer that bore the great cast bronze Olympic bell west towards the Grunewald. Now the crowds that had lined the avenue – cheering, the children lifted up on their fathers' shoulders; the women tearful, waving handkerchiefs – had gone home. It was late evening and the café was full with broad men in fine uniforms, accompanied by their gilt and silver mistresses. 'Let's get out of here,' said Valenti. 'They say they have microphones under the tables and in the lampshades and no doubt in between the bosoms and up the fannies of all these delicious creatures. Who knows.'

We caught a cab.

'Isn't it grand though,' he said, peering out of the cab window at the debris of celebration now being meticulously cleared away by workmen. 'Look at it all. Hey driver,' he said loudly. The driver glanced at us in the mirror. 'Isn't it grand?'

'I haven't stopped all day,' said the driver in that tough guy voice all the Berlin taxi drivers had. 'God knows what it will be like when the foreigners come.'

'You'll earn a fortune,' Valenti shouted. He got the driver to go north and stop at an ordinary working-class bar.

'This is where life is, eh?' he said paying the fare.

'Everyone to his taste,' said the driver.

The bar was full and happy too, but with a different, rougher happiness. The lights were dimmer than in the city restaurants, the clothes poorer, the accents harsher and the laughter with an edge to it I had almost forgotten.

We sat in a corner. Valenti amiably shooed away two girls

who came to the table. 'Later, later,' he said. 'A bit of business first, girls.'

We had gin with beer chasers.

'Salut,' he said chucking the first tumbler down his throat. 'I learnt to drink up here. I can't quite take society now. Know what I mean?'

'I know what you mean.'

'Yes,' he said. He leaned forward over the table looking keenly at me. 'You do. That's the trouble.'

'What on earth do you mean by that?'

'What on earth do you mean by that,' he mimicked. 'What I said to you in the café. It's time to wake up.'

I looked into my beer.

'I gave you this job. You're good. The pictures you take. But you know what Nielsen said about your last lot of shots? He said they looked like a Bolshevik's. I told him, he's an artist, man. Yes, you are. God help you. He just looked at me. Being an artist – that's not too good, now. I made you into one, didn't I, Walther? I took you up on the mountain and showed you the earth. And you grabbed it – as everyone should. Well – perhaps I didn't. You made yourself into one. You do things I can't. But all these uncommon angles – this light and shade and shadow. I couldn't do what you do. No, let me finish.'

He snapped his fingers, smiling, at the harassed waiter. Same again.

He nursed his second gin between his fingers and went on.

'You take the piss. You give the salute like a comedian and mumble out the words. You smile at me when Nielsen gives his little lectures. You think it's not noticed. These people are sensitive. And your pictures take the piss too. You've seen all these things that I have seen. All the artist photographers who've fled away and have got nice billets in London and Paris and New York and you think you can do what they did. You can – *there*. Not here. Faces in close up. Faces obscured by shadows. Faces in half. Multiple exposures, the over-exposures so that you get one of those white-faced tarts there and bleed her face into the white wall so that only her eyes are showing. Negatives. Reflections in distorting mirrors. Streets shot from high up. Buildings shot from low down. Pictures of beautiful fucking eggs. Of stones. Hands. Feet. Feet in mirrors. Surrealism. Realism. Ultra-realism. It is not wanted. It is not fucking wanted. It can get you hanged. You understand me?'

I understood. I argued. Passionately. What harm was a mere image?

'It's the way. The way things are now,' he said. 'I'm trying to protect you. Take those pictures for yourself, if you must. For yourself. Not for the agency. You are in danger.'

'Don't you feel ashamed saying this?' I asked coldly.

He took his beer and looked hard at me. Then he reached his hand over the table and gripped mine.

'Why do you think all these other people left? Not because all of them were Jews or Reds. They couldn't see straight. You know what I'm trying to tell you. Right? Now let's enjoy ourselves. I watch your back. You watch mine. We're mates, OK?'

But I was still angry with him.

'This won't last,' I said. 'Art is stronger . . .'

'Keep your voice down, you idiot,' he said in a low, equable voice. 'Yes, it will last. People want it to last. These people, in this bar – look at them. Are they going to lead a revolt for Art?'

I looked. The ex-Socialists, and union members, and unemployed and tarts and young thieves and their drunk fathers and uncles and mothers and others – all drinking as if there was no tomorrow – perhaps in that hope.

'Look – this is how you do it,' said Valenti patiently.

And he told me how to exist in this present climate. How you must act as if you believed. He hadn't believed. But there was something happening here. It was a great deal more powerful than anything known before. He wasn't one to bend the knee. I knew that. Surely. 'I've always been a rebel, Walther, always will be, but you can't get away from the fact that the country has been turned around. That now we are heading somewhere.' He thumped down his glass of beer.

'What happened to Mitzi?' I asked sometime later, in a drunken haze.

'Who?' he said. 'Oh her. God knows.'

I went on photographing the Games, and the city coloured and enriched by tourists. We were all on our best behaviour; one of my Jewish neighbours remarked that now things could never go back to the way they were. The sun shone, the crowds roared, a German girl dropped a relay baton, the Führer cried. Duly chastened and impressed, hastening away with news of the great experiment on hand in Germany, the foreigners went home.

The festivities over, we began to prepare for war.

I worked hard. My pictures of the Games were impeccably dramatic in the correct, heavily shadowed, sculptural way. My relations with Valenti were outwardly friendly; inwardly the conversation in the café had signalled the end of his hold on my mind. I saw him frankly for what he was; an energetic, ambitious, coarse, youngish man on the make – the things that I shared with him I disliked in myself; and what I thought different in myself I saw had to be protected from him. The fact that he was cynical about the state of affairs made him more dangerous. True believers could not reach into my soul, could not read my mind or look through my eyes. So, I divided my mind. There was my public work. And there was the work I would do as an artist. I didn't of course see that such a division is impossible; that one will leak into the other and that both will in the end be spoiled. The artist becomes too wedded to self-expression, the entertainer too cynical.

5

The telephone rang at about eleven in the morning. I didn't recognise the voice. The woman insisted. 'It is Marthe. Marthe! Herr Klinger.'

Marthe? I couldn't reconcile the voice with the use of the telephone. She must be holding the ancient instrument that stood in the hall at grandmother's and had never been used by anyone but me or Karl during the time I had lived there.

'Your grandmama,' the voice clanged. 'You must come at once.'

'She is ill?'

'What? You must come.' Obviously Marthe had difficulty with the idea of two-way communication on the apparatus.

'My grandmother she's ill?'

'Your grandmother is very ill.' The instrument was abruptly put down at the other end.

I took a cab. The day was very bright; the journey seemed interminable. At the house, the front garden had been freshly tended. The front door was locked. I knocked and rang the bell. It opened on the guard chain and Marthe's face looked up at me. For the first time I saw expression there; the eyes were red with weeping. It seemed unnatural that an old woman should weep. As she let me in she began talking quickly. 'As the mistress required I took the book from her table and the number just inside the front cover, Master Walther if anything should happen in there . . .' She hung back at the door.

My grandmother lay in her chair. It seemed at a great distance across the room and she looked very much smaller. Her head lolled back on the cushion rest and her blue eyes were wide open and her mouth too and a little caked blood ran from one corner and stained brown the edge of her lace collar. I knew of course that she was dead, but for form's sake and because Marthe was watching me from the door I took my grandmother's left hand and felt for a pulse without really trying to locate it. The hand was – a cliché, but they tell the truth – as cold as stone. The occasional table at the side of the chair had been knocked over and letters and photographs were strewn across the floor. One of the old photograph albums had slid from her lap to rest against her right leg. She was now an object to be labelled with sides and directions.

When had she been found? I asked Marthe. An hour or so ago. She had been told not to come until called, but the mistress usually took breakfast about nine. At ten Marthe had grown worried and had knocked and knocked and at last dared to open the door without any summons, to be met with this sight. The bureau stood open; papers and letters had been taken from the drawers and pigeon holes and stacked untidily on the writing top. The untidiness was uncharacteristic, as if my grandmother had been desperately searching for something.

'Did our family have a doctor?'

'Doctor Heyden.'

'Have you his number?'

'Why no.' Marthe stared into the room as if its walls had been removed and the world outside and the universe beyond that had disappeared from view.

The number was in the book that lay by the hall telephone.

The doctor's secretary said that he was visiting and would not be back until the afternoon; was it urgent?

No, I said. No. It wasn't urgent.

I had seen the wounded lying in the street after a battle, seen a man with his leg shattered by gunfire crawling like a crab across a street and screaming as he was then beaten by the police. I had seen the waxen faces of the victims of murderers in police photographs, of accident victims – but never had I seen this complete vacation of a body, its aspect of hardening stone. I sent Marthe away to make coffee. I closed the door quietly and went out to the garden and smoked a cigarette. I ground the butt under my heel and went with a steady stride to the kitchen. I questioned Marthe again as gently as I could.

She had not heard her mistress come to bed.

She herself always went to sleep as the clock struck twelve. She had since she was a young woman, she said proudly. She was in that state of slight delirium that affects people close to a death, where they chatter and memories and whimsies rise to the mind and are expressed without constraint. Some people joke inordinately and badly. Marthe dreamed aloud about the hours and days of her mistress and the years they had been together and every slight ritual that had grown between them. I listened patiently, becoming a little bored. I wondered again where exactly Marthe slept in this house. What was her room like? Her face composed itself into expressions and planes before me; her lips worked as if they were not used to speaking and were growing looser and looser. And all the time in both our heads was the image of my grandmother's white-blue face staring at nothing, the mouth – once set in a precise but mobile line – now gaping, fouled and for ever silent.

The doctor, arriving at last, gave the time of death to the best of his estimation as about midnight the previous night. I was glad Marthe was not in the room to hear that. The doctor advanced into the room, eyed the body with a quick bright sideways glance as he put his bag down, said, 'Oh dear, oh dear,' and tended to his examination with brisk hands. It took very little time. No, he could not give an absolute cause of death. An autopsy was needed. Perfectly standard. The police would have to be informed. The undertakers. He would arrange all that. There would be a fee. The undertakers were excellent men. He flicked a card out of his top pocket. It was the card of the undertakers who had done business with my late Uncle Karl. 'I know them,' I said. 'They seem to be very good at this sort of thing.'

'Somebody has to be,' said the doctor.

I saw him to the door. We shook hands, he clicked his heels in the old manner and walked to his car parked at the gateway. I turned and Marthe was drawing the curtains in the living room. As I say, the day was brilliantly sunny.

We buried Grandmama in the vacant lot beside her husband. The stone letters were freshly chiselled, giving her name and dates.

The funeral brought my mother to the city for the first time since her marriage. 'It has changed a lot,' she said. I burst out laughing at her innocence. 'It has, certainly,' I said.

She had come alone. Peter was too busy with his engineering studies in Bonn it seemed. Mother wanted to put up in a hotel, but I insisted we both stay in the house at Dalhelm. She agreed, but not too happily. The night before the funeral she entered the hall of her mother-in-law's house – how lost and unhappy she appeared among all the heavy furniture and bric-à-brac. I remember ringing and ringing for Marthe to come. And Marthe's look of contempt for my mother, still dressed in her outside coat, perching uncomfortably on the edge of Grandmother's chair.

The next day, after the funeral, my grandmother's old friends – all female – convened in the house. Also, two sisters and an invalid brother in a hooded bath-chair, Grandmama's lawyer, and cousin, Herr Schuckler, and my mother and I assembled in that living room and drank to my grandmother's memory. I was glad Peter was not there. The others seemed grateful too for the absence of the young, according me symbolic status as the one young person present.

My mother was ignored – or rather, she sat outside and subtly excluded from the physical circle these female and sexless relatives made for themselves. They were like a circle of lizards in the sun. Every now and then, out of a punctilious sense of fair play and good manners, the lawyer's voice would chime through to her; he was allowed this part because as well as being employed by the family, he was also a part of it. A man in a beetle-black suit, his silver hair crisp as snow, his long, sensitive, fine features seemingly bred from centuries of scholarship and law – in fact his blood came from the same line of industrialists and peasant farmers made good as the rest of us. In his beautiful, hardly accented English he asked what did Frau Klinger think of this or that international event, of the dangers of war, the impossibility of it occurring between their two great countries England and Germany? My mother's replies were timid, ill-informed, evasive. I felt ashamed for her. And angry with the rest of them. For none of that circle of relatives broke its inner spell by turning to hear her answers or to question her further. There was only one Frau Klinger for them and she had just been interred in clay. The conversation was steered away from politics and entered those minutiae of long-gone family reminiscence from which I, as a youngster, and mother, as a stranger, were debarred.

When they filed out again into the bright sunshine, their stiff clothes rustled like moths reawakening from spring, the bath-chair creaked as regularly as a metronome as the wheels turned. I half expected to find broughams and berlines drawn up outside and the sweet smell of straw and horsedung in the air. Instead there was a chauffeur-driven Mercedes, a hunch-backed, two-seater American coupé – the lawyer's – and three taxi cabs which had been instructed to return at this time of just half-past three.

I raced upstairs and, concealing myself behind the curtain of the window that opened onto a small false balcony, I proceeded to photograph the old women going towards the cabs, their brother, my great-uncle, being lifted like a bundle of firewood into the back of a cab; his chair being strapped to the roof. My mother raised one hand in faltering farewell, her shadow cast brokenly up the steps into the house.

My mother collapsed with a sigh onto the sofa in the drawing room. 'Oh, they are very nice, Walther – but I am so glad they've gone.'

I'd told her that Grandmother had left me the house, and that her allowance was protected by the will.

'That was very good of your nanna,' she said. 'The allowance gets smaller every year, of course. But I don't know what I'd do without it.'

'Why don't you come and live here?' I said. 'I don't want the place – I have a flat in the city. And you'll be out of that horrible town – it's not the same, is it? Not now. And you'll have Marthe here. And Peter can come too. You can live here for nothing – you know that.'

'That's kind of you, Walther. But I couldn't. Not here. This is another woman's house. A woman who didn't particularly like me, I think.' I made to interrupt, but she went on doggedly. 'And I shan't be going back to the spa. It's right what Herr Schuckler was saying here today. There is going to be a war, sooner or later, and I think I'd rather be at home. Did I tell you that I wrote to my sister?'

So she had been deciding for me all this time.

We talked it over that night. She surprised me with the clarity and the thoroughness with which she had thought everything out. She still had her British nationality.

'Well, I'll come with you,' I announced.

There was no need – of course, if I really wanted to . . .

'I'm twenty-five years old,' I said, 'and I've never been anywhere.'

I didn't tell Mother that there was a girl with whom I was involved it would be well for me to avoid for a while. A trip to England would be just the thing.

Poor Paula. My girl, just then. I hadn't been very good to her, I'm afraid. She was a painter – or she had been. She was at a loose end when she met me. Her last lover had gone abroad for his health. I think she had become an artist when she was young because that was the way to meet interesting people. She could still paint and draw, for her own amusement. So she'd stopped. She wasn't good – or bad – enough to persist in the face of adversity. I wouldn't have dreamed of telling her. She came of a good family which frowned on my profession – or lack of one. But I visited her home, and she visited my apartment. We didn't live together. Those things weren't done now. Everyone knew of the party officials with their girls in flats across the city. That was a time-honoured practice for that sort of girl. Not for Paula. It was Paula's feeling that I might marry her that helped to propel me abroad. Not that she was not an enthusiastic lover, and an excellent model. I still have somewhere in my trove a picture of her beautiful conical breasts.

I was glad to get away from her.

6

Berlin to Brussels by train. Brussels to Ostend by train. Ostend to Dover by steamer. From Dover the train chugged through the countryside to brilliant, anxious London. The sky was an addled egg white in the late summer evening. September '38. A fellow passenger's newspaper announced that Mr Chamberlain was to visit Herr Hitler. The Herr registered as a shock. Such an ordinary plebeian title would have been out of the question in my own country, a patronising insult; here it was meant to convey respectability. Outside the station, newspaper sellers compounded it by crying it as 'Her Hitler'. The placards in front of them spoke of war.

In the week that we stayed in the capital my little camera clicked voraciously. I was astonished, for all the talk of war, by the civilian aspect of the place. The lack of uniforms, the tawdriness and dullness of shop windows, the appalling food, the sugary syrup that passed for coffee, the general drabness of clothes, the gust of bad breath from a bus conductor; above all by the fact that no one looked young or well. If they did it was because they were rich, and rich young men and women flashed across streets and in and out of doors like fabulous birds, their hair thick, their colour good, their clothes rich; but for the rest – they were the inhabitants, the workers of a city, its levers and cogs. They were like Berliners and not like Berliners.

The light was better, the sky somehow brighter and higher, as befitted a large straggling city on the banks of a broad river. The air, compounded of traffic fumes and coal smoke and peoples' bodies, was subtly, and utterly, different. These two – the signatures of light and air – are what determine a place. The light I tried to capture – but I had brought my own light with me and the London shown in my photographs is a strange place. Like all immature artists I was attracted by extraordinary juxtaposition; extremes of expression; the darkest of shadows. The London I shot bore no resemblance to any city on earth, except the one in my head.

We left for the west country. The engine trailed its brown-mauve smoke through an anthology of British landscape paintings. That late September was fine, the trees feathery, the fields lushly green in pasture, and shining gold where the harvests were being taken, the hedges rich and round as bolsters on a bed, the towered churches the colour of owls, the Bovril- and Guinness-postered stations, brown and black and flowerbedded at each end of each platform . . . This Arcadia would not last long. I had only a three-month visa. Officials on both sides had pointed out that I would be deported back to my own country if I overstayed my time. Did I intend to stay in England? If I could have done, I would perhaps. I was forced back to my own country then? That would be a facile excuse. I've said already that I'm no rebel.

A small town, this one to which my mother returned. A place of miniature, glassy charm, with its shallow river running down a series of water steps that descended through the town's park-like heart and entered, in twisting, fast flowing rivulets through the sandy beach, the sea. Swans on the river were negatives, black on the silvery water. Ale-houses on each side of the gardens and the river were smoke-ridden and sour-smelling; their residents spoke in a slow indecipherable burr; only out in the street did you hear the quick, irritable rattle of the few middle-class residents.

My mother's sister lived in a neat white curved corner cottage with curved walls, curved windows, and a flat front door. She welcomed my mother home as if she had been released from prison. 'Oh, you made it safely, then,' she cried. 'There's going to be a war. Oh dear. Oh dear, I'm sorry. I didn't mean,' catching sight of me looming large in her doorway.

There was going to be a war. But Mr Chamberlain was going to sort things out with Herr Hitler. After all, how could good young men – myself – be pitched against other good young men – she pointed to the window, to the deserted street. My aunt made much of me those first few days, though with sublimated distaste – I was half-German, a sort of chimera produced mysteriously years before by her sister and brought back like a sinister gift in a fairy tale.

The great news came on the radio. We all hurried off to the local cinema at the weekend and watched the newsreel of Chamberlain, who, like a grave, moustachioed parrot in a long coat held up his hotel bill and said it had been countersigned by Herr Hitler – there it was again, that touch of the lower orders that Hitler could not shake off in foreign eyes, like a suspicious mothbally scent about the clothes. Mr Chamberlain said there would be peace for our time. The whole audience in the cinema cheered and clapped. My fame as the German had gone before me. Beefy farmers' sons craned round in their seats to see me.

My hand was seized and pressed warmly. I half expected to be carried through the streets in triumph. 'Thank God for that. There'll be no war,' said my mother quietly when we got back to my aunt's.

The place was insufferably dull. There was obviously no future for me in the cottage. As the days passed I could see my mother settling more and more into the routines of her sister. My aunt asked, 'Have you a nice job then, back home?' She spoke in the quick, refined accent of the bourgeoisie. My mother's voice, absent for so many years from intimacy with its own language, sounded mellower and firmer and perhaps a little out of time.

October, November – my time was nearly up. The truth was that I was excited by the thought of going home. If there was to be peace perhaps the whole situation would change. I had my work that I had neglected, my rooms, the house in Dalhelm, a life that this sleepy town knew nothing of. I was, I was astonished to find, homesick.

I will skip the farewells. My mother was settled, probably for life. I went home in November.

7

As soon as I put my case down in my apartment the telephone began to ring. I was tired. I'd spent the day before in the train to London, then a taxi out to Croydon from Waterloo to catch a night flight, or rather a wintry evening flight to Brussels. I had

had to wait for a connection and finally we took off before dawn and flew into the cold white round of the sun rising behind cloud. I had slept in the taxi from the Berlin field. I let the phone ring. It was probably Paula. I had said I was going away, but not for how long. She was annoyed. She had probably been ringing every day of my absence. It rang and rang. At last it ceased. I went into my bathroom and stripped and started to run a bath when the phone began again.

Cursing I put on my robe and marched across the studio floor. I picked up the receiver. 'Klinger. Yes?' I said irritably.

It wasn't Paula.

'Walther? Lotte Abrahams.'

I'd met Lotte many times. She was in her late thirties and had been the most famous fashion and society photographer in Berlin – until the new connoisseurs came along. I hadn't seen her for a year. I knew that things were not good for her now, but she still managed to put on a show each autumn and I spotted her work in the magazines that came in from abroad. I'd gone to her shows, though the numbers daring to attend had dropped off as her friends disappeared abroad and others thought it wiser not to be seen at a Jewish event. I'm ashamed to admit that I hadn't turned up the previous year. She was still about, but I didn't quite know why. Why on earth hadn't she gone when she could, with the others in '33 or '34 or '35?

'Lotte – how lovely to hear from you.'

'I got your number from your agency. I hope you don't mind?' It was strange for Lotte to sound in the least apologetic about anything. 'It's just that last night I was working – then you know. I locked myself in the studio here . . .'

'Why – what happened last night?'

'You don't know?'

'I only got back from England this morning.'

'England?' She made it sound as far away as China. She began to laugh. 'Some luck. Take a cab. Come to the gallery.' She gave me directions to the back entrance. 'And knock, don't ring, so I'll know it's you.'

'What in God's name happened here?' I asked the taxi driver as we came into the centre of the city. Many shop windows had been smashed. People skirted round the glass that still lay on the pavement. In pairs the police, the ordinary Schupos, looked on silently as here and there a man brushed broken glass towards the gutter. A fresh, furious rash of anti-Jewish slogans had been scrawled and painted on walls and whatever remained of the windows of stores and businesses.

The driver stopped at the traffic lights. He looked back over his shoulder and weighed me up in that way all cab drivers have. 'They took after the Jews last night,' he said evenly, coolly. There was no hint of triumphalism in his voice; also none of condemnation.

Lotte's gallery was on the Kurfürstendamm. Her professional name, *LOMA*, stood in two-foot-high chrome letters above the long front window with its chrome surround, the glass black except for a clear eye shape outlined in the centre, a black focal cross quartering the pupil. Through the eye you could glimpse white walls and framed photographs, perhaps even Lotte herself, tall and thin, her black and white clothes making her seem a moving, elegant portrait. It must have been a sitting target of course – and sure enough as we drew level I saw that the whole window had gone. The glass had fallen backwards and lay in large black shards on the fawn carpet; in the middle a path had been made of glass shattered into tiny fragments where the front gallery had been invaded. Pictures had been daubed with swastikas or their frames ripped from the walls and trampled under foot.

'Here?' said the driver.

'A little way on.' I'd seen an SS man looking with interest at the cab.

Untouched shops stood self-righteously among the broken windows and the goods tumbled out on the pavement. Bizarrely, although it was a cold day in November, and after all of this, a couple sat wrapped in furs outside a café, drinking coffee and chattering brightly. Quite a few shoppers were about, hurrying this way and that, seemingly oblivious to the destruction on each side.

'Turn here.' The corner of the department store curved into a side street. A little way down was an alley for delivery and service entrances.

I paid him off and went down the alley. From the higgledy-piggledy backs it was hard to judge which smart frontage belonged to which steamed-up window and air vent and peeling door. I counted as best I could and came to the block that housed Lotte's studio. A yard half full of trash cans, a row of three steps to a door with a long tally of brass and wooden tablets listing obscure companies with grandiloquent names – *The Atlas Mercantile Trading Company, Intercontinental Securities and Bonds, The Adrienne Clinic for Herbal and Astrological Remedies*. Dirtied white strips of card pushed into brass holders gave the names of private residents in the flats above; engraved black in a silver-coloured square plate, *LOMA*.

I pushed open the door. Inside the hallway was a nest of postal boxes, like pigeon coops one above the other, faced in netting with a slot for the letters.

At the end of the corridor was a typed notice above a bell push: '*LOMA – Deliveries. Please Ring.*' As instructed, I knocked.

Strange, but I didn't feel afraid. We had grown so used to the abnormal being presented as normal in those days, that all this seemed somehow inevitable.

Her voice came through the door. 'Who is it?'

'Walther.'

The sound of a bolt being drawn back; the door opened.

Lotte. Beautifully dressed, unflustered, not a hair out of place, but in the cold bare electric light of the lobby into which I stepped her face was cruelly exposed, her eyes too large, the skin on the sharp cheekbones stretched too tightly.

She bolted the door behind me and led me into the dark-room.

She'd been working in here, she said, when she'd heard the first shouts outside; the running footsteps in that sudden concerted way she had come to know too well; the sound of large, hard-bodied men in a joyful rush to licensed violence. She'd drawn the curtain between her and the room where she had been developing and opened the door to the gallery – just at the moment when the front window was smashed in by truncheons. In the shadow, and with the storm troopers' own excitement – 'They do get terribly excited doing these things, you know' – she hadn't been seen. She had shut the door, a heavy one as luck would have it, bolted it and then locked herself in the darkroom. They had clumped about, amid sounds of splintering and tearing and shouts of triumph. The door had been tugged at and pounded, but they had no reason to believe anyone was in, and after a couple of minutes a whistle had blown and they had moved off up the street.

She tried to light a cigarette, but her hands were trembling. I took the matches and did it for her. She didn't care about herself, she said, but what if they were arresting all her friends? She hadn't dared risk ringing any of them. It was impossible to ask them to come here anyway. She knew I was a friend. A fellow artist. And I could get about the city. I didn't mind, did I? If I was in any danger, of course I must leave immediately. She would quite understand. These things quietened down. Come nightfall she might be able to leave.

She sighed heavily and looked around helplessly, avoiding my eyes.

'But I don't even know if I can go to my flat. I rang there and my maid answered, terrified, and said they had been there. I just don't know where to go for the best.'

I felt flattered that she had chosen me. She was perhaps exaggerating the danger, but I must help. She could not go to my flat – Kurten, the block warden, was already convinced that I was a loose-living Bohemian type to be watched. I had no doubt that I figured high on his painstakingly assembled weekly report to the Gestapo – written, I imagined, on cheap, blue-lined notepaper, in schoolboy copperplate.

'I have a house out at Dahlem. My grandmother's old place. It's been empty all summer. I meant to let it when I got back. You can stay there until this blows over.'

'I hate even to ask,' she said.

'I'll arrange for the front of the gallery to be put right, and make sure it's secure.'

'Ah, Walther – you are a godsend – but I think that might be beyond even you.'

Marthe had left the day after her mistress's funeral. I wouldn't need the house, she said, nor her. She would go back to her home village in Pomerania. It astonished me that Marthe had somewhere to go to; I had never imagined any existence for her outside this house. I pressed some money on her as she stood in the kitchen doing up her coat, a shabby, roped-round suitcase by her side. I told her I had to rush into town. She would let herself out, she said.

When I came back later that day she had gone. The money I had given her was beside the household keys on the table.

So the house was dark and shuttered when a cab deposited Lotte and me in the driveway.

Lotte was there for just over two months, until early in '39.

I have the pictures she took; she left them with me for safe keeping. They are unlike any she had ever done before. Her industry in those two months shamed me. I saw how a true artist works incessantly in any surrounding. I knew then that I had been merely playing; a gifted, fortunate amateur. She taught me a lot – about everything. How much I have retained is another matter.

'Do you mind if I photograph your house?' she asked. 'I have no other material.'

In her pictures the house has been minutely photographed,

as if an insect with its multi-lensed eye had crawled into every corner, over each item of furniture, over every square centimetre of carpet or woodwork or wall. Only now and then does a window give a glimpse, a sliver of the world outside, and always, though I may be being fanciful, with the suggestion of a barred window at the edge of the photograph. But that sort of sentimental symbolism would not have occurred to Lotte. Occasionally a mirror catches glimpses of her, the side of her face, oval, fearless, animal, behind the rectangular camera; but always the camera's one blank eye stares out, not at her own image, but at the object of her intense scrutiny.

Sometimes that was me. Sometimes Lotte.

It could be understood from the pictures that what existed between us was a sexual affair. A strange one admittedly; not the subservient one that exists sometimes between a model and an artist, but one where the roles of artist and model were interchanged as the dark box was handed from one to the other.

So, in the pictures – I have some of them here, others are in envelopes in that locked room at Dahlem – Lotte comes on stage. Clothed. In candlelight. In the light from the north-facing windows upstairs, her face clowning and deadly serious and smiling and staring straight at the camera – no artifice – though there always is artifice, she said, just by the pointing of the camera by the taker, the preening of the takee.

And Lotte is here, in my head most vividly as the woman of the photographs that I was privileged to take. On some she wrote on the back in red crayon with an ironic exclamation mark, *'Exhibit!'*

She ordered me to take her as I wanted. She insisted that if

I had the camera I must tell her what to do, but all the time I knew she was the true mistress of the light. We consulted on how far or near her body should be; her merest gesture. She had become all of her models and none of them – simply Lotte. As if there was anything ever so simple. In any human being.

Lotte, like all women, looked utterly different out of her clothes. A thin, tall woman, but yet her pear-like breasts and large hips were a surprise. She insisted on scrubbing her face before the photographs and I was astonished to meet through the lens the pale rather plain, beaky features of a professional art school model. Lotte asked me to take her on the double bed she had found in one disused room. I knew at once that this must be the original bedroom of my grandmother and grandfather. I was surprisingly timid, puritanical – no, I did not wish to disturb their ghosts. Might she sleep in this room, then?

And reading over that passage above I am suddenly aware that the word 'take', like the word 'shoot', has of course another meaning. There was no question of 'taking' Lotte in the sexual sense. As I say, the pictures we both took would almost certainly tell to a stranger the story of an affair. But, read by me – and I am the only one likely to see them now, I fear – they tell a different story. There are the two of us in the house that first night. The second night I make a dinner for her. When I come in from the kitchen with a bottle of wine and lean over her shoulder and pour the pale gold into her glass she looks up at me and smiles and I lean down and kiss her gently on the lips. My hand is on her shoulder.

After a little while, perfectly judged by her, she withdrew her mouth, as a servant withdraws his hand from the table, his body through a doorway. 'That was very nice of you, Walther,' she said. 'That was very nice in itself, my dear. Sit down.' I sat at the right-hand corner of the long table and she at the head. 'The food is appalling. The wine is gorgeous. You are most attractive,' she said sipping at her wine, laying her fork gently across the pale and hard grey-fleshed fish I had misprepared – 'But you must know – I simply don't take men as lovers. Give me your hand.'

So then, knowing that I could not know her in that way – language is slippery, 'take', 'know', 'shoot' – the only thing she could teach me was how to make an image in the camera – to take her through the lens.

She lay on the bed in the room that was once Karl's – I had no sentimental objection. Her body, rotated through the lens in the meagre light of a December morning, the trees outside bare, our neighbours' brown-tiled roofs under the brown Berlin sky, the oil stove burning in this room – the secret of how the house was warmed and fed had disappeared to Pomerania with Marthe. Her body. There was nothing remotely pornographic in these shots – though I suppose you could say that by their very remoteness and cold beauty they would appeal – to whom? I thought of those southern-venturing Germans at the turn of the century, with their Capri albums of slender youths with enormous dangling genitals. Would they find Lotte beautiful? No – they were trapped in male beauty like flies in jam. There was no possibility of beauty in growth or decay for those boys. You would have to have loved Lotte to love my pictures of her.

So, here is Lotte, as taken by me. Shot from head down, her body dwarfish – or from huge feet upwards, her knees like boulders, her sex plum-like, closed, thinly haired – now covered by her fingers, by her whole hand. She simply wished to appear as her own animal on that bed. Those pictures have gone. Somewhere in Dahlem. I hope my brother doesn't find them. In the pictures of Dahlem I have with me, Lotte is clothed most elegantly.

In my grandmother's room, Lotte stands, smiling beside the newly opened left-hand curtain. The furniture looks more ancient than I remember. Here she is in my own bedroom, on my single bed, clothed, reading, or smiling with a broad triumphant grin at the camera. And by some paradox, these pictures of her are far more erotic, in that she seemed so perfectly an easy part of my room, as wives or lovers are a part and the whole of their rooms, so that they enter into a room, belong to its light and furnishing and the room as no other room and the lovers and the room share a mutual regard. I have two of these pictures and can fill in the time between them. I linger over them.

Would I have wanted to have been Lotte Abrahams' lover? I was in love with her, in a new and peculiarly subtle way that disturbed and made me happy at the same time. I would have loved her and protected her for ever. Of course, I would. Only life doesn't arrange itself that way.

Does it, Life?

For that is what we all worshipped, the Nazis more than most. Life, with a capital L. The body as a temple of light and muscle and cleanliness. The brain as an enormous, clangorous hall, resounding with shouts, paved and walled with engraved absurd, absurdly observed rules, with offices off here and there inhabited by scholarly homunculi endlessly carving fresh tabuli – and behind, somewhere hidden in the walls, the groans of the broken-ribbed, smash-toothed, perfectly bloody nuisances. And the broad, paved corridors of this building lead to the entrance of a vast arena, hung with flags, the topmost tiers of seats so high that they were plagued by clouds . . .

I look at them now, and see that in my pictures of Lotte there was for the first time human warmth. She was looking at her lover, the camera, and she was happy with what her lover recorded.

Here she is dancing in a parody of Isadora Duncan, a long, unfatal silk scarf trailing across the room like silver vapour. Eating a meal. Looking out of the window at the garden. She could not enter the garden; she didn't think it safe. She wasn't afraid for herself – she didn't want to compromise me.

Then another woman comes into view; tall, dark-haired, extremely beautiful. And now Lotte has the camera – I was away – I must have been away, I never saw this woman in the house. Images of this woman in the kitchen, the dining room, my darkroom, standing calm, self-possessed, the mistress of her image in the eyes of her beloved, a thin stream of grey smoke rising from the cigarette she holds in the hand posed elegantly away from her hip.

And Lotte has carefully written the date and time of taking on the back of each of these pictures: 13-XII-1938, 10:42; 14-XII-1938, 13:20, so that one could arrange the pictures in order and trace like a story the woman's progress through the house and the state of the light and the weather through the glimpses of windows behind her.

The woman disappears.

From then on Lotte's pictures change. There are no more pictures of the house. Instead endlessly repeated examinations of simple objects; a white plastic conical lampshade, a steel coffee pot, a tennis ball, a pencil – not taken with all the usual trickeries of light and angles and perspective such as you find in the manuals of photography – '*How To Become A Most Original Artist This Afternoon*' sort of thing. No, quite the opposite. She seems to have selected the objects for their essential banality and made no attempt to redeem it by artistry. She used the north-facing room that was my studio and these photographs, dozens of each object, vary only with the state of light outside the window; and in her favourite barest brightest light cast by the snow outside they seem to shrink and shiver away from their own banality. What were they for, these pictures? 'When all this is over I shall hold an exhibition,' she said. 'In Paris. I've had enough of beauty and the rich. Won't they be surprised.' She looked at her pictures and she said, 'It is all nonsense, this idea of art, Walther.' She talked of the impossibility of art existing as an abstract quality, to be determined by its practitioners. Art was created by artisans, not artists, she said. The masons of the cathedrals. The Chinese potters; the Japanese book illustrators. Bach and Mozart were journeymen. Michelangelo, a man employed to *make*. The negro trumpeter we had both heard at a club in 1932 had no intention of creating angelic sounds. All of these were workmen, producing work. I had shown her one of Paula's paintings. It had no talent, she said with an irritated finality. Looking at it again, I had to agree, and felt sorry for Paula. And for Lotte. She knew it was too late for art; too late for Paris; all those frontiers were closing for ever.

She was bored with being a kindly treated prisoner. She wanted the city back. She announced bluntly after Christmas that she could stay no longer. She was earning no money. She would get a room from friends near to my apartment block in the city.

All her money had gone into the shop that she was no longer allowed to own. We cooked up a plan before she left. I would buy from her the remaining lease of the shop and the existing company. I couldn't possibly give her the true value of her goodwill and reputation and contacts and this and that . . . but she would get everything back when the present madness ended. I would run the business as her front. 'I trust you, Walther,' she said. I had a document drawn up by a neighbour in my apartment block, a Jewish lawyer. It had no legal validity, but I insisted on it as some sort of moral declaration. It laid out that I was not in reality the owner of the business but that it should revert to Lotte at any time she requested. It was purely cosmetic – but it made me feel better.

I had to get official forms re-registering the business to an Aryan. When I took them back signed by Lotte, the clerk smiled at the cash price shown. 'A bargain, sir?' he said, banging at the papers with his fine array of inked stamps. 'We'll make them pay, eh?'

Lotte and I returned to the city, in darkness, to her new home in the apartment she had arranged. She would write. I would write. She would phone – even the most ingenious of the Nazis had not yet devised a way of dividing Jews by voice alone – though the public call boxes were forbidden to them. We wouldn't meet – many of the new cosy arrangements were being monitored to make sure that Jews derived the minimum benefit from the theft of their businesses and property. 'You could go to prison, Walther.'

I had the gallery redecorated. I used the studio, the darkroom. Soon I built myself a clientele of the new society who came to have their photographs taken. The new society of party bosses. I took a delight for a time in thinking that a large percentage of the fees they paid me was going to Lotte, a Jewish woman making her money from the portraits of men showing off their new uniforms, decorations, mistresses. It was the sort of irony that Berlin was full of – and the sort that encouraged what false and deadly optimism there was, that the system could be thwarted, parodied, guyed in a hundred different secret ways. Never was optimism more horribly misplaced.

Now it must surely be a bombed ruin, that shop. And Lotte? God help us all with what became of her.

This is what I have found necessary to tell.

The time for, of, the personal is over.

BOOK II

1

Major Preidel painted the sea in careful water colours on thick white cartridge paper. He rendered it as a series of limpid pools with the gliding red-spotted plaice that abound off the coast pinned like butterflies under washes of pale green.

Lieutenant Klinger felt superior. He knew that the true sea did not interest Preidel; that Preidel probably never saw anything, only these sentimental renditions.

Below the cliff on which the guard tower was built the water came into a shallow, white, inaccessible beach; the high tide beat against the grey and black rocks and spray went spitting halfway up the tall cliff. In the shallows of the bay, when the sea was calm, the water appeared to be variously coloured but only because of the white or green or deep blue stone it covered. In a series of clearly demarcated lines going away from the beach, the sea was at first a thin, pure, yellowy-blue, further out a pale aquamarine, then, after another curved line, a deep royal blue, and then the chopped and heaving waves absorbed whatever colour the sky made overhead. Klinger had tried to photograph the sea many times but the results had been always unsatisfactory: colour film misrepresented it subtly but totally; black and white turned it into a series of compositions that seemed too studied, too artistic.

There was plenty of leisure, and boredom, to be artistic. Otto List, his fellow lieutenant, was translating Ovid. *The*

Metamorphoses. 'We are all in exile, Walther,' he had said to Klinger – what could be more appropriate than to translate a poet who died in exile. Klinger had said nothing. He wondered if Otto was being deliberately provocative, as people were to catch you out. He knew him better now.

The Captain, Wahl, was writing a history of the neighbourhood and its customs. He had no fondness for them, but he had been an anthropologist before the war – at the Society for Research and Teaching of Ancestral Heritage – and so he noted intently the legends and rites of the local area and its people. He intended, as he confided to Klinger, to publish his findings in at least one great, footnoted volume, perhaps two, with his own sketches, and Klinger's photographs – 'if, of course, you are willing'. And Klinger had said, yes, of course, if he could be of any help – and thought that Wahl had no more sense than to imagine that these things, these idle, fatuous studies, had any value, that they could still go on in any possible way, given what faced them in the next few months. The odd thing was that they did go on . . .

Dietrich, the political officer, had no cultural pursuits. He drove from the tiny port where they were based into the nearby town as often as possible. Klinger knew that Dietrich didn't like any of his fellow officers; he suspected their belief in final victory, their loyalty, but even Dietrich had to have some relief from patriotism. He had a widow in town. He went quite openly to her house and was obviously confident that not only did none of his fellow officers know about the woman, but the local inhabitants were also ignorant. The local priest had dared to warn Wahl that Dietrich might be in danger. Wahl told Klinger this, shaking his head – not because of the danger, but because of the dark hair of the woman, her immorality. No one had told Dietrich. He was disliked, but what was the point in antagonising him? The war would be over in one, two years at the most and they would lose. No one said this; no one dared say this. Klinger only ever talked about such things to Otto.

They'd discussed the war while walking on the cliffs one evening soon after Otto had arrived at the unit. Klinger asked, tentatively, testing the new man, how did Otto think that things were going. The East . . . ? It didn't look too good, did it? To his astonishment Otto had said, in his clipped, precise but pleasant manner, that they had already effectively lost, in the way at least that there could be no conclusive victory; the question was how they might honourably extricate themselves – meaning their country, their army, themselves – from disaster. And Klinger, skirting round such direct talk still, said only, perhaps there would be a negotiated peace. There was too much that stood to be lost in people, in things, if the Allies insisted on unconditional surrender. The whole could not be destroyed. Otto looked at him, then smiled. 'You haven't been East,' he said.

They walked on in the spring dusk; white and blue butterflies lurched from clover to clover. 'One thing that struck me,' Otto said. 'My last posting was in a POW camp for the British. I was censor for the prisoners' letters. They talked, they wrote incessantly of what they would do after the war. None of our men ever do that, have you noticed?'

Klinger looked round carefully and said, 'That's because some of them want it to go on and on, and for the others there seems to be nothing else but to go on – they can't see any other outcome.'

Klinger would have liked to sit on the grass at the cliff edge but they were officers, and the men looking down from the armoured tower would have seen them. So, when Otto didn't answer, he remarked that these were just like the cliffs over there, the same flowers. Even the grass was the same.

'They were joined once,' said Otto. 'A few thousand years and geology have robbed us of victory.'

Klinger didn't know if it was safe to laugh. He looked at Otto and Otto was smiling. Then he asked how Klinger knew about the other cliffs. He had been over there in '38, Klinger explained. Didn't Otto know that he was half-English? His mother came from the south coast of England. 'Don't tell Dietrich, for heaven's sake.'

'He'll know already,' said Otto. 'Dietrich knows everything about everybody. He keeps files on us. It's his job. And we know about his little *amour*.'

'It isn't the same thing,' said Klinger, frowning. 'Not of the same level of importance.'

Otto asked him for a cigarette. He'd pay him back when they went in again. The little flame of Klinger's lighter fluttered in the breeze and he cupped it in his hand, the perforated steel shield growing hot as his new friend bent over and sucked at his cigarette.

There were any number of ways to feel fraudulent. Klinger's disability, his excuse for soft duties, was passing. He had been in Brest where he had been photographing for *Signal* the gallant recovery made after heavy air-raids. He had had the camera to his eye when a delayed-action bomb burst in the middle of the day. The effects of blast can be most peculiar. A man sitting in a car had his head taken clean away. Another, whom Klinger had posed three metres in front of him, holding a piece of an American plane's wreckage, had his uniform and body shredded with glass and wooden shards. Another, standing on the sea wall, pointing down to the submarine pens, was left completely naked, looking with surprise where his left arm had been detached, and then falling forward, dead. For Klinger himself, the blast passed round and through his head with the sound of an enormous door shutting. As if a huge bell clanged once and its reverberations ever more slightly vibrated into silence. For days the sounds of the world were bafflingly absent; then slowly, like a mouse squeaking, the world began to return in his right ear – the left was entirely useless. Klinger didn't say how much he had recovered in the right ear – one thing the army teaches is that any advantage that can be wrung from it is to be prized. He hadn't asked to join the army; the best thing was to remain ignorant of its commands.

The underground hospital was only a quarter full – it had been built to prepare for the invasion – and he was soon released. But where to put him? Although in uniform, he had been effectively a journalist. There had been a diminution in their numbers anyway – the market for good news from France had withered with the eastern reverses. There was little point in sending him home, it was explained; the army was not short of men; nobody wanted them at home. He had a trade. He was a photographer. He was sent up the coast to Major Preidel's outfit.

They were called an Auxiliary Surveying Unit.

There was something wrong with all of them. Major Preidel, their immediate commanding officer, was almost sixty and an engineer by trade. He had been wounded in the last war and sympathised with Klinger's condition. He always spoke loudly and clearly, and Klinger cocked his head to hear him. The Major confided one night over brandy, his voice dropping so low that Klinger had to hunt after it, that when he had first come home from the trenches he had refused to have a telephone in his office, as the sudden ringing would cause him to tremble and feel faint.

Otto was the youngest. Slightly built, wispy fair hair, round wire-rimmed spectacles, a ruddy face, a limp to his right leg. He had been in Russia, which gave him credibility as a soldier. Otto was their cartographer. Klinger knew from his glowing enthusiasm what great comfort Otto took from seeing the world in maps. The abstractions from reality where a country's inhabitants disappear and the unruly, sprouting land is pleasantly reduced to pale shades of brown and green, hills are the whorled fingerprints of giants, trees are deciduous globes, or evergreen cones, the habitations of men, women and children become tiny hollow boxes, a watermill a star, a lighthouse a candle, a ruined round of battlements a Greek key pattern, a church a crucified man. He had too his Ovid, *The Metamorphoses* – finding more comfort in that rich, racing language put into cool German couplets. And, despite his unathletic build, Otto was a surprisingly good swimmer and sailor. 'The sea is the one element a cripple can conquer,' he said to Klinger.

And there was Wahl, who had no obvious disability besides being in his early fifties, and slightly mad. And Dietrich, coastal defence expert, artillery man, had a steel plate in his back from the Battle for France; thirty years old. He looked across at Klinger and Otto with a sort of leer whenever they talked together in the mess, calling out, 'Can you hear me, Klinger? Oh you can, eh?' and then turning back to his companion, laughing and mouthing something Klinger really could not hear.

And Klinger's position in this crew?

He was the photographer and artist of the unit. Not an artist in the sense of the war artists whose work he had seen in London before the war. Nevinson. Wyndham Lewis. They, although attached to active service units at the front, had had great freedom and produced dark, mechanistic anti-war images. No, Klinger's gifts were employed by the army on a strictly utilitarian basis. The object of the unit was to survey the coast, to search for weaknesses of advantage to an invader, to identify the cracks in this neglected and strategically unimportant part of the Atlantic Wall. So, every morning, Wahl or Dietrich, as briefing officer, stood in front of the large map in the ground-floor room of the tower and pointed out the section where Klinger and Otto would work that day – which was one square up from where they had worked yesterday, and the next square was where they would work tomorrow. Where Klinger must photograph and sketch, and Otto map and report on, the beautiful, alien coastline.

This was only Klinger's third week into this duty with Otto. They shared a billet, and he felt already that he could trust him. It was necessary, more than necessary, that one learn to ask the right questions of one's companions and be able to judge the answers – given the oblique and coded way in which they were obliged to speak to each other.

Klinger hadn't told Otto everything about himself; but then we never do tell quite all that is discreditable to our own selves. Otto had an innocence and openness about him that was rare and perhaps dangerous and which Klinger could not resist. How he had kept that innocent quality Klinger had no idea. Otto was open too about his writing, but Klinger hadn't felt able yet to tell him what he had written down in the long winter nights of last year, in the notebooks he kept hidden behind the headboard of his bed.

Klinger had written in cheap exercise books easy to fold and hide. There were none covering the present. They were his past – those he had marked *The Age of Gold, The Age of Silver* – he had added these titles after Otto had talked to him about the classical divisions of time. He had reached *The Age of Bronze*, but had written only one sentence in the past few months, 'The time for, of, the personal is over.' Perhaps there would be a book too for *The Age of Iron.* For the Future. If there was to be a future.

THE AGE OF IRON

1

They took out the small fishing boat, the *Star of the Sea*. Both of them wore jerseys and corduroy trousers, not uniforms, so that passing enemy planes would mistake them for fishermen. With Otto in the wheelhouse, they puttered up the coast and stopped off at the day's allotted patch. This morning it was a small, horseshoe-shaped, silver-sanded bay. There was no pill-box on top of the cliff; it looked quite sheer. When they pulled in a little closer Klinger saw a very narrow gap between the cliffs. A diagonal cleft that might hold a steep path and only gave itself away where the base of the cliff opened in a triangular spread of fallen scree. Otto got out his French pre-war maps and the latest army charts. There was no sign on either set of the break, nor of a path on the cliff above. The French sheet showed an isolated farmhouse about half a kilometre inland set among emblematic trees, with a dotted track leading to the coast road, which ran away a fair distance to the next village. The house looked substantial; a black L-shape with smaller squares and rectangles indicating barns or outhouses arranged in a square. Their own army map had the track and the surrounding wood, but no house was marked. 'Lazy bastards – they must have thought the track led to the cliffs and not even bothered to go along it,' said Otto. 'If I can get up that path, I'll have a look later,' said Klinger.

The sun was high. Klinger took out one of the sheets from his portfolio and began to sketch the coast. His brisk pencil censored its impulse to elaborate and invent, drawing first the undulating line of the cliff-top, here and there spiking in bushes and wind-twisted trees, then he hung, like a stage curtain, the surface of the cliffs themselves, down to the base, broken by the rocks that ran along the top of the sand. He marked the drawing into segments, each of which he would photograph later.

Klinger waded ashore, holding his pack above the water. The boat stood off and anchored. He found that the crack in the cliffs was a complete if narrow path upwards. It was steep and rough going; loose pebbles tumbled away under his feet and added freshly to the outspill at the bottom.

Coming out at the top, Klinger waved down; Otto waved back and then sat in the shadow of the wheelhouse, took out his book and bent his head to read.

On the cliff Klinger couldn't hear the sea. The cry of gulls came to him in a distant tinny way. He wasn't cured yet, thank God. It was hot already. He sat and laid the waterproof pouch that contained his camera and notebook carefully on the short dry grass. About a kilometre inland, a discontinuous line of short scrubby bushes and trees showed the coastal road. Across the fields was the wood that hid the buildings shown on the map. He had no inclination to go over there just yet. Soldiering is largely a matter of boredom aggravated by intrusion; moments of such wonderful, airy privacy were rare. He stretched, resting after his climb to the top. He folded his arms round his raised legs, chin on his knees, smelling the rough sweet tarry cloth of a non-uniform. Directly in front of him, over a bare patch of sandy ground, a colony of ants crossed and recrossed, intent on their tasks, sometimes avoiding each other, sometimes scrambling blindly over each other; one struggled at a tiny pebble, turning it under its legs like an acrobat on a ball; the ant fell, and scurried on its way, unperturbed, under the interlocking shadows of a blade of grass and a cinquefoil the size of a cathedral.

Klinger lay back. At such moments, for a self-absorbed man, an artist, a fulfiller of his own destiny, a half-crock, a lazy soldier, it was possible to forget the war. High above in the cloudless sky, he saw a formation of silver darts, a long vee of twenty or so planes, all silent to his ears. Enemy, American, going to the ports again. He let them go. Their vapour trails slowly disintegrated into woolly lines. He willed himself back into the state of grace he thought he deserved.

To the north the grape-purple, the green and white breaking sea sparkled. Silent countryside to the south. Ahead of him, distant to the west, Ushant, the ancient edge of the world. At his back, the most of France, the all of Germany, and over the interminable plains of Poland, Russia, the continent endlessly dropped further and further into the east, evening, and night.

He got up, and walked back to the edge of the cliff.

'I see your wood,' he shouted down. 'I'm going to look for the house.'

Otto shouted back. Klinger couldn't hear him. He pointed to his bad ear. He held up the map and camera case. 'It'll take me an hour or so.' And Otto shouted back again, cupping his hands round his mouth. 'Dangerous' – that was the only word

Klinger caught. He smiled down and waved. 'Wait for me,' and he stepped away from the edge and out of view again.

Of course there were Resistance people here, but the flat, sparsely wooded country was not good territory. Things had been quiet for a long time. Perhaps the bastards were saving their powder for the invasion; or perhaps the hostage-taking and shootings of last year had stilled them. It was amazing how quickly one accepted such barbarities – if one of your comrades is shot, you shoot ten men – your comrade is more valuable to you than ten other men. There was nothing he could do about it. And even Klinger felt, however he rebelled against it, a sense of comradeship. *Esprit de corps*. You are encouraged to value your comrade above all others, and he must do the same. So you wish revenge for the loss of your comrade. It is what armies are organised on. Today Klinger was happy and immortal. The war would end soon, or it would not end soon – an hour is enough for happiness.

He left the uncultivated edge of the cliff and came to ploughed fields full of spring crops. He had to make a dog-leg down a strip between the fields, then turn and walk along the low sparse hedge that led directly up to the wood where the map showed a farm.

He photographed the wood and its fence from twenty metres off. As he came close he saw that some of the fence palings had rotted and fallen in. He stepped between them and made his way through the trees. The tall oak wood was an illusion. It was no more than three trees deep. Behind its screen was an orchard; plum on one side of an overgrown grass path edged with grey irregularly sized stones, apple on the other. The apple trees' trunks were twisted and bent almost horizontal under the weight of bearing fruit for so many years. The plum trees were thin and wizened, their trunks lined with flaking, striated bark. Ahead was a high brick wall; in it a wooden door. Cresting the wall a farm, a manor house faced with grey stone.

Klinger photographed the orchards, for their ancient beauty. The sunlight lay like a warm, still liquid varnish on the leaves and the brown, barely grassed soil beneath. He came to the door in the wall. It was a little way ajar, its hinges rusted. It creaked and stuck and the wood bent back rottenly so that he had to force himself between it and the jamb.

A flagged courtyard; two stones' width leading to the house had been cleared meticulously of weeds, but on each side grass had forced itself up in thick tufts between the thinnest cracks. To Klinger's right was a stable with three halfdoors, a peaked roof, a round window circled with bricks of a deeper grey. The house mounted to four storeys where it abutted onto the stables, but for most of its rambling length was only three storeys high. The windows of the lower storeys were mostly neatly hung with patterned curtains, but the uppermost windows were bare. Two doors into the yard. One, he supposed by its deeply worn step and the blank windows hung with copper and tin pots, led to the kitchen. The larger door had an almost freshly whitened step, the paint just beginning to be worn in the middle.

Standing alone in the yard Klinger, the conqueror, felt like an intruder. He marched – or, rather, attempted to ease his learnt military step to the large door. He knocked, loudly but not, he hoped, coarsely or peremptorily, again assuming a mix of the civilian and the commanding.

'Yes. What do you want?'

The response came from the side. From a stone wall that met the house at a right angle, in an open wicket gate he had not noticed, standing below the level of the yard, was the top half of an old man.

'The occupier? You perhaps, monsieur?'

'You want Madame Denez.' The old man came up the step. At the top he looked not very much taller.

He behaved with that studied lack of grace that most of the peasants adopted. Klinger thought that the man probably imagined that age excused his lack of courtesy. Klinger would have been ashamed to tell him the truth. That neither age, nor the quietude of such a place, could have kept the old man or the place from harm if Klinger wished it. The old man's enormous, blue-veined hand twisted the ring handle on the door.

He entered with no sign, but Klinger followed him in.

The hall floor was of bare oak boards. Against one wall stood a huge oak dresser lined with plates; centuries of beeswax had been applied so that a glow seemed to radiate from somewhere under the surface of the wood. On the opposite wall was hung an oval-framed daguerrotype of an elderly woman with a bush of silver hair.

'Your business?' said the old man.

'To see madame,' said Klinger, amused.

'Wait here.'

He opened the door ahead. A glimpse of more heavy wooden furniture, of a view through a window of a small, walled flower garden. The high back of an armchair, its cloth fabric displaying a pheasant in the curling branches of a stylised covert. A cabinet full of polished glasses and plates.

'One of those people,' Klinger heard him say.

'Well who?' The voice was a woman's. Some other words were muttered that Klinger could not catch. Then, 'You better show him in. And wait a moment.' The voice was educated. The French inflected with an odd accent.

The gardener, or whatever he was, came to the door and his hooked finger beckoned to Klinger.

The woman was in her late twenties, he guessed. A blue and white polka-dotted dress reached to just below her knees. Her face had a slight spring suntan. She stood, leaning forward slightly to tap a cigarette end on a porcelain dish on the table. A book, Malraux's *L'Éspoir*, was tented on its face beside it.

'Klinger. Lieutenant Klinger.' He held out his hand.

Surprised, she hesitated for a moment, then shook his hand briefly and limply. Her fingertips were cold, the nails bitten. 'Julia Denez,' she said.

She screwed the butt of the cigarette into the dish. For the first time she looked him fully in the face. Her eyes were large, and a most beautiful grey-blue. An artist friend had once told Klinger how he had experienced an almost overwhelming erotic shock, like a powerful orgasm, that had instantly suffused his whole body and mind – by simply meeting the eyes of a woman, a complete stranger, as they walked in separate directions through a shop's doorway. Klinger had laughed – and was astonished now to feel a sensual thrill jolt his body, as if a current had passed into him from this woman. Embarrassed, he fumbled his officer's pass book from the breast pocket of his guernsey and handed it to her. She examined it briefly and gave it back.

'Ronan said you were German,' she said. 'You look more like a fisherman. Something like a fisherman anyway.'

'Forgive me,' he said. 'Your accent? You're not French?'

'I married a Frenchman. That makes me French enough.'

'Not English, surely?'

'Oh no. Quite definitely no.'

Still feeling awkward, he smiled at her. 'Well?'

'Irish.'

'Perhaps you'd rather we spoke in English,' he said in English. 'It's better than my French.'

'Yes, it is. Ronan, ask Thérèse for some coffee for myself and the gentleman.'

All of this time the old man had stood stone-faced by the door. He went out without speaking.

'You'd better sit down.'

'It's a great surprise to find you here.'

'I've all the correct papers and permits,' she protested. 'If that's what you've come for.'

'That's not my job . . .'

Recovered, Klinger fell into the frank manner that had always gone well for him with women.

'Your husband – he's here too?'

'He's missing. I presume – as they say – that he's dead. It's been a long time since I heard. They say I would have heard.'

'I'm sorry.' He examined his hands for a moment. 'I have to come here. To look over any buildings near to the coast. I'm not a policeman.'

'You want to turn the place into a fort or something?'

She picked another cigarette from the pack. They were the cheap issue to the German troops.

'I have to record every building. Not its occupants.' He reached into his haversack and placed the Leica on the table to get at his notebook.

'You photograph everything too?'

'Yes, officially. And for my own interest.'

'They're different – yours and theirs?'

'The two don't get confused.'

'Why is that? Your English is very good.'

'My mother was English.'

'Must be confusing for you, that. I don't particularly like the English.'

'No?'

'Anyway – your photographs?'

'I was a photographer before the war. Now I record for the army.'

'We were all something before the war. Oh God – you weren't one of those godawful fellers under the hood at a wedding, were you?'

'Not really.'

'Well, tell me – I'm interested – the difference. Between the ones for the record and the ones you take for you? What do you take? The people? The land?'

The maid, Thérèse, brought in the coffee. She was a tiny, bent-backed woman. She fussed around madame with the jug of hot milk and the cups and pot and went out again without once looking at Klinger.

'But then,' she said, pouring into the cups, 'you don't have to worry much about the difference do you? You are the victors. I mean, don't you find it awkward? You look, well, forgive me – normal at the moment. But I suppose you clump around in uniform like the rest.'

The coffee, thin brown, leaving a circling scum in the milk, was German too.

'I clump around – I suppose I do.' He laughed. 'But today, I'm just a surveyor. I have to know certain details of the property. That's all. You know you're not even on our maps?'

So – apologising for this, for that – he asked her what he said were necessary questions. In fact, they were an excuse for him to spend more time with her. How much land? How many rooms? Were the stables used for anything? He filled her redundant answers in his notebook. And every time he lifted his head to ask another question, he questioned her body too. She was thin-shouldered, small-breasted, rather broad in the hips, her legs were stockingless, the long thin feet with delicately raised veins in a pair of rather worn town shoes.

She lived here alone. Well, almost alone. The farm belonged to her husband's parents. The father was dead. The mother was here, but bedridden. A bad heart.

Klinger murmured his sympathy.

She shrugged her shoulders. They didn't have much in common. Then there was Thérèse. The old man, Ronan, had a cottage up on the coast road.

She herself had run out of money in Paris and come back to wait for her husband. She'd been here a year or so. Time didn't mean a lot. There hadn't been anywhere else for her to go.

The farm? Most of the land was rented out to the neighbouring farmers to cultivate. The stables were shut. The horses had been taken by the other farmers. Did he want to know what animals they had? The number of chickens? He would have to ask Ronan.

No, no, he reassured her, that was another department entirely. No concern of his.

He put his notebook away

'But you'll report the place – or something about it?'

Not unless they asked, he said. He had no cause to.

'And my presence. You'll report that?'

Why should he? To whom?

Thérèse had appeared in the doorway.

'Madame – madame . . .'

'I'm sorry,' she said to him. 'There's something I have to attend to with my mother-in-law . . .'

He stood up. 'I must thank you for your co-operation.'

'I suppose your people will be back?' she said.

'Which people?'

'The people you report to.'

'I've no interest in that.' She was about to leave the room; he must seize his moment. 'I'd like to come again,' he said urgently. 'May I come again? Is there anything you need?'

She looked puzzled, then said, 'If you want to.' She hesitated. 'Yes, come again. I try to keep myself away from it all – the war and things. We have no phone. You'll just have to turn up, I suppose. Thérèse will see you out.' Her voice was not unfriendly, but an uneasy mix of candour and a slightly nervous, mocking tone.

He gathered up his pack.

He crossed the yard. At the gate he looked back. Thérèse's face was small and white, staring out of the narrow window at the side of the door.

He went back across the fields, along the cliff-top and descended the rough path in the cliff.

The tide was beginning to go out. He waded to the boat and climbed aboard.

Otto's pad was half full of lines of poetry, smoothly written with hardly any corrections.

'Anything?' he said.

'A wood. A ruined manor,' said Klinger. 'Nothing of interest.'

2

He kept the rolls of film separate from each other. One was the official roll he had shot of the coastline. That he developed in full and handed the prints into Wahl, together with his drawings and Otto's written report on the day's outing. The other was of the manor and its wood. From this he developed and enlarged several photographs. Then he labelled the film '*The Manor*' and placed it in the hiding place with his notebooks. The images on that roll were for him. There was nothing intrinsically dangerous in them. Not in the pictures themselves; half of the troops had cameras – for taking photographs of each other lounging round tables, their arms across each others' shoulders, beer bottles and glasses and cigarettes on the tables in front of them. Or with the local girls on the coast, the girls hugging close to them; half-ashamed, half-brazen. All those were innocent. But his pictures of trees and house were dangerous in another sense; they were personal. They excluded his comrades. They were a potential betrayal. He must go back to that house. To Julia.

It rained heavily for the next two days and there was no

chance to take out the boat. On the third day of inaction Klinger was up at six as usual, washed, had had breakfast and was back in his room by seven when a soldier appeared at the door. Major Preidel would like to see Lieutenant Klinger.

Preidel's office was hung with his seascapes, expertly mounted in gilt frames. The major smoked his pipe and gazed placidly out at the rain. 'Ah, Klinger. At least they won't come in this weather, eh?'

The invasion had been rumoured throughout the spring. If it came, it would hit way up the coast. By the time they were called in, Dietrich had said, the Allies would be back in the sea and they would have missed all the fun. 'Not your sort of fun, anyway, is it, Klinger,' he called across the mess. 'Our little deaf and dumb artist . . .'

'Awful bore,' said the Major, 'but they want an official photographer in town for some function. Would you mind obliging with your camera? Something to show to the locals. You are our photographer, after all. You can go with Wahl – he's dropping in the reports. See Captain Lasker.'

Wahl was waiting beside his saloon car in the courtyard.

'Do you like her?' He patted the bonnet. 'My little chariot.' He told Klinger for the fifth time how he had bought her from a farmer who couldn't get petrol or a driving permit. 'Absolute song. Of course – it was all correct.' Wahl was always correct.

On the way, clutching the steering wheel as if it was about to come away in his hands, taking the corners with exaggerated care, spurting forward on the open road, then slowing to almost a crawl, Wahl explained in his painstaking way that he could now get out to the standing stone circles and other sites. He had been sketching them for his study of the ancient religion that once had all of Europe in its grip. The Pan-Germanic religion that pre-dated Christianity and the Romans. The religion that was still in their blood. Not in the head. He tapped his head and veered towards the ditch. Why, only last week he had found an ancient fertility symbol, a statue of a woman with enormous breasts and – 'you know, Klinger, the other bit'. The statue, knocked about but perfectly recognisable for what it was, had been hidden among the old piled gravestones at the back of one of the local churches. The priest had known nothing about it. Wahl had had it winched upright and placed beside the entrance to the church. 'That's where it would have stood in the old days. Before the church was ever erected, of course. You see, the alignments of the sites sacred to the older pagan religions were chosen for just that reason. The Christians simply appropriated them.'

He began his usual amiable, insane diatribe against the Christians and their forebears the Jews.

'Though it's not done to say so,' he said, *sotto voce*, looking at Klinger quickly sideways as he shifted gear noisily, 'and without confirmation of my research, but I have good proofs that Christ was not Jewish. This is a thing that has always been stated by the Christians. That Christ comes out of the Hebrew tradition. Now, if they do not give way on this point; well, drastic steps may be taken. It was hoped at the start that all the pastors could be brought into line, but there are so many fools among them. And the thought that this whole Christian thing has been a total imposture on our good will for two thousand years. It's frightening to think about really . . .'

He kept this up all the way to town. Fortunately Klinger

was not required to join in; Wahl had the happy autonomy of thought of the monomaniac.

They drove between the gates of the Kommandantur in the requisitioned Hôtel de Ville – the mayor had had to move to smaller quarters across the square. As he parked, Wahl asked, 'Are you going to be long? I have to go over to Saint Poule.' This was how he pronounced Pol – it sounded as if he was about to visit a prostitute. 'The priest there has some rubbings for me. What have you to do?'

'I've no idea,' said Klinger.

'Unless you are delayed I shall see you here at ten. Or perhaps you prefer to go straight back.'

It suddenly occurred to Klinger that Wahl would have to travel up the coast road. 'No –' he said. 'If I may come with you.'

'Delighted.' Wahl beamed.

Captain Lasker was waiting in the guardroom. With him was a sergeant wearing the uniform of the Field Police and two men in civilian clothes. In bad French, Lasker introduced them as a representative of the mayor – Monsieur Duhamel, a tall, embarrassed-looking, florid-faced man in a black suit who bowed his head stiffly – and an inspector of the civil police in the province. The inspector carried a small portfolio under his arm tied up with blue ribbons. His face wore a sour expression.

Lasker turned to Klinger. 'You have your equipment? Then let's get on with it. Sergeant.'

The sergeant opened the door behind him.

A short corridor. A bored-looking soldier sat on a stool against the blind wall at the end. He stood smartly to attention. On either side of the corridor was a cell door, each with a Judas hole covered with an iron iris hung on a nail and below that an iron trap with a sliding shelf to allow food to be passed into the cell without opening the door.

'These gentlemen wish to view the prisoner,' said Lasker to the sentry. 'Well, come on. Let them see.'

The soldier laid his rifle to one side of the door, bringing up a key on a chain at his belt.

'The peephole first, blockhead.'

The soldier, his face reddening, put his right forefinger to the disc on the door and swung it back. Lasker invited the mayor's representative forward. He applied one eye to the hole, studied what he saw for a few long moments and then stood back. The inspector looked next.

'That is the man?' said Lasker curtly.

'Yes, I have the papers here.' He began to pull at the blue tapes on his portfolio. 'Countersigned by my colleague as necessary . . .'

'They won't be necessary.'

'And by your own regional assistant civilian liaison officer.'

'I said, they will not be necessary. This man is to be dealt with by military law.'

'A civil trial . . . that was agreed,' the policeman protested.

'The man will be dealt with now,' said Lasker. 'He has admitted his crime. He is – or was – a soldier in the German army. He has disgraced that uniform. He will be dealt with forthwith.'

'Monsieur Duhamel.' The policeman turned to his companion. 'I understood this was a criminal matter.'

The mayor's representative thrust his hands deep into his pockets. 'I don't know . . . Whatever.'

'I have the document here authorising my conduct,' said Lasker, thrusting a piece of paper forward.

'I can't read this. It's in German,' said the inspector. 'This is not what was agreed.'

'A translation will be furnished. Everything is in order. Open the door.'

The key grated in the lock. The door swung outwards.

'Klinger,' said Lasker. 'You will enter with these gentlemen. This man is to be photographed and a copy of your prints and any subsequent prints that I authorise will be given to them. Any other film is to be surrendered to me. Understand?'

The man in the cell was young, perhaps eighteen, if that. His uniform was not clean. All identifying badges had been picked off, the threads hung out as cleaner, grey filaments where they had been. He stood up awkwardly. His left leg was manacled to the foot of the iron bed frame.

'Heil Hitler,' he shouted in a loud, farm-boy's voice.

Lasker ignored the salute.

'You may photograph him now.'

'Stand at attention,' the sergeant bellowed behind them.

The boy was rigid, his thumbs down the seams of his buckled-up trousers.

Klinger wanted to take off his greatcoat. He felt suddenly clumsy, as if his movements were impeded in the small cell. He fumbled in the pack and brought out his camera. He avoided looking at the boy.

'Read out the charge, Sergeant,' Lasker ordered.

Klinger raised the camera. 'There's not a very good light in here.' There was only one tiny window in the wall high above the bed. 'And with the greyness of the day outside . . .'

'What you have will have to do,' said Lasker irritably. 'Sergeant.'

'That Private Wittau on the night of the twentieth of April 1944 did abduct one Emilie Anne Lefort, aged thirteen years old, and did violate . . .'

'Switch on the light in the corridor.'

'. . . and strangle until she was dead the said French citizen, being a minor, and contrary to German military law and French Civil law as enacted under . . .'

Klinger met the face of the boy through his lens, focusing him sharply. The face in his lens was unremarkable, pale and square; dark, arched eyebrows under the blond hair gave it a childish appearance. The sergeant's droning expressionless voice went on and, with no particular dramatic finality, ceased. Klinger clicked off two frames, hesitated, checked his exposure again, raised the camera.

'There's no need to be bloody fancy about it.'

Lasker's gloves rapped against his arm. 'Sentry. Undo the manacle.'

Klinger found himself backing out of the cell, into the guardroom office, with the two Frenchmen. Another two soldiers clumped through and went into the cell. Lasker came out.

'If you would follow me,' he said to the Frenchmen. 'And you, Lieutenant.'

He led them down a corridor to the back of the building. A door was open to a courtyard. The rain had stopped but cloud hung heavy overhead. Towards the north the sky was brightening.

'I must ask what is happening,' said the policeman.

'Justice will be done. You will see it done,' said Lasker.

'It will be necessary for you to photograph this also,' he said to Klinger.

There were two cherry trees in a rectangular plot in the middle of the yard. A little away from the brick wall a stake about two metres high had been planted – one of the paving stones had been removed to allow it to be driven into the earth. Four wooden railway sleepers had been upended and laid against the wall behind the stake.

The two Frenchmen had come out. When the tall one – Duhamel – looked at Klinger he gave a quick silly smile, then straightened his mouth under his moustache with a stiff finger and frowned and gazed up into the air and then down at his boots. The policeman glared fixedly ahead.

Now here came the sergeant and his two men, holding the boy between them under the arms, half running him across the yard. His hands were tied behind his back. Klinger shot his progress.

'There's no need for that,' snapped Lasker. 'When I tell you.'

At the stake they had to unbind the boy's hands. His eyes looked on the two men's ministrations with something like gratitude. They were not rough, but expert and disinterested as they placed his straight back against the stake, and refixed his hands behind, a thick large belt around his midriff. The sergeant approached, pulling something from his pocket. The boy bent down and the sergeant slipped a white hood over his head, obliterating the face. Then he placed a woollen scarf round the neck and said something softly and the boy obediently put his head back against the stake and the sergeant tied that at the back. Now for the first time the boy's body twitched, he struggled to be free, but his bonds were so efficient that only his shoulders were able to move. The sergeant said something else close to the hood and the boy was still.

A squad of six men marched from the open door at the other side of the yard. Their boots were very loud on the flagstones. They marched in single file and turned, to orders, in a line about ten metres from the figure at the stake.

Lasker stepped forward and read from a document; a repetition of the charge, the finding of the military court. The sentence to be carried out immediately.

'Carry on, sergeant,' he said, stepping back again. As he did so, he said to Klinger, 'You must take this.'

Klinger found the figure in his lens, focused and pressed the button. He wound on. He heard more orders shouted. He stepped back two paces to get in the firing party and the stake and pressed again. The rifles were raised. He pressed again. He adjusted for the light. The bolts clicked back. Every sound seemed to exist within its own bubble of time. The noise of the rifles firing was terrific in that enclosed space. Klinger took the shots rapidly. The jerking upwards and backwards of the chest. The sudden sack-like slump of the torso. The loll of the head a minute fraction afterwards. The snapped marionette strings of the legs. The spreading stain on the front of the trousers. The blood on the sleepers behind the stake.

He made his way into the main square of the town. It was a quarter past nine. He had seen Lasker sign the Frenchmen's papers, and then sign his. Lasker said, 'So you see, gentlemen, justice has been done.' Klinger had promised the photographs would be sent down by messenger that evening.

The great ugly church, with its twin conical spires and triangular front, dominated the square. All round were the offices of lawyers and merchants and banks and shops with three, four, five storeys of apartments above. There was a café directly opposite the church. It was for the locals, and not for the army, but at the moment he needed a drink.

There were the usual two or three men gathered up at the far end, where the owner sat behind the counter. The other men who used the café early had long gone to their work. These were old men. Their conversation halted as he came in and stood halfway up the counter. He saw himself in the mirror in his greatcoat and peaked cap.

The volley of shots must have been audible in here.

The bar was utterly silent as he drank his calvados.

3

Almost a week later, Klinger walked along the lane towards the wood that hid the manor. He carried a thick brown paper bag. He was bringing gifts to the Irish woman, Julia. He believed, or wished to believe that he was falling in love with her.

Wahl's car disappeared round a bend in the coast road. Wahl had been puzzled and slightly annoyed that Klinger had asked to be let out here. It was most irregular for an officer to be put down in the middle of nowhere, on his own. Dangerous too. Was he sure he wanted to be dropped here? Yes, Klinger said, he had to finish some surveying work on this stretch. There was a guard post beyond the wood, he lied. If Wahl wouldn't mind picking him up on his return from his own business? He would be about an hour.

'Very well. I shall be back at two,' said Wahl huffily.

What Wahl had been annoyed about, Klinger thought, was the lack of his new boon companion, someone – the only one among the staff – to take an interest in his scholarly preoccupations.

The lane from the road petered out at the wood's edge, and a spur of trees hid a dirt track to the farm. The image of the boy came to his mind.

Julia answered his knock on the door. She stared at him. He pulled off his cap.

'You said I might call again,' he said diffidently, in English.

She stared at him.

'I came by boat. The fisherman – don't you remember?'

'Oh, yes. I didn't recognise you. Not in uniform.' She stood back. 'Come in.'

She led him into the sitting room.

'Your mother-in-law – she's better?'

'No, actually she isn't. She's not here. She's at St Pol – the doctor said she was to go to the hospital.'

'I'm sorry. I do hope it's not serious.'

'It is. She's not well at all. And she's not so old, I suppose . . . I'll go and see her later in the week – but she won't want to see me.' Her voice was cool, almost off-hand. 'I'm her son's wife. Women don't get on if they've a common interest. She's got Thérèse – she doesn't need me. Anyway . . . Please sit down.' And she sat, folding her hands in her lap.

They sat like this for a long moment, looking at each other, then she said, 'You know I feel most peculiar with you here. You don't mind me saying that? For all these four years, I don't think I've sat in the same room as one of you. The Germans, I mean.'

'Please – it's not an official visit. Despite this.' He touched his uniform.

He reached down to his camera pack.

'I wanted to show you these. May I . . . ?' he asked, clearing to the edge of the table a glass paperweight, a small dish and a book.

He laid out some of the prints he had brought, twisting them to her as she bent over the table.

'I hope you don't mind. I took them when I came last time, walking up to the house.'

She picked up one print, then another, slowly leafing through them. Then she said, 'Why – they're beautiful. These are the orchards as I see them. As I think I see them, anyway. How clever of you.'

She smiled across the table at him. 'No, really – they're wonderful. These aren't official photographs, surely?'

'No, I printed them off for you. If you'd like them.'

'Oh yes – of course. That's really kind – you're sure?'

'As I say, I did them for you.'

Now, for the first time, she looked at ease with him. She tidied the loose prints into a neat pile, stood up, smoothed her skirt and said, 'I don't know what I can give you in return.

Would you like some coffee? Thérèse is in town. It won't take more than a few minutes.'

He looked at his watch. 'I have an hour before I'm collected. If you can put up with me for that long?'

'You've paid for your coffee,' she said and smiled again.

While she was away in the kitchen he went to the window. Above the trees the sky was starting to drive its rainy load away from the coast, but over the sea it was still smeared with a thin brown wash.

'I think it may get fine again,' he said when she came back in. 'It's hard to tell.'

'That's the sea. It changes so fast here.'

He put the paper bag on to the table. 'I hope you will not mind. I have brought you some other things.'

He placed a packet of English Players cigarettes on the table. A bottle of good Bordeaux. Two illustrated magazines. Two bars of chocolate.

She frowned at the offerings. 'Is this how you do it?' she said.

'What?' But he knew what she meant. Stockings and chocolate were what the soldiers gave to their local girls.

'I can't take these from you. The photographs – they're different. I thought they were different.'

'I'm sorry. I've upset you. I know what you mean. They were intended genuinely. I have insulted you.'

Her eyes were fixed on the cigarettes.

'We're not short of food here. Or wine.'

'I'll barter them then,' he said. 'I shan't take them away.'

'Isn't that against your law?'

'Legality is a fine concept in our present circumstances.'

'I'll give you some ham,' she said gravely. 'For the cigarettes. Some butter for the magazines. Will that be acceptable – ham? What's the going rate? A pound of ham for the cigarettes?'

A most meticulous transfer took place a few minutes later. Klinger stowed the greaseproof paper-wrapped packages in his bag.

'One other thing I wanted to ask. A much bigger thing,' he said slowly. 'It's not illegal, anything like that, but it would do me a great favour.' She said nothing, and he went on. 'I need a place where I can store my work – not my official work. A small space – anywhere; one of your outbuildings, perhaps, to use as a darkroom. There's work I can't do, or get done, in our headquarters.'

'Your own work?'

'Yes.'

'I suppose you can. Yes, you can. You won't be disturbed. Ronan and Thérèse are trustworthy. They don't speak to anyone. They hardly speak to each other.'

'Of course, I shall pay you for this.'

'There's no need. What's there to spend it on?'

She offered him one of the Players, and asked where he had got English cigarettes.

'A friend of mine bartered them from prisoners when he was a guard.'

'Do you really dislike all this?' she asked.

'Dislike what?'

'The war. Everything.'

'Yes, I do.'

'In a way you're worse . . . I'm sorry, I didn't mean that. What I mean is, it's ridiculous to sit here with you in that uniform and to be having a civilised conversation. Why are you sitting here?'

'I wanted to talk. I had to do something unpleasant – is that the word? – last week. I needed the company of someone who wasn't anything at all to do with that.'

'What was unpleasant?'

'I had to photograph an execution.'

She stroked the end of ash from her cigarette on the side of the tray.

'A Frenchman?' Her voice was again perfectly calm.

'A German. A German soldier. He was executed for murder. Of a child. The photographs were for the French authorities. I have never seen anything like that before. A death in the family. Bodies in battle, following our troops at the start of the war. Never that.'

She didn't speak, letting him go on.

'I didn't mean to talk about it – I don't know why I did,' he said.

'Perhaps it's upset you. Would that be a bad thing?'

'No.'

'Tell me about it . . .'

He did, bringing the images freshly up in his mind.

When he had finished, she looked at him for a while and he looked back, then down, and fiddled with the side of his boot and then handled his cigarettes in his pocket and decided not to take them out, and let his hands flop on his knees and once again looked at her. What was that word, he thought – disingenuous? A lying picture; a true picture – who can tell the difference after a while? He very much wanted to make love to this woman. Julia. That was her name. To make love gently – not from necessity – though it had been a long time since he had lain with a woman he loved – and all the stuff in between was soaked away in the cigarettes and wine and work and rough blankets and the dreadfully cold winters that accompanied this war, and the drizzling spring, the whores in the cramped, damp-smelling house in St Pol who were so pleasant and unpleasant in their professional way that no one could want to know them more than once.

She was saying how dreadful that must have been and that – as if to rescue him – they should go out into the orchard. The rain had stopped. 'You took such beautiful pictures of the orchard.'

'Yes, of course.' He got up. He bowed, totally unironically, as she carefully skirted him in the room and went out. He followed her through the hall and over the yard.

Now the sky was blue over the sea; cloud driving rapidly inland. It suddenly uncovered the sun and light flooded between the rain-glistening trees.

'I didn't hear a car,' she said. 'How did you get here? By boat again?'

'Another officer gave me a lift.'

'He's picking you up?'

He didn't understand the phrase.

'He's collecting you?'

Yes. He mustn't keep Wahl waiting. He might need him again.

They walked in the orchards, circling the house slowly so that the trees seemed a continuous wood. She walked in front. It seemed to him that she made sure she outpaced him so that, although she appeared to be guiding him, she also remained apart. As they went he unbuttoned his camera pouch.

'A moment,' he said. 'Julia – may I call you that?'

He had the camera to his eye, knowing that she would turn, looking surprised. As she did so, he took her picture; once, twice, then she shook her head and put her hand in front of her face, laughing, and said, 'No – no. That's enough. I don't want them. I hate myself in pictures.'

'They're not for you. For me,' he said.

She didn't answer at once. She glanced at her watch. 'Your friend – when did you say he was coming for you? We'd better go back.' As if she'd led him into a deep wood and suddenly discovered the path out, she stalked back through the trees.

I am in love with her, he thought, as he walked back up the wooded, uneven lane.

Promptly, to the promised minute, Wahl's car bounced into view on the coast road.

Otto was sitting at their small table, with his Latin dictionary, his Ovid, his notebooks, his pencils, pen knife for sharpening them, precious eraser – 'Everything is precious. We shall lose it all,' he had said morosely to Klinger.

Klinger rolled over on his bed. By having his good ear buried in the pillow he was able to shut out the barely audible noises of Otto at work. He dozed and then slept, dreaming of the orchard and the house at Dalhelm. Karl was pouring drinks for them, a small Japanese boy at his side kept tugging his long nineteenth-century coat and demanding, 'When am I going to see the pictures you promised . . .'

There was a special briefing the next morning.

Major Preidel had news for them. The news was good. The news was bad. Almost certainly, as they had expected the invasion was due. It was most likely in a couple of months, in June. There was no prospect of this being the area chosen for the Allies to make their attempt. The distance. The seas. The rocky coast. No, the invasion would most probably happen in the Pas de Calais; there were the major ports that the Allies must seize for their unloading and fuelling facilities. They had been asked, however, to be extra vigilant. Nothing like a successful landing would be made. The fortifications that had been erected, the calibre of their men – the Allies' attempts would necessarily fail. 'This, I am to inform you on highest authority,' said Preidel in his quiet way, 'could well be the turning point of the whole war. An invasion successfully repelled, would bloody the British, weary the Americans in the west' – his hand swept inappropriately over the lower reaches of the map of Europe on the wall – 'and allow us to finish off the Bolsheviks in the east.' He began to read from a paper, holding it at arm's length so that he could focus on it. '"Your unit." This is a message from headquarters, gentlemen. "Your unit will play its part in the grander design, the ultimate defeat of the Marxist bandits and English and American International Jewry. There is no place for failure in our plans." I have no doubt, gentlemen,' said Major Preidel, laying down the paper, 'that we shall prevail. We must. There is no alternative for our army but victory.'

Klinger thought of the whitewashed message he had seen scribbled on a wall during his leave home in the autumn of last year.

4

The train to Berlin had burrowed its way through the night like a great halting grunting badger. The creature stopped occasionally to ingest passengers in the dark, leaf-strewn country stations. Sometimes these halts were swift. The train pulled out almost as soon as it arrived, only the banging of a door somewhere announcing leaving or joining. Then again they idled for ever, the carriage light, dim already, growing dimmer, so that you could look at the bulb above the door and actually see the filament go down to red then revive a little to orange, then the dimmest yellow. And in these long halts when the light went down, the conversation too halted in the carriage, the calls in the corridor of the crowded train became single and embarrassed at themselves and died away, and Klinger, by the window, would lift the blind a little away and see the vaultings of the station, the dark and silent country behind, or, if they were on the outskirts of a town or city, the slow searchlights vaulting the sky, the fierce orange or red glow of burning buildings, the arced tracer fire falling well short of any plane, the bursting beautiful stars of the anti-aircraft shells. Then the blind dropped back, and he was in the crowded train again, with the almost welcome but then almost insanely wearisome slow drumming of the wheels . . .

He reached Berlin at noon. The sky was bright, but with a darker tinge lying in a bar across the north where fires had burned out. He had been here last six months before. There had been many raids and much damage then, but now the city was badly mauled. He began to walk from the station to the Ku-damm. He was astonished at what was ruined and what left standing. On a wall was chalked 'Enjoy the war – you won't enjoy the peace'.

Lotte's gallery, boarded up, was in a relatively undamaged block, though a row of shops a little further down had fallen into a huge pile of rubble along with the apartments that had been above them. He unlocked the front door. There was a slew of letters and packages that he pushed aside with his foot. The rows of his own and Lotte's pictures that he had displayed last year, as a quixotic gesture – he had no one to run the shop or to take orders – were still there. But when he went through to the back he saw that the rear door had been forced and all the photographic equipment had been taken, that the cupboards had been forced and his and, worse, Lotte's cameras and lenses had been stolen – as had every last, least valuable item, right down to her battered kettle and coffee pot. The only things the thieves had left were his and Lotte's photographs. Coffee is more important than art.

He carefully relocked the front. There were no cabs to be had; he walked a long way. The streets were covered with a fine glassy dust. Still-standing walls were pock-marked by shrapnel. Men and women dug at sites that had presumably been made the previous night; as they moved away rafters and beams the banked rubble stirred up dust like smoke. The block where his apartment had been was gone, the site brushed clean and flat, as though by a giant broom. He went on a few streets. The tenement where Lotte had her apartment was untouched.

A letter had reached him last year, saying that she was having to move. Things were not so bad – she would forward an address as soon as possible.

He walked through the archway and into the well of the courtyard. Clothes hung out to dry on the window ledges. The windows were smeared with a sort of grease and criss-crossed with paper tape. The sun couldn't get into this courtyard except for the brief time when it was straight overhead. Now it fell, an angled slice of bright light on the high lead guttering, like a knife opening a can. Children yelled through the archway across the yard, and ran away to the main road beyond. He crossed and found on the inside of the arch a door with a plate that had 'Block Warden' on it in Gothic letters.

He knocked. A shout from inside made him enter.

The man sitting behind the small desk was the type Klinger expected to find. These jobs did seem to impose certain restrictions on human intelligence and attractiveness – and it was obvious that this man had found his level. He was tall, thin, his eyes enlarged behind spectacles, his full head of grey hair parted on the right, brilliantined down and cut very short so that it sat like a beret on top of his head. He wore his warden's armband on his sleeve. On the wall behind him was a picture of Hitler wrapped in a cloak and a cloud, and a certificate stating that Herr Meissner had performed an heroic act in saving several persons from harm in air raids during 1942. As Klinger entered, a woman, presumably Frau Meissner, looked out suspiciously from a tiny sitting room, scowled and shut the door on them. Klinger was glad he was in uniform. The man saluted with a fierce 'Heil Hitler'. On the desk before him was a small, cheap notebook of butcher's paper, and a long typed list of names against numbers, which Klinger guessed must be a list of the residents.

It was no good being honest with this man. Klinger concocted a story on the spot. He had taken over a business before the war, Herr Meissner. It was Herr Meissner? The warden bowed. He had some legal details to sort out with the late owner. He had known this as her last address. Her apartment number he didn't remember.

'What was her name?' The warden picked up his notebook in his left hand and with his right wetted a pencil end on his tongue and hung ready.

'Abrahams. Lotte Abrahams.'

'That's a Jewish name.' The pencil point drew back sharply from the notebook.

'I know it is.' Klinger looked the warden straight and insolently in the eyes. That was a mistake.

'There are no Yids here. Not now. No. You should know that. None here.'

'I had some business to finish . . .'

'No – there are none here.'

'Do you know where she went?'

'Where they all went. They all went east.'

'They were moved out?'

'Yes, east. Where have you been? You're infantry, aren't you? What do you want with those people anyway?'

'You can't help me then? You have no forwarding address?' said Klinger.

The man's lips parted and his upper lip drew back in a broad and horrible smile.

'Forwarding address? They don't leave forwarding addresses.

They've gone. Just gone. I think you had better explain precisely what you want, Lieutenant.'

'You can't help me – I'll leave you to your duties.' Klinger opened the door on to the cobbled alley.

'Not so fast. I have to have your details.' The warden gathered up the notepad and pencil once more and came round the desk. Klinger backed out. He began to walk briskly forward to the street beyond the arch.

He heard the warden's voice calling out: 'I must have your name. For the record. For the record.'

He got away. There were not the police there had been once on the streets. The city was one of old men and women and children with absolutely no interest in him at all.

The house at Dalhelm was untouched. There had been bombs dropped here and there in the suburbs, most likely as the planes unloaded on the last turning for home. That was the particular gamble of the middle class – that in every society or neighbourhood they got just about the best of it, with the occasional hit of misfortune. For those in the working-class districts chance was becoming certainty. Those in the tenements and mean houses buckled down to suffering; those in the big houses among the lakes and quiet roads tut-tutted at the noise and distant upset – between them the almost incredible government machine felt and fumbled and tumbled like an incompetent circus troupe; but as always there was no revolution. Mass hangings and soup kitchens; grave speeches and Beethoven on the wireless; oompah bands on street corners; the huge coloured posters on the front of the cinema – a man riding a cannon ball – announcing *The Adventures of Baron Münchhausen*. The thought, any thought, of Lotte was reduced to its absolute minimum, as he looked through the photographs in Dalhelm. That night he heard for the first time the peculiar coughing cry of foxes somewhere in the wood that mingled the boundaries of his and his neighbour's gardens. The house was his; but he did not feel that he had any right to it. It was his grandmother's. And now he had only a small part of it.

He had leased the house to a Party official and his family two years ago – on the condition that they allowed him to keep a small suite, including his old room and the room he had used as his studio. They had been as good as their word. And, from the look of it, their maid had discreetly polished and dusted so that the rooms were cleaner than he remembered leaving them, and not another thing but the dust had been disturbed.

After the city he was almost glad to renew his acquaintance with Dr Peppler and his wife, Magda, and the charming teenage children. When he came in tired and depressed after that first day in the city, and sat with a brandy, the doctor had knocked on the door and politely, warmly, very genteelly, gently, let him make no bones about it, asked him down to sup, as he put it, with the family tonight. 'I don't know how long your leave is, but if you have the time to spare, we would count it an honour . . .'

He would be honoured. At what time? At eight.

He gathered up the photographs and put them in a file. He shaved again. He put on a clean shirt. He combed his hair in the mirror. He looked at the case on the bed – the case that contained his camera and lenses. He felt suddenly weary of the whole damn thing. Then he looked in the mirror again, shook his shoulders back, gave himself an ironic army salute. And, at one minute to eight, he descended his grandmother's stairs to these strangers.

Dr Peppler was standing at the foot of the stairs. He had changed from his black suit into a wondrous blue cloth and gold-braided uniform. As Klinger appeared, and the doctor signalled, Frau Peppler struck up on the piano in the drawing room – the instrument that Klinger had never heard played before, a piano he had thought incapable of sound, a useless ornament like a bowl of wooden fruit – a triumphal jangled version of the 'Ode to Joy'. And the three children, the fourth and eldest was missing in Russia, the two boys and one girl, all in youth uniforms, joined in the song.

The meal was pleasant. There was not a great deal on each plate, but they had obviously gone to much trouble to produce this chicken, these fresh vegetables.

Dr Peppler hogged what passed for conversation . . .

Now was the supreme testing time. Stalingrad had been a severe blow – but perhaps a blessing in disguise. Everything had gone too well up until then. They couldn't expect a clear, unclouded run, whatever their strengths. It had given the generals time to clear their thoughts. Now – this was the true situation – the Allies were stuck in Italy. But the Russian front seemed to be holding and it could not be long before a counter-attack. And there were weapons under development – obviously he could not talk about them – of such a secret, devastating nature . . .

And as Klinger listened – nodding politely in agreement here and there – to this round, bald-headed man – whose brightly winking spectacles completed an odd resemblance to Mr Pickwick in the pictures in his mother's green buckram-bound set of Dickens – he became aware that this genial, family man actually believed what he was saying. That the ten-year-long intoxication was to continue, that it was at its most intoxicating now – that there was no prospect of any awaking or sobering up.

The youngest male Peppler, with a shock of fine brown hair that Klinger thought would most probably go he same way as the good doctor's, sat listening intently to the conversation of his elders. The two girls talked in whispers with their mother about household matters – as far as he could gather from stray words in the midst of Doctor Peppler's ripe monologue.

After the dessert, Peppler produced the bottle of cognac that Klinger had given him on arrival. 'See what our brave warrior has brought,' he cried, waving it in front of his wife. But Magda was not given a drink. The son was given a small liqueur glass-full, well-watered. The daughters and their mother retired with the dishes to the kitchen. All men together, Peppler asked him about the situation in France. Klinger mentioned shortages, the resistance of some of the local population – 'Ah, the devils,' said Peppler. The compliance of others – Peppler nodded. Klinger tried to sound a modest, busy soldier. He hoped Peppler would not recommend him to the Eastern Front.

Then Magda came in and sat at the piano again. Peppler got up and stood beside the instrument, leaning his elbow on the lid. Dutifully, as if rehearsed, the three children ranged themselves so that the son stood beside his father – Peppler's other hand resting on his son's hair. The two daughters stood on the other side of the piano. They all faced their audience of one. They sang and Klinger sat, intensely embarrassed, not knowing whether he should join in, deciding it would look ridiculous when he had not done so straight away, and so sitting stiff and trying to appear charmed and delighted by their singing.

And really, it was quite charming. They sang folk songs; in a rather reedy tenor the doctor sang 'The Erl King'. The two girls performed in duet a Schubertian conversation song he didn't know the title of. Then, in a moment of intermission, while Magda fussed with her music, they heard the unmistakeable crump-crump of bombs falling some miles away on the city. Peppler raised his voice and began to sing, without the piano at first, 'Wir fahren gegen England', in a loud, defiant voice, and the children's voices joined his and they sang louder and louder, and at last Klinger too joined in, their voices and the clangour of the piano drowning out the dreadful noise of the bombers.

5

No more Berlin.

But he was due a week's leave. He had been determined to take it in Paris. What was the point of swapping one garrison town for another when you could go to what was still a sort of paradise? But now he couldn't get Julia out of his mind. He had to see her. It was difficult. He couldn't for ever rely on lifts from Wahl. And Otto and he had had their coastline reconnaissance cancelled. There seemed little point in defending the high cliffs, and most of the mobile guns were now slated to move eastwards up the coast. They – especially Preidel's unit, the Cripples' Circus, as they were called – were not wanted. So the boat was out of the question. He would have to do a trade with Wahl for the use of the car. His mind formulated and reformulated his plans for what would happen when he next met Julia.

In all the years of war he had had only three mistresses and none of them had he loved in whatever sense that word made. Now he was sure he was in love with Julia. So, he was a romantic? But an artist gave his heart only to his work, didn't he? It was part of the deal. And that was also romantic. And what art? He thought with dissatisfaction of the propaganda photographs he had taken for *Signal*; of other, technical photographs of war machines and weapons – though those, paradoxically, he liked better; in their neutral show of cold practicality, the necessity the subject matter imposed of operating within the exactness, the coldness, the purity of the image.

He had entered France in 1940 riding in the cab of a truck full of infantrymen. He was the official photographer following the advance spearhead at Sedan. Every unit had one – and every second man in every unit seemed to have a camera, too. But Klinger was the one with the bag full of lenses, the head full of images – the authorised eye on the deserted towns and villages they passed through. These, it seemed, were inhabited solely by dogs who followed the men around in melancholy, tail-dropped expectation of scraps of food. They made good pictures – they could be used in the family magazines back home. Unlike the others he took, where soldiers got drunk in abandoned cafés, both officers and other ranks, because, victorious or not, they had all fought and were dirty and dishevelled and the drunkenness was sheer relief at having come through alive.

'Where is everyone?' Klinger asked a doctor who had stayed behind in a hospital deserted by all but the dying.

'They fled.'

'Did they think we were going to eat them?' asked Klinger's commanding officer.

'The threat of bombs and tanks – those are quite enough,' said the doctor.

Klinger went back to the column halted in the centre of the town. Six streets, arranged like the spokes of a wheel, led into the main square. At the far end of one street he saw figures flitting from one side to the other. They were dressed in white and blue striped nightshirts. A woman with long filthy hair ran into the Place, an empty dish in her hands. She halted in front of the leading scout car, and invited the soldiers to dine. 'God', said one of the men, '– are all the French like this?' They laughed and the woman started laughing too. Then she ran away up the street. One of the forward patrols returned and said that these strange people were the inhabitants of a lunatic asylum on the outskirts. Their attendants had upped and left them and the town and fields around were full of them. When they pulled out again, what they called a lunatic squad remained to take the escapees back to the asylum.

Klinger photographed lunatics and dogs. He saw little fighting. The smoke of explosions from shells ahead, the droning of planes going westwards, an occasional dog-fight overhead between their planes and British fighters, buildings burning after the Allied bombers had passed.

Everything went quiet one day and they were told over the radio that the French had surrendered. Klinger was able to have his first bath for days in a hotel. Staff officers appeared on the scene to lecture that there would be no more drunkenness, no looting. They must be correct in their behaviour. France was part of the New Europe. The population should respect them. The people here were not Poles. What resistance there was would be quickly mopped up. Not even by them. They had more than enough volunteers from the local population.

Klinger went to Paris the day of the victory parade. He photographed the happy crowds that were intended to represent the welcoming French; in fact the front ranks at least were composed mainly of German civil servants and their wives who had been drafted in to run the city. Maybe the strained faces behind were the French.

In the next week the buildings that had been bombed began to heal, a blizzard of black and white and red signs, bill-boards and posters appeared on every wall; injunctions, prohibitions, exhortations, traffic signals . . .

The Führer himself arrived at six one morning, and was driven, standing up, along the slightly misty, empty Champs Élysées. Behind was a car with a movie camera, and behind that another car with a photographer, and behind that another car with another photographer – Klinger, photographing all of these, in a recession of images . . .

Well, now, Julia, Klinger thought – these things were needed: transport, the promise of future transport, the effective planning of his leave, the transfer of certain goods to the farm to aid his work, his art – he would enjoy using them away from the view of the army, the snooping of the Field Police. The snoopers hadn't much to do at the moment and that made them doubly a nuisance. The local Milice rounded up the Resistance and what they called the Resistance – half the time they pursued their own personal dislikes and vendettas. There was little for the truly unpleasant German to do except plague his own countrymen.

The news from home worsened each week and the lists of dead in the newspapers sent from Germany lengthened. Too often came news of wives or children or parents killed by the air raids. There had been half a dozen suicides among the troops in their sector that year alone. There was never enough to eat these days, and what there was almost uneatable; worse, the supply of cigarettes had become erratic and a few days without those was enough to bring complete misery. And with the promise of the Allied invasion to come . . .

The first thing to do was to see Wahl. Wahl's leave was due the same week as his.

Major Preidel sat in a corner reading an old copy of the *Frankfurter Zeitung*; he nodded to Klinger. Wahl was alone at the table in the corner laying out, in what looked like a complicated game, many small feint-lined cards all bearing tiny squarish handwriting, symbols, and small odd-looking drawings.

'Captain, may I . . . ?' Klinger was motioned to sit down; Wahl's eyes returned to his cards, his hands dealing one to this pile, one to that, removing one here to replace it there, dealing another. 'Your researches . . . ?' asked Klinger delicately.

Of course, then there was no stopping Wahl. These cards were notes of investigations of local church sites. He had hoped that the lieutenant would have been able to accompany him when he had asked him last, said Wahl rather petulantly. What with the present military disruptions, who could know what chance there might be to conclude his work. Wahl gazed off into the distance, far away from the room in which they sat, to the future where his two, three, four handsome volumes bound in black leather with red, gilt-lettered labels on their spines, and silver swastikas stamped on their fronts, opened their thick creamy leaves displaying his words, his knowledge, his genius . . . accompanied, at a respectful distance, by sketches and photographs by Lieutenant Klinger.

Klinger said that he would be delighted, indeed, honoured, to contribute to such a work.

Wahl leaned forward. His hands passed slowly over the cards on the table, moving from the sides to meet in the centre and then parting and passing back to the sides again, as he whispered, 'When all this is over – this is what will last. Believe me, young man.'

It was settled. Klinger would accompany him and photograph, to Wahl's instruction, his latest expedition to a set of standing stones up the coast.

Early the next morning they drove east into a mist curling like a blowsy, half solid wave over the cliffs from the sea. Wahl was glad that the Lieutenant had agreed to help. It was so difficult now to find people with a genuine interest in important matters. He was off on leave himself next week, back to the Fatherland, and hoped to take some preliminary results with him to show to a friend at the Racial Institute. He would be grateful if the Lieutenant could have all the prints from today's journey ready tomorrow to take with him.

Would the Captain be going in his car?

'No, no of course not, by train.'

Would it be possible for Lieutenant Klinger to borrow the

Captain's car? He could obtain some additional petrol rations for official duties . . .

Wahl frowned; he looked at the steering wheel and then the bonnet as if inspecting a daughter before she leaves home for the first time on her own. 'Well . . .'

The Lieutenant would of course be delighted to help the Captain with any future work when he returned from leave.

'Well . . .'

They came to the field of stones. Klinger was impressed with their strangeness; if not for the same reasons as Wahl advanced on the way back.

He had agreed to the loan of the car reluctantly, hedging it about with provisos about not eating sandwiches please, and not entertaining women, if you please, and was in full stride now that he had earned his audience's attention with his favour, about the significance of the stones:

'. . . and while we cannot know the true import of the stones, or why they are aligned precisely the way they are, we can say, I can say, that their purpose is truly mysterious. Does that sound paradoxical to you?'

No, said Klinger to himself. But he was quite happy now, and this was the price he must pay. 'I think I see what you mean,' he said.

While Wahl chattered on about lines of astral force, the significance of placement of stone against stone for drawing down lines of power from sun and moon, Klinger remembered Wahl's figure, soft and perishable, among the tall, frowning stones and the fantastic shadows of their figures that the sun threw on to the grey, dissolving wall.

Yes, Yes, I see, Ah, he said to Wahl in as many varied

expressions of interest as he could manage, as the car bore them back to more madness.

6

'Would you come for a drive?'

She laughed. 'Yes – I suppose. Why not? Can we go along by the sea? As far as we can? Is it your car?'

'A brother officer's. I did him a favour.'

'How long have we got – when do you have to be back?'

'I'm on duty this evening, from six.'

'Wait there . . .' And she went out quickly and he heard her cross the hall and enter the kitchen. He heard her say something to Thérèse and Thérèse's cracked voice muttering something. He looked at a book, put it down, examined a shell on the mantelshelf, twisted twice round on his heel, glancing at the room; a haven of glassware and solid wood and fabrics, the view from the window, the books, all that was familiar and Julia's . . . He lit a cigarette. Picked up the book again. He read a little at another place. Put it down again. It was astonishing how difficult it was to fill time. The house had gone pleasantly silent, with only murmurings from the kitchen, the song of birds through the open window. Perhaps ten minutes later Julia came back in, swinging a basket in her hand. 'Lunch,' she said. 'A picnic.'

As an excuse to visit her, he had brought the equipment,

a suitcase full of negatives and prints, a box of developing equipment. 'It is most kind of you. I really have no room,' he'd said, struggling with all this up the stairs behind her. To a white-washed room with a high window that faced through the topmost branches of the trees to the dirt road and the coastal plain beyond. Another room in his life. 'There are things I can't keep in the billet. Because of the lack of room. I have to share. And for other reasons . . .'

He didn't elaborate. She didn't question him about the contents. He hoped that she would look in the suitcase when he had gone. That she would admire his photographs alone; without the necessity of him demonstrating, however modestly, their admirable qualities. An artist should not be modest, he thought, but a lover should. A putative lover, Otto would say. Why all these words? The words got in the way with their hidden snares and pitfalls.

He had almost brought over the manuscript he had written. He had rehearsed a speech: I have written about myself. Please read it. It will tell what I am. Who I am . . . But he had read it through himself the night before.

Self-serving, vain, callous, with a surface charm, like a shine, to his actions, not particularly pleasant, though, when revealed thus. It was too honest by far, he realised.

Besides, he had lost the taste for writing about himself. What had passed the time in last year's long bitter winter seemed redundant now. The past was redundant. No doubt he could have found a way to continue, but difficulties were mounting daily. Earlier in the month a unit of Todt Organisation people had descended on them. They were to oversee the repair of fortifications along the coast. There were always people passing up and down the corridor outside, opening the door by mistake. And he didn't want Otto asking, 'What is that?' and being forced by friendship to show Otto the story of his life. Now he decided not to show it to Julia either, for different and more important reasons. Perhaps when he knew her better. If there was time. Like everything else, time was becoming a commodity in short supply.

He drove some ten kilometres west. He turned the car into a narrow lane, burred each side with brambles. The windows open, the warm sea-charged air streamed over their faces and lifted Julia's hair. She was silent all the way, leaning her elbow on the sill of the window, smiling into the breeze. He respected her silence; there was a conventional pattern of events and their order which must be obeyed. To have her here; to then have her smile – she would be happier to talk later, away from her home. He slowed and pulled into the side as a private soldier rode round the corner on a bicycle. The soldier wobbled and almost fell off as he looked down into the car and tried to salute Klinger. Klinger touched his cap cheerfully. He passed the grey pill-box from which the soldier must have come. Just after it the lane petered out. He pulled onto the cliff-top and parked under some blackthorn, just out of sight of the slit of the pill-box. 'There's a pleasant spot below here.'

'You've been here before?'

'I know the whole coast.'

Her skirt billowed about her knees as she came down the steep sandy path behind him. The path led onto a tiny beach of silvery sand, enclosed on each side by a table of huge boulders drying where the tide had gone out.

'We can sit up there,' he said, pointing to a ledge.

He sat close to her. She rested her hands on the basket's covering white cloth. It seemed that she was unwilling to look at him now that they were truly alone. He let her gaze on the sea for a while. Then he said, 'I'm sorry again for this.'

'What?' She did now face him, brushing her hair back with one hand.

'The uniform. There's nothing I can do about it, I'm afraid.'

'Well.' She turned to him. 'You could always desert,' she said casually. 'Don't people ever desert?'

'Desert?' He frowned, then laughed. 'I'd be shot. Besides, I'm an officer. Officers don't desert. It's only poor ploughboys and kids from the slums who do that. A lot have people at home who've been killed in the bombing. They're usually picked up trying to get back to them. Then they're shot.'

'You haven't anyone to run home to?'

'No.' And that is where he began to tell her about his life. What he told her was not so different from what he had written down, but he spared himself. He was, in his way of talking, modest, amusing; not everything he said was calculated; he could not speak of what he regarded as his art without passion . . . After this bloody war was over he would travel, my God he would. To America, South America, China – Africa – there was the place; an illimitable ocean of light. He knew that when all of this, this war, was cast off – his right hand gestured the war away – then he might be a great photographer. Even if no one ever saw his work, his work would exist as a record of what his camera had witnessed. Not him. It wasn't a personal thing. Art was impersonal. Lotte's face came to him. She spoke through him. The artist is nothing – his skill is learned, his material is whatever is common to everyone – his skill is all. He would cast off every chain that had been loaded on him, purge every compromise he had been forced to make. He would, at last, function as an artist should – solely in the service of the image, the subject, the outer world. He no longer believed that art was a means of self-expression. That was a despicable, masturbatory activity. Art – if he was capable of such a thing – was the making of a work of art; the world as a single expression. The illumination, the drawing out of the secrets of the world. What was the self compared to that?

His excitement mounted as he talked. He stopped, as if embarrassed by his passion. 'Well, enough of that –' he said. He reached behind him for his camera. Might he take some pictures of her, down there, on the beach, against the sea?

He posed her in front of him on the beach. He took several shots of her from three, then two metres. Coming close in to her, he said, 'Could you just put your arm up, your right hand against your hair?' He took her hand in his and, now that they stood very close together, leaned forward and kissed her on the mouth. There was no resistance – but her lips were cool and remained shut. When he stood back, she said, 'I don't think I should be doing this.'

When he had finished photographing her they lay on the ledge. He was in his shirtsleeves. They had finished the meal of ham and cider. He said, 'I have leave due. I'm going to Paris. Will you come with me?'

She was silent for a moment, then she smiled, and said, again stroking her hair back with the blade of her hand, 'What would you want to be taking a woman to Paris for? The place is full of beautiful women.'

'Not the one I want to be there.'

She looked away to the sea. 'No – I won't come. It's good of you to ask me. But I don't want, to be plain, to go as a German officer's woman. I saw a lot of those when I was in Paris. I like you. I don't want to be like those.'

'I go tomorrow. I have a week. I should have looked forward to it.'

Again she smiled, but a little differently, with a slight slackening of confidence in her response.

'I have my rail warrants already made out for that time,' he said. 'I can't change them. The army doesn't like you to change your mind.'

She was silent.

'What about your husband?' he asked, desperate that he was losing her. 'Have you heard anything about him?'

Then she told him, pulling the dry, grey grass with little tugs of her fingers, her legs folded beneath her, the skirt tightened round her thighs, that she and her husband – well, they had not been happy for some time. At first she'd worried about what might have happened to him – and worried again when he began to drop out of her thoughts, so that it had become almost a duty to remember him. She couldn't even sometimes quite assemble his face in her mind.

They'd married before the war. She had been working in the Paris office of a New York paper, as a way of killing time after college in Dublin. Her father's connections with relatives in New York had got her into the bureau. She came of the good Irish stock, she said with a smile, the sort that had founded half America. But Ireland was a tight little island for the young. The Church was God, if he saw what she meant. The English?

The English were admired, regretted, envied, distrusted. No, she'd had no particular political views before the war – she picked them up from those she liked. She thought the idea of Paris was perfectly wonderful. Paris would be full of writers and artists. The newspaper was very conservative, a Republican stronghold, but all of the bureau people she met from the States were left-wing if they were under thirty; right if over that. So she went Left. Left, Right – she couldn't give a damn; it all seemed a game. She didn't really understand – she was twenty-three in 1938. She had a degree, not a very good one, in English. She had left the clumsy suitors – that was really the only name for them – of collegiate Dublin far behind, and her head fairly hummed in Paris. Politics were a part of life. It just seemed that all the young men, the best-looking young men, the most intelligent and dynamic young men, were on the Left. 'It was a biologically determined sort of Marxism.' She laughed. Her fingers ceased plucking out the grass and folded about her knees and she rocked slowly, staring out to sea. Klinger sipped at the wine.

She was left-wing too, she supposed. That is until she met Maurice. He was a journalist, but of a very different sort. A French sort – there are no others like them anywhere else in the world, she said. He was vastly charming, knowledgeable, well-connected – almost a parody of the handsome Frenchman, and she had fallen instantly in love with him. He was also a Fascist. Her friends had told her this. At first gently, then ferociously, saying that she must be mad to consider such a man. He was vermin; an anti-Semite, a Nazi – she could have nothing to do with such a man. Which, of course, made her all the more determined to cut herself off from them, to float free of these friends. When the call to return home had come she had ignored it. She had married Maurice in April 1939, on a Paris spring day, which was the best spring day you could have, in a beautiful outfit he had bought for her – only then had she sent a cable to her people back home to tell them. Her parents had been thunderstruck. Her father had come over and tried to face Maurice down; and his voice and anger had foundered in front of his daughter's sweetness and happiness and Maurice's serious-faced agreement with him, so that in the end they both turned on her with a mock-severe chastisement of her unthinking behaviour, of the heart-ache she had caused her family by her thoughtlessness.

Her father had urged them to move over to Ireland. There was obviously a war coming. Maurice too knew that there was a war coming. He hoped to benefit in other ways. He was very clever; he had correctly foreseen that his country would crumble. He had reckoned that there would be good pickings for those who believed in the New Europe that would emerge after a swift German victory. Obviously, she knew what this meant in a sort of abstract way. But it wasn't politics that absorbed her then – it was the discovery of his affair with a friend of hers.

'It's strange,' she said. 'His most revolting views – they made me uncomfortable; they struck me as barbaric, obscene. But it was his affairs, they were what really got through to me – and the fact that I believed in love and he showed me he didn't. It doesn't matter. Men think women very silly for believing in love, don't they? They get very philosophical and pragmatic and want to sleep with their secretaries and say that the word doesn't mean anything. It does . . . Anyway, all this is after the event . . . Are the Allies going to win?' she asked him suddenly.

Klinger grimaced, shrugged his shoulders, and felt himself a character in a book performing these actions. 'Yes – I think they must – in the end.'

'I think that he knew that – my husband, Maurice – I think everyone knew that in their hearts. And they made their decisions on that basis. Does that sound too fantastic? I think Hitler and Churchill and every soldier and airman always knew that and all through these horrors everyone knew what the end will be and we must go through this, all of this terrible thing, because it is here – do you think that? Do you think it can go on for ever, though? That might be what I mean. That would be truly horrible. To know that something has an end, and no end comes.'

'No,' he said quietly. 'I don't think it will go on for ever.' He felt disgusted with the war, the beach, the tiny rust-blue and brown limpets in grey reliefs on the rock behind them – but mostly with himself, with his tawdry small plans. He took a sip of wine, then tilted back the glass and finished it with a long, coldly lavish swallow.

It was simple, and endlessly complicated, to fall in love with this woman, which is what he realised he had just done, when he had felt fury and resentment at the thought of her first husband, the casual mention of other men.

They drove back. He asked if he might go and arrange the equipment in the room she had given him upstairs in the farm. 'Yes. Of course.' Her voice was easy, intimate. The drive back had been one of ease between the two of them. Thérèse peeped at him round the kitchen door for an instant as he set his foot on the bottom stair. Her head flicked away.

He looked out through the window as he arranged objects and books and papers on the chest that rose above the window ledge and cut a portion of light from the room. The landscape was flat beyond the surrounding trees, the square, uninteresting, gardeners' fields; the land of daily labour and the entrance and exit of seasons and regularity, of peasant boredoms and intrigues and frustrations and endless accommodation with the land, with what could be done, what had always been done, what should be done – and he knew that he was not part of that, either here or at home. That Julia was not a part of that, though she had buried herself here. They were citizens of a new world that was not here. As he laid out his belongings they became the first citizens, the first colonists, of this new world.

When he came downstairs she was standing in the living room. She turned and smiled.

'I have to be going now.'

'You're going to Paris?'

'Yes – tomorrow.'

'I wonder, could you – would you bring me back a copy of *Les Enfants terribles* by Cocteau. It's impossible to get books here. And Fitzgerald. Scott Fitzgerald. Any of his.'

'That's one thing Paris has. They have no ham, but they do have books.'

She came to the door with him.

'Have a good time,' she said, holding out her hand. 'You know – this is absurd – but I've never called you by your name. Your Christian name.'

'Walther.'

'Julia,' she said, and released his hand.

He was even willing to sacrifice Paris for Julia. Not that the city was such a bargain nowadays. At the Soldier's Home he was allocated a tiny plywood compartment on his own. A Luftwaffe officer, sitting at a table in the dining hall, drunk, at noon, informed him that he would be wise not to go out on the streets in uniform. Some of them had taken to wearing civilian suits coming in and out of HQ because of the snipers. 'The silly bastards don't seem to take any notice of reprisals any more. Why should they?' It was a bright sunny day, but where, last year, the sun had streamed through the high windows brightening the long, narrow, officers' restaurant, now these windows had been boarded over and they sat in pale yellow artificial light as if it were twelve at night, not noon. There wasn't much to eat, the rivers of wine had lessened from a flood to a mere trickle. There was nothing coming from the Fatherland, and little enough left in the capital after everything had been looted. The carcass, said the blue-uniformed, blue-chinned airman, had been picked quite clean. Klinger longed for the countryside of Brittany, seeing its flat fields in the face of the drunk who went on talking to him. 'But everything is so beautiful, isn't it – the women, my God the French women might have been bred like greyhounds for love. But don't go to the big brothel.' He named a house on Rue Lauriston. Klinger had heard of it. 'Unless you like your meat a little high,' said the Luftwaffe man, grimacing, twisting his mouth like a mule's in what could be pain or laughter. And, again, in a tone of mingled disgust, humour, lust, foul language and sentimentality, he told that there was a torture chamber under the brothel. That while officers were entertained above by the girls, below in the cellar Milice and Gestapo half-drowned naked men and women in a high walled bath; hung others by their wrists or ankles and whipped and beat them. Sometimes if the wrong door opened, you would catch a scream, or worse, that sort of sound cats make – you know, that high-pitched whimpering . . . Only, some poor bastard would be making that sound.

The Luftwaffe admin-man stared into the distance, considering in turn his own humanity, his grace, his immortal soul, the deplorable state of his socks, his need for another cigarette, another cognac, the need for victory, for defeat, for him to survive; the strategic necessity of cruelty, the equal necessity of shedding blood for the Reich; the pathetic fate of such a one as he was in ending up in this dusty, boarded-up hall, the things he could have done, the town he came from, the street, the house, the flush that mysteriously appeared, disappeared, and reappeared, like the blood of Christ, in the corner of the priest's eye as he bent to administer the host to the line of boys at Easter, his hand on Stefan's shorts, which the other boys all saw and giggled at afterwards . . . 'Have you a cigarette, Lieutenant,' he asked, casting the past away. 'I'm out. When I get up for another drink, I'll buy some.'

But when he came back, Lieutenant Klinger had gone.

What in God's name had happened to the rest of the people in the world? Klinger asked himself as he swung out of the door furiously, sadly – his mind numbed by the drinks he should have refused.

He stayed in the capital only long enough to buy the presents he wanted for Julia. The books she had asked for, and half a dozen others; perfume, good cognac, silk stockings. As he bought these things, he realised how much he missed her; but how right she'd been to say she wouldn't come with him. Before the war, perhaps even after the war – but not now.

The railway lines being bombed out, travel was disrupted and difficult; he hitched a lift in a car going north with three Signals officers.

They'd had a great leave in Paris. As they told of their Homeric exploits in the brothels, Klinger couldn't keep out of his head the images of men and women naked in the upstairs room, making love – well, the men making love of a sort, the women making money – while in the cellars naked bodies were introduced to terror and pain. What the hell – these men didn't know. He hoped they didn't know.

They were all happy in that car, travelling north, as if they were going to a football match or a dance. 'If they do come – then we shall see . . .' was the general attitude to the invasion. And if they did keep them out, why then there would be nothing for the Yanks to do but negotiate a peace of some sort – then they could finish the Russians off in the east. There was agreement to this, except for the youngest of them, a young man with a cropped yellow poll and a red startled face, who said, 'But who wants a peace with the New York Jews?' 'Oh, fuck the Jews,' said another. 'They've had enough. They won't bother us again.' 'I'd just like it all to stop, so that we can have a bloody good meal again.' And the conversation turned happily to a sort of Land of Cockaigne fantasy, where houses were built of sweets and gingerbread, roofs of marzipan, the fences made from sausages, the cocks on the churchtowers plump and feathered and to be had, where the roads were giant slices of bread and the rivers milk and beer and champagne, and the bridges halved and hollowed cheeses, where the pigs ran about with slices carved out of their backs and oranges in their mouths – a land of happy, well-fed fools and drunks. The sun flashed across them as they went under trees. A bottle of cognac passed from hand to hand and mouth to mouth. Klinger thought again how they were all living in a particularly vivid dream – that there was no prospect of waking from it, that that was the only thing to be feared – the waking from the dream.

The officers dropped him at the railway station at M——, with great expressions of sadness, much shaking of hands, then the car spurted away, hands waving in farewell, forgetting him already. It was early evening; the train was so late that he did not cover the ten kilometres up to St Pol until almost midnight.

Wahl's car was parked to the side of the station in the little wired-in compound for the German vehicles. A sentry opened the gate for him. He placed his parcels on the back seat. He was stopped only once, leaving the town's outer suburb. A nervous sentry played a torch over him; a very young man, with only one companion, the same age, on their own, in a dark flat land which meant them nothing but harm.

He turned off the coast road towards the wood. The sky was crowded with clouds pressing in from the sea; here and there the moon sailed, and was again drowned. The farm was asleep. He had wanted to arrive earlier, while there was still light. He knocked. It sounded very loud. To his surprise, the door opened almost at once. Only a little way. The light of a candle wavered in the hall behind Julia.

* * *

He stayed for the last three days of his leave. That first night he slept on the old couch in the room she had given him. The second night he went to bed with Julia. He didn't give her half the things he'd brought from Paris, in case they should seem to be bribes.

They made love urgently, and he said, and she said with him, as if they were learning a lesson, Why oh why must there be this stupid war. We are not part of it, not now.

He'd brought trousers and a jacket in Paris. He felt at first like an actor adopting a role, dressed in civilian clothes after so long. In the day he wore his jacket and sat and talked with her in the room downstairs, again like actors in a play, both of them knowing this, that there was no way that these scenes could be extended into what was called real life.

On June 5th he returned to the barracks. Wahl came back that evening and Klinger gave him the keys to the car.

7

'They've landed.' That was the one sentence that everyone, French or German, came out with that day. Every sentry along two hundred kilometres strained his eyes to the sea horizon to see the enemy. Nothing. Not for them. The real invasion took place up the coast.

In the evening, after they'd heard the news, Klinger and Otto, standing in the courtyard, fancied that they could hear the sound of heavy guns, but far away. It began to rain. They went indoors.

The radio said that 'they' had established a beachhead, but reinforcements were rushing to throw them back. Day after day, the news was still the same; the Allies were pushing a little inland here, being mightily repulsed there. The weather was unreasonably bad for the time of the year, which was taken as a good omen. But still, twice in a week Allied bombers bombed the railway siding to the south-east of the port village; a few men killed, all civilians. A bar down by the station was renamed the Half a Twitching Dog, for the reason that Otto had seen on a bomb site near the bar the front half of a dog twitching its front legs convulsively, its back ones blown clean away.

And, as always in armies, the revised situation, the post-invasion set of nervous responses and anxieties, came rapidly to be normal, so that one couldn't imagine what they were like before. They adjusted to the new pattern of air raids; to actually using the shelter in the basement of the tower. Then the raids eased.

Otto looked at the map with Klinger. He plotted the positions of the Allies on the Normandy beaches. He saw at once that when they had reached a certain position they were bound to take the Cherbourg peninsula; but that they would be held at Avranches. If they burst through there, there would be nothing to stop them taking the whole Brittany coast.

'Except us,' said Klinger.

He expected Otto to laugh and agree with him that they were a pretty sorry lot to be defending the whole coast.

'We shall have to be enough,' Otto said.

* * *

Alone, employing English as his spoken language, using a phrase of three words, one word of which was the soldier's universal adjective, another a noun that was too huge and pretentious to include him, Klinger said aloud, 'Enough fucking History,' and drove down the dirt road towards Julia's farm.

She was excited. This meant the end, didn't it – sooner rather than later?

Yes – it was the end. How long it would take, no one knew; but now that the Allies had survived the first days . . . yes, it was over. He felt traitorous, telling her this, but she probably knew far more than he did, from listening to the BBC.

'What will you do?' she asked – as if he were a free agent faced with any number of possibilities for the future.

'What I'm told, I suppose,' he replied. 'I am a soldier.'

And she told him not to be absurd. He didn't believe in the cause for which he was fighting. He was an artist. He had something to give. Her face shone, her mouth twisted into an odd shape.

'If you stay, you'll be killed,' she said bitterly.

If he stayed? Where on earth was he to go?

'Come here. You can stay here,' she said. Her husband's mother was dying. There was nothing that could be done – she would never be here again. She had sent Thérèse away to town for good, and paid Ronan off. She had told them she was returning to Paris.

He laughed. 'They won't believe you. They're country people. They'll know you're still here. They know where everything is when it's necessary for them to know.'

'It doesn't matter,' she said. 'They don't know when I'm

going. We could simply shut the place up, hide the lights, never be seen. I've food. Wine.'

'You mean that I should actually desert? Hide here?'

'Yes. Until it goes away. Until they come.'

'And what if they don't? What if we push them back? I couldn't hide here for the rest of my life.'

'I haven't anything else to offer,' she said. 'How long would your life be anyway?'

Klinger had driven a bargain with Wahl for a share in the use of the car. He'd bribed him with the only thing which would interest Wahl – not cigarettes, or calvados, or black-market ham, or a woman – but an offer to continue with his photographic help, and also to sketch professionally the artefacts that Wahl had collected on his travels. He flattered Wahl outrageously – 'What a handsome work it will be, Captain, just think of it . . .'

With the invasion, Wahl had become paranoid about the fate of his researches. His rough notes filled two suitcases, which travelled with him in the boot of his car. To be further on the safe side the first draft was in a bulging briefcase which he stuffed under the driving seat. Whenever he drove into the yard, these cases would be carried to his room, Wahl hurrying after holding the briefcase, and all of them would be stacked beside his door ready for immediate evacuation if need be.

Almost two weeks after the first landings, when the enemy was consolidating to the east, though the Americans were still being held, Wahl came up to Klinger in the mess hall.

'Have you heard – there's a rumour we're to go down the coast to the naval base at Brest and hold that as a fastness until relief comes.'

Did Wahl really believe in that relief? From his urgent but unpanicky appearance it seemed he did.

'But that's fifty kilometres away. We're just going to cut and run?'

'I don't know about that,' Wahl said impatiently. 'But you know what this means – I shall have to leave my research half done. God knows what the armies will do to the sites. It's most important that I fill some gaps before we have to leave. In the present state of unrest we really could be moved anywhere at a moment's notice.' A look of slightly pained confusion came into Wahl's eyes. His obsessions were colliding with his duty. He had demonstrated himself to be a good Nazi, if of the eccentric breed of believers in long lost races of blonds making their way up and down the mountain paths of antiquity to, and from, liaisons with maidens, also fair-headed, whom the repulsive small dark people had somehow missed seducing – 'The origin of dwarfs – and gods, you see,' Wahl had said to him cheerfully. Wahl had been researching a Pan-European religious symbol – a swastika carved on the back of a corner niche Madonna – 'but the figure is earlier, much earlier, you see, predating Christianity.' Klinger hadn't the heart to tell him that the swastika had probably been carved deeply and ironically by some terminally bored sentry on a long night watch. And it must be, Klinger thought, that the Captain desired the victory of his cause, but he was heartened to see Wahl's individual madness winning out over the greater one. There was the ridiculous and abnormal in his nonsense – but, embodied in his upright, strutting pouter-pigeon form, it became almost innocence, compared to some of the forms it could have taken.

What forms? He had put to the back of his mind, as much as he could – until he began to believe and not want to believe – the rumours of what was happening back east, far away in Poland. The stories had grown that there were places where locomotives backed into birch-woods carriages and trucks full of human freight and came out empty and went in again full, and came out again empty and did this over and over again – these were surely just soldiers' nightmares. Except that Lotte had gone. All the others had gone . . .

8

'Goffic says, in his book,' said Wahl, 'that the Pardons are in fact the last vestiges of the pagan festivals, absorbed into Christian ritual, but with many of their original features obtruding, as it were.'

Klinger glanced round at Otto in the back of the car; Otto grinned. It was barely believable, but Wahl had managed to scare up enough petrol for this trip. He must, he must see the Pardon in the village of St Anne – it might be their last chance. It might indeed. Supplies of all sorts had dried up. The Allies were stuck at Avranches, but their advance now seemed inevitable; Allied planes frequently strafed the roads; their own were rarely seen. And the three of them were off to view a religious procession. Wahl had the blind courage, or rather blind lack of fear, of the obsessive. The other two had come along to map and photograph – in return in Klinger's case for past favours, in Otto's case for friendship, and out of sheer boredom. They had been waiting for two weeks now for the order either to join the forces eastwards up the coast, or to retreat towards the west and the coastal ports.

'. . . of course, before the war, they were much bigger occasions, the Pardons. Every village and hamlet has its own Pardon, though the more popular saints recur time and again. But at the larger ones there would have been a huge fair and food and drink stalls, perhaps a wrestling match for the men. Certainly at, I think it was, the Pardon of Fire, two villages would contest physically. Actually do physical battle for the possession of the holy banners, believing that on their possession by one village rested the chances for a good harvest . . .' Wahl chattered on, informing Klinger and Otto of what they were about to see.

They had driven west from the port; the fortress at Brest was some fifty kilometres away; the stabilised front at Avranches almost two hundred; Klinger took great and guilty comfort from this thought. On the way they sped past the road to Julia's farm. She was no longer there. All the outlying farms near to the coast had been cleared and their occupants moved into town in case the farms should be needed against more invaders on coastal raids. Julia had taken a room in the only hotel not taken by the army.

He had visited her there; at least two other officers had their mistresses installed in the place. She said that she loved him, as they lay in bed together. That was the easy part.

'I must leave when the others do,' he said.

'Stay, I will hide you.'

'Don't be silly – where can one hide from an army?'

'In the farm. We can go back to the farm,' she said. 'Your men will be going to Brest – you told me. They won't come back again, will they? It's finished. You must see that.'

They said the same things over and over . . .

'I'd have thought that was a job for autumn or spring rather than now,' said Wahl suddenly. 'Typical of these French.'

'I beg your pardon, Captain?'

'The two men we just passed, mending the hedge. A living hedge made by cutting and bending the trees and shrubs in the row – I've seen it. But not at this time of year, surely. These people are stupid.'

Klinger looked back. One of the men stood up in the ditch looking after the car, mopping his forehead with a handkerchief.

Well, thought Klinger, once again watching the road ahead run towards them, God alone knew what would happen now; presumably they would, and sooner rather than later, be sent to reinforce the front. The garrisons here and in Saint Pol and the other towns around had already been bled dry of experienced men – there were only the crocks left. Broadcasts announced in cheerful lies that the enemy had been thrown back, then reversed, then held; that they would soon be cast into the sea; but the fall of the Cherbourg peninsula meant that a huge landmass had been opened for the Allies – 'However,' Preidel had said, demonstrating on the map at that morning's briefing, 'If our troops can once again advance on Caen here from the east, and on Avranches from the west, the Allies are caught in a net.' The cheer raised was half-hearted, their faces glum as they looked at the blackboard. The Allied push was bulging southwards. Only yesterday, the 19th of July, they had heard that Caen had finally fallen; it could not be long before the pressure on the western front at Avranches was intensified by the Americans.

As they came to the top of a rise in the road, Wahl slowed the car. 'The church,' he announced.

A small square tower, topped by a conical spire tipped with a glinting gold weathercock, rose from a fold in the rolling and dipping, gorse-covered heathland. A few houses could be seen perched about the hill facing the sea. In front of the car women in traditional dress and men in what looked like goatskins were walking steadily; on the hillside opposite, other locals made their way down towards the church. They drove on slowly, the sides of the narrow lane cutting off their view; the villagers they passed very close to did not look at them. Only the children, on a level with their windows, looked in. A boy, his hair plastered back, thin body tight in his communion suit, stuck out his tongue. Luckily, Wahl didn't see him. A hanging offence.

'We're riding in a glass coach,' said Otto, and laughed.

'Eh – what's that?'

'Nothing, sir.'

'Then don't speak if you have nothing to say,' Wahl snapped.

The village was no more than a hamlet, made up of the few scattered houses they had seen. There was no centre to it, but the lolling field of coarse grass in front of the churchyard's low surrounding wall. The field was now rapidly filling with people. Wahl swung the car to the side of the road and bumped it to a halt.

'Safe enough there, I think.' He studied the church on one

side, the near hedge on the other. 'They won't try anything today. It is one of their holy days.'

They got out. A few people at the edge of the crowd stared at them, then shrugged and turned away to face the church.

'You stay with the car, List,' Wahl ordered. 'These peasants will steal the boots off our feet if we don't watch them.'

As Wahl began to study the church, Otto grinned at Klinger. Wahl took out a notebook from his pocket. 'While we are gone you may occupy yourself by drawing a plan of the church and surrounds. You have pen and paper?'

'Everything necessary, sir.'

'Well then – you have your camera, Lieutenant? We may gain a better view up here.' Wahl climbed stiffly up the rise that overlooked the church.

'Stand by me – here. We are waiting for the banner. I have read about these events. The great banner leads the procession. Did you know that the church's lower foundations are composed mainly of an earlier Roman building – probably a military installation? What awful thieves these Christians are! And that St Anne herself, whom they come to worship – the legend is that she was originally a Queen of Brittany in the very ancient days. That she somehow annoyed her husband and – with child in her belly – took a ship they call a ship of light, with the wings of an angel for sails, from these shores to Judaea.' He pronounced the word with a thick, disgusted *Yu* sound. 'And there she gave birth to Mary the Virgin. So the queen Anne brought up the child to be the mother of Christ and all that took place thereafter, you see, has been falsehood, and the true origin of Christ's forebears has been ignored or concealed,' Wahl said impatiently, waving his hand in front of him as if to finish centuries of concealment. 'Then Anne grew old and restless and wished to see her native land again and the same ship came back, only this time the sails were black, her lord, the King, having died the meanwhile. She settled here, on this very coast, and became the guardian of the sea. And, so say these ignorant folk, Jesus himself and St Peter and another of his disciples – I really can't remember which – came to ask her blessing before his crucifixion. And that Christ himself consecrated the ground for a church – they say that Christ stuck his staff into the earth and a fountain came forth – but then this is the land of fountains and calvaries, as you must have seen. Ah, here is the banner. Your camera at the ready, please, Lieutenant.'

From inside the church, which glimmered with the light of many candles, through the Norman arch of the front door a pole protruded. Three men were needed to guide the pole and the banner that hung on it through the doorway. As it came out, the pole was raised upright and the banner fell straight, showing the figures of St Peter and St John – their names embroidered at their feet. A thickset middle-aged man who must have been immensely strong took hold of the trunk of the pole all on his own. It must have been four metres high and four white cords from its top, held firmly by young women, steadied the pole as the man walked forwards.

After the banner came the priest, settling the embroidered cope over his thin shoulders and beginning to read in a monotonous roar from his missal. An altar boy swung a censer on one side of the priest. Another boy, also carrying a censer, scurried out to catch them up, so that in a moment two blue trails of incense followed the settling, lazy swings of the censers, the odour sweet and heavy and mingling with the summer smell of heath-land and sea as they came out from the churchyard gate towards Klinger and Wahl.

'Are you taking this?' Wahl asked sharply.

'Ah, yes.' Klinger began to photograph the procession as it came out of the church, the yard, towards them, turned, and started down a path towards the sea. After the great banner came smaller standards carried by men in black suits and white shirts and tightly, tinily knotted ties; and after them came the women in splendidly starched dresses and many-coloured shawls, and the children, shining-faced and restive; and last, four venerable men, each with a thick white moustache, carried a wooden stretcher on which there stood upright a rather dumpy statue . . .

'There – you see,' said Wahl rather loudly as the statue passed. 'That is St Anne. The legend I was telling you – the local priest recounted it to me – it is held sincerely by the older people – that after their visit Christ and Saint Peter – and the other fellow – returned to the Holy Land. Anne sickened and died. A great mist came over the sea, and when they went to look for her body it was not to be found. Then came the news that fishermen had pulled up in their nets a statue and that it was the very image of the sainted Anne . . .'

The procession was now past and the other villagers began to press down the narrow lane after it, a few glancing up at the Germans with those blank faces that were somehow more contemptuous than any overt expression of hatred.

'We shall let them go down, I think,' said Wahl studiedly. 'It would hardly do for us to become caught up with them. Now – do you see the importance of this legend? You don't?'

Klinger did his best to look puzzled.

'No? I must say that it took me a while to realise its true significance. It is amazing. No? It ties in with all the other facts I have gathered about a common Aryan religion that spread over all of Northern Europe. More, it accords with Professor Bergman's *Twenty Five Points of German Religion*.'

Klinger walked slowly beside him as they followed the procession. The lane was so overhung with grasses and brambles that they almost met in the middle above their heads.

'Bergman's point number two,' Wahl said excitedly. 'That Christ was not a Jew – but a Nordic. Betrayed and put to death by the Jews but actually a warrior, the son of a king and a queen. Because if his mother was daughter of a queen, and if we take the virgin conception into account, then the lineage of Christ is purely Northern European – in other words it has no trace of Jewish blood whatsoever. That is why this rite, so small and insignificant as it may seem, and so little understood by its ignorant participants, is of the utmost significance.'

'That is quite fascinating, Captain.' Klinger had the sudden feeling that he was walking with a lunatic and that the hot summer day and the high banks of this lane and the clouds and the smell of the sea and flowers were all illusory for this man; that Wahl lived in a sort of perpetual worm-cast of thought, where he could not move any of his limbs but his round, pink smiling face and mouth opened to pour out this rubbish; that this tube of enclosing earth was one from which all sensation and thought was excluded except the senses of warmth and constriction; where there was no light, no poetry; and where, in the world into which the captain's bald, pink head obtruded, every object, idea, personality, was hung with an arbitrary nonce-name that bore no reality to its actual identity – a world of idiotic surreality, where the simple beauty and piety of this procession was mixed in with Grendel and Thor and torchlight parades and black uniforms and children's books that spelled out the word Jew beside a caricature of a monstrous rat-faced man, and where men tortured other men under a brothel and others with patient, delicate, dedicated fingers measured the skulls of the living and the dead.

'The Führer was right of course to stigmatise Christianity as a religion for the weak and stupid and Jewish in its origin – but not in the person of Christ. On Christ's example – there we can truly say that the Führer is the New Messiah, and that this older, purer, Nordic-Aryan religion links Christ himself as a precursor . . .'

'Excuse me – I must get some photographs while this goes on . . .' said Klinger and made his escape as the crowd spilled out onto the open cliff-top. He was able to circle round, to be closer to the priest and banners, leaving Wahl on the edge of the crowd, scribbling in his notebook.

The service was beginning. The four old men bore the figure of the saint to a cairn of stones almost at the edge of the cliff. Klinger felt intrusive. Almost automatically he shot the pictures Wahl would want, then he sat down on a rock, took off his cap and let the wind blow back his hair.

The priest intoned prayers; the villagers made their responses. Now they were lifting the figure of the saint from the stretcher and placing her on the cairn, her blind stone face to the sea.

Klinger knew that any picture taken from the point of view of the crowd itself would show the two Germans as almost warders or sentries; occupiers overlooking the rites of their captives. But the worshippers, with an unspoken, glancing contempt, seemed to whisper, 'Your day is nearly through. Look, we have preserved this and this. What have you preserved?' The two of them could take out their revolvers and shoot into this crowd and the crowd would panic and run for cover, the priest would dive comically behind the stone cairn; they could break up this ceremony and perhaps smash the statue of the saint in an orgy of resentment against their loss – but they could only wound these things now. Wahl could not see, in his intellectual fantasies of blood and will, that the small stone figure was the true victor. Wahl regarded such things as signs of weakness. It is all nonsense perhaps, Klinger said to himself, but these people have the more powerful nonsense. He put a fresh roll of film into the camera and began to take more shots for his own pleasure, keeping his distance though, not wishing to offend. He put the camera into its satchel before he strolled down, and along the edge of the crowd, back to Wahl.

All most correct.

'I think it best we go now,' said Wahl. 'The service I think is nearly over. I wish you to take some photographs of the church.'

As they went up the lane the crowd behind them began to sing a hymn. Its sound was rather weak and quavering against the low roar of the sea below and the raucous cries of the gulls . . .

The car bumped up the lane. Otto sat in the back, slotting his sketches and map into Wahl's briefcase, as instructed by Wahl, shouting back over his shoulder. Klinger leaned his arm on the sill. He resented having to go back to the billet, to discipline, to an increasingly irksome life – perhaps he would even welcome a move up the line. Then he remembered the dead and, worse, the wounded, and he thought differently. But still – something must happen.

Up on the coast road they travelled for only a couple of kilometres and then slowed for a halted convoy of an armoured car, half a dozen trucks full of troops and a staff car. Two junior officers stood beside the car consulting a map.

Wahl drew up and with great condescension offered his help.

The convoy needed to go through St Pol; they weren't sure if they'd taken the right turning at the last crossroads. They had been sent along from the most western point of the coast to proceed to the front. All the men in the trucks looked relaxed and tanned after a summer, or more than one, among the rocks and bays of Finistère.

There were more coming up behind.

'Well, we shall lead you in as far as St Poule . . .' said Wahl.

He let them get back in their staff car and then spurted forward ahead of them.

'By all that I hold holy,' he said. 'I wish I was going with these fellows.'

Look, Klinger almost said, feeling so relaxed and happy in the summer wind, look, there, ahead, just ahead, you can see, drawing nearer, the little wood, the trees growing ever so slightly taller, the wood that hides my mistress's manor . . . He dropped his cigarettes in the seat well and bent forward to pick them up.

All sense of motion ceased. He could not be sure afterwards what order these things came in, but there was a flash of blinding white light, a great sound inside his head, a blackness that shut out completely the dome of bright blue sky that again began to become very slowly visible through this perplexing, thick mist of floating dust and scintillant particles of glass.

To his astonishment, Klinger could move. There was, for some reason, no more roof to the car, only that blue sky, opening between lids of dust, and sails of white, which blew away, leaving only the wonderful sky. He looked round and Otto was sitting in the rear seat, a little slumped to one side, as if thrown there, but smiling. Then Otto's smile faded, his face went grey and he said mildly, 'Oh God. Oh God.' Klinger hauled himself round in the seat. Where the hell was Wahl? The door on Wahl's side was missing and so was Wahl. He looked down to where Otto was pointing. Otto's legs were no longer there, not from the knees down. There was a mangled hole in the floor of the car and some strips of cloth from Otto's trousers and now a lot of blood.

Then there were hands reaching him out of the car. Hands of kindness. He looked another way from Otto. On the road the figure of Wahl, seemingly unscathed, was executing some sort of dance up and down the verge, calling in a high maddened voice, 'My book. My book,' as he snatched at scraps of blackened paper that floated in the air. Klinger sat with his legs in the edge of the ditch at the side of the road and someone offered him a cigarette and he said thank you very much and when he took a drag and pulled it away from his lips he saw that the end was soaked with blood and his fingers found the cut in his lip and he moved his hand over his face and those were slivers of glass embedded in his forehead.

He asked the man who had given the cigarette about Otto.

'The other lieutenant?'

'Yes.'

'I'm afraid that he's dead.'

Why afraid that he was dead? Why afraid that any of them were dead? That was their trade, wasn't it?

9

A small landmine. Probably of English make. Intended for the convoy coming up behind. They had been lucky, said Preidel. Except poor Lieutenant List. He wondered, he could not help but notice that Klinger and List were friends. Would Klinger perform that painful duty of a fellow officer and sort out List's obviously personal effects to be held for his relatives? Although, as Preidel said, it was practically impossible to send them through to the homeland, transport being what it was. He, Preidel, would write the necessary official letters.

Klinger had been kept for only one night in the field hospital. The place had been a school room. Wounded from the front had not reached them yet so the place was half empty. Klinger's life had been saved by bending forward in his seat. He had a bump on his forehead; impacted glass from the instrument panel had been removed and the wound stitched up with black thread. The hospital was no more than a few streets from Julia's hotel. Wahl lay in bed at the opposite end of the room; he was still in a state of shock and only when he slept did he whimper from the many small pains that visited him from the hundreds of fibres and tiny fragments of steel and wood that had penetrated his back from the car seat. The doctor told Klinger that Wahl was in no danger. But Klinger sat by his comrade's bed that night and listened to him dream. Wahl was by the stone circle. Wahl was writing. Listen, said Wahl to himself, listen, the book, you must keep the book and my papers and all these things – the artefacts, the photographs, the notes, the endless notes – these all must be kept . . . The drugged Wahl held Klinger's hand, not knowing who he was, and squeezed hard. 'Tell the adjutant to make sure that the boxes are full,' said Wahl firmly, and squeezed again.

And poor bloody Otto was already in a box somewhere . . .

So, the next day, when Klinger got back to the billet, he had an unpleasant task to perform. He opened the door of their room – the evening light made the room warm, a deep rose suffused all the walls and furnishings as if seen through a red filter. Otto had been such a quiet, unassuming, gentle man to share with – when you consider what thugs and idiots the army could – did – delight in doling out as room-mates. A large farmhouse wardrobe had served them both for hanging clothes. Otto, he knew, stored – had stored, that was – his more personal belongings in a cupboard beside the wash-basin. There was a canvas bag on the bed holding what had come from Otto's pockets yesterday. Klinger opened the neck of the bag – inside were a few Occupation marks, bloodstained, a pocket watch, its face smeared with blood, an identity card, a pass to the harbour, a letter in a small blue envelope; petty things, common to them all. The notes were too bloody even to be stolen by the orderlies for drinking money. Better to destroy those. He put the bag down beside the wash-basin. He would give it to Preidel in the morning. He turned to the spare uniform, the shirts, the neatly rolled socks, taking them from the wardrobe and laying them across Otto's bed.

He went through the pockets of the spare uniform. A couple of centimes; another letter. He didn't want to pry; he opened and glanced at it, trying not to read any detail, just to find out who the sender was. It was from Otto's mother. With that guilty but irresistible fascination of looking into a side of life of another that is normally closed off to the outsider, he read it through. Nothing of interest, except to Otto. About keeping warm – it was dated last January – was he getting enough to eat? Things were hard in the city, with the bombing and shortages of this, that and everything, but – God willing – they would all come through and she wished her beloved Otto home as soon as God could spare him, but she supposed he must do his duty and be brave. Do write back soon, your loving Mutti.

He put this letter on his own bed – another of the things he must give to Preidel. The uniform would presumably go back to stores.

There remained the cupboard.

Two shelves. On the first a tin of biscuits and a packet of issue cigarettes. Two magazines for Otto's automatic pistol. Hairbrush. Shaving lotion. A bundle of letters in small blue envelopes. Klinger did not read these, knowing with the cruelty of the living, the sad banality of the repeated simple emotions put down on paper over months and years; affecting singly – but unbearable if read together in a short space of time. Simplicity, he knew, was the basis of great art. Why was it bad art when it was real? He pulled the other things off the shelf. Shoe brush. Clothes brush. A huddle of small tins of boot polish, tooth powder, Russian Lice Powder . . .

Below, in the bottom of the cupboard, were Otto's spare boots. And a pair of black civvy shoes. A small pile of notebooks lay on the top of the Latin Ovid, and under that the huge, two-volume Latin dictionary lugged all the way back from a Paris leave. Klinger took out the top notebook and opened it. It was one of Otto's translations. Perhaps done on the boat or some time ago, somewhere in the long boring nights of a barracks. Perhaps in that POW Camp where Otto had read the prisoners' mail.

> In the centre of the world, between the land and sea
> and heavens, is a place where all of their three
> boundaries meet. From here, all that is here or anywhere
> can be seen, and every single voice calls to its ear . . .

Page after page was covered with thick black script. There were hardly any revisions. On the left-hand pages Otto had doggedly transcribed the Latin text in blue. Klinger put the notebooks on his bed with the letters. Pushed back into the right-hand corner of the bottom of the cupboard – what was this? A camera case? He pulled the case out and opened it. A good old-fashioned miniature Ermanox, he saw with delight. The very type of camera, if a slightly younger model, that Lieutenant Marivaux had lent him in the spa nearly twenty years ago. One of the first 35mm cameras. Behind the case, a large leather wallet.

It was stuffed with photographs, seven or eight centimetres square. A few a little larger.

He sat down on Otto's bed and took out the larger pictures. They were the usual family shots; engagingly amateurish, the camera being passed from hand to hand. This must be Otto's mother and, he presumed, the girl at her left side must be Otto's sister, and on her right, gangly and thin, bespectacled Otto as an adolescent – only too recognisable as Otto still. Well, not still. Here was a picnic in the country. And this one – the father no doubt, with Otto a small boy, perched on his shoulders, pulling the man's hair up like horns. Huge grins on the faces. A dog lying with his front paws on the lap of the mother. Otto, sombre, with another girl, not a sister, her left hand through his right arm, his right hand laid tenderly on her hand, best suit, studio – engagement? He knew that Otto was not married. Who was she? Where had she gone? He looked closer. She was conventionally pretty – in that way that goes off rapidly with marriage; a merely biological disguise to assist the . . . What the hell do you know about it, Klinger? said Klinger to himself.

The other, smaller photographs formed a thick square bundle. As he took them from the envelope he saw the number 15 scrawled on the back print; shuffling them, there were numbers in descending order on the backs of each. He turned them over.

The first picture – not terribly well taken, but for its size clear enough, in a greyish black and white – is of a row of trucks. People, civilians, are climbing down from under the turned-back canvases at the rear of the trucks. They are overlooked by soldiers holding sub-machine guns, and a single officer; his silhouette on top of a ridge of earth – peaked cap, long nose – one arm outflung, directing his men. Picture

Two: the men are all out of the trucks and stand, scruffy, in open-necked shirts, without shoes, in semi-military lines being seemingly counted by an army sergeant, whose hand is raised like a conductor's. The officer is now standing tall and stiff, his hands clasped in the small of his back. Picture Three: an earthworks, a sunken path being excavated by a mechanical digger, leading into a sort of amphitheatre, its banks made by piles of its own earth. On the top stand three soldiers, dressed in greatcoats, their sub-machine guns held against their chests; the arena is empty. Klinger knew this was somewhere in the east, by the light, even allowing for the poorness of the photographs, the sheerly grey consistency of the light, the flatness and treelessness of the landscape, the thin, hollow-cheeked, high-cheekboned appearance of the civilians, the largeness of their eyes, the cheapness of their clothing. These were the creatures of a million exhortations, warnings, diatribes in the papers and on the wireless. The terrible Slavs, the dreadful Untermenschen. Picture Four: the first of these men appear at the head of the declining ramp; they are taking off their clothes and laying them in heaps. There are more sentries around the raised perimeter. In Picture Five, the naked men advance, their bodies white, their pubic hair and hanging genitalia somehow overemphatic, claiming too much attention, as in a pornographic photograph – the ones Klinger had seen, he thought inadvertently, were of the same awful standard aesthetically. But their purpose was different surely from these? In the one great work of art he had seen in the erotic field, the only such work that had been redeemed by the force of personality of the subject, there was presented a woman, taken from below, foreshortened on a divan – a West Indian woman presumably, or Mauritian perhaps, this being a French photograph; not African, though of course that in origin, and you looked at her sex, that wavy line of flesh and hair, but then, as if she compelled you to do so, you must look at her face. Its mature beauty gazed out with contempt at the voyeur looking in; her eyes directed you to the necklace that lay above her breasts; a pearl necklace with the pearls and their gold links painted in on the daguerreotype so that they shone . . . He looked at Picture Six. The men march three abreast down the ramp; there is one who looks straight towards the camera, whose dark eyes hold an unplumbable depth of pity and contempt. The sentries have parted in the next picture. They are setting up machine guns on the edge of the ramparts, the guns turned inwards. The first files of men have been conducted into the earth arena. The next batch, the men at the top of the ramp, are undressing. There are perhaps two hundred or more men in the arena . . .

Klinger had heard rumours of these things at the front; massacres, reprisals against the dreadful war the partisans were waging, and that must be waged against them; he was willing to think that the beings portrayed here looked more ridiculous than pitiable with their clothes taken away; he was unprepared for the pictures that followed.

Kindness to the mind. After he had seen, in excerpt, one batch of men lying down, contorted one over the other in the ditch he had not noticed before, dug like a great notch, or orchestra pit, or prompter's box or first row of the stalls, in the forefront of each small picture, and presumed that they were not acting in some charade, but had been shot down, he was quite ready for the next batch to be driven down. Here is interpolated a picture of Otto, holding his camera in both hands against his chest, he and a row of comrades in uniform smile at whatever photographer is shooting them, the two officers on each side of Otto rest friendly hands on his shoulders; the ramp glimpsed behind. Also to be seen, heaped corpses. Otto too is smiling, that charming, warm, lop-sided grin.

The rest of the photographs – well, what was to be expected? The scenes were barbarous and obscene – what did such words mean any more? It was simply that Klinger had never seen death treated as an industrial process. The bodies lay piled on top of each other. In the last picture a bulldozer was breaking down the parapet of earth so that it fell and covered the bodies below . . .

He put the photographs in his pocket, feeling them there as an excrescence of his body, or something added to his side, like the pack of devil's playing cards in the old story.

For the first time that year he got out his notebook and wrote again, addressing Otto:

> I find these photographs and I don't understand. Of course, I've glimpsed such things before, passed round by men who have served in Russia and Poland. I have always walked quickly away, making some excuse not to look, not to hear their comments. I think the reason I liked you, Otto, was that somehow your conduct, your manner, gave the impression that the world was not all bad, that all men were not beasts, that there was an essential core in you that was uncorrupted, perhaps even incorruptible. But these pictures. When did you take them? Where? But, you know, the question that really tortures me, that I cannot ignore, is why you took them?

And I find myself blaming you doubly because you were no photographer. Not like me. Because then there would have been the artistic imperative for recording these events, wouldn't there? I would have been obliged to have stood in the place you did – perhaps though, moving closer, or to another position to improve my vantage point. And what is my vantage point? To achieve the best picture? Yes – I am an artist, after all. I am a twentieth-century artist, which means that much must be forgiven me. And for whom would I have been so conscientiously recording these events? For myself? The expression of my self – the raison d'être of the artist now? Or to bear witness? Or to do what I fear and dread that you did, Otto. To record with careful prurience horrors to examine at leisure later. It is the very care you took – typical of you, my friend – that so pains me . . .

For, after these things have been witnessed – and reproduced – what place is there for artists? If Bosch from his imagination conjures visions of hell and puts them on a canvas, what place is there for small, banal images of real hells? Surely there can be no more artists, only historians – and all of us liars. After the example of your photographs, dear Otto, there will be no more stories, no elaborations, no fables, no transformations. Your manuscripts, left in the dark of a suitcase under a bed, at the bottom of a cupboard, will slowly fade and cease to exist simply because no one will be there to look at them.

The detailings of desires and obsessions – what is the excuse for our abstraction of one image to another but the desire to falsify? Even – especially – the pure, the morally neutral image I have sought through the machinery of the camera, the steel iris, the perfectly ground glass – my reliance on, my machine's need for the miners of sand and silica, of iron ore, the steel workers, the makers of plastics and rubber, the melters and blowers and cutters and grinders of glass, the endless refinement of tolerances to the smallest fraction in the steel parts, the lathes and milling machines and sanders, the factories that produce these, the craftsmen taking pains to perfectly achieve the concave of glass, the elimination of the tiniest flaws and specks in their creation until they can only be seen by God, the setting of all these into this box to admit the light of the world and then to extinguish it, to reduce it to paper, to the illusion our eyes reconstruct taught to read this version of creation. All to print the dead.

Not the memorial I wanted for you, Otto.

He took his suitcase from under the bed. He placed in it his notebooks, Otto's photographs, and Otto's translations. He pushed the suitcase back under the bed. Then he went to visit Julia in the town.

This time, the moment of entering her hotel was a parody of stepping back into the past and going up to see Mitzi and Valenti in the small hotel in the spa. The summer light was almost the same, the sun flooding across the dusty lobby. There was no one else in the lobby. He went straight up and along the blacked-out corridor with its one dim bulb over the landing.

She was alarmed at the wound on his forehead; she produced some precious cognac and they sat on the bed together. Now it was as if they were adolescents; the lack of space in the room made them awkward; whenever they moved, stood, walked to the window, to the sideboard, they apologised softly to each other. No, she would not make love. When he pressed her gently, she told him that it was her time. They drank a little more. He told her of the explosion. His friend's death. He was glad she wouldn't make love. To sit with her and simply to be tender was enough for now.

He stayed for only about an hour. No pretence – they had been ordered back into barracks by nine because of the increasing terrorist attacks and invasion alerts.

10

At about a quarter past twelve that night, just after he had fallen into a light skimming sleep, which dropped into and out of a dream in which he spoke with Otto and Julia in the same room, a long interminable conversation about where they were to dine that night, he was woken by an orderly first knocking loudly on the door and then opening it and letting the light from the corridor onto his face.

All officers were to report to the command post. In full uniform, please, sir.

He went across the pitch-black courtyard. An air raid was in progress near the rail yard.

He pushed aside the black-out drapes. Dietrich, grey-faced, waited in the small hallway. He snapped his arm up in the Hitler salute, and said, 'There is terrible news. There has been an attempt on the Führer's life. We must all now listen to the wireless.'

In the room were Preidel and the Todt officials, and two other officers he didn't recognise. Preidel asked, 'We are all here, gentlemen?' and nodded to Dietrich. Dietrich turned on the wireless set – a tall whitewashed box.

There was grave, martial music. An announcer. Then the voice – not heard for a long time. It sounded a thousand years old, as if it was coming from the stones of a tomb rather than a human throat, but it was still, indubitably and awfully, alive.

'If I speak to you today it is first in order that you should hear my voice . . .'

None of them looked at another; they stood, almost at attention, facing the wireless.

'The bomb placed by Colonel Graf von Stauffenberg exploded two metres to my right . . .'

Dietrich closed his eyes and muttered something to himself and to heaven.

'I myself sustained only some very minor scratches, bruises and burns. I regard this as a confirmation of the task imposed upon me by Providence . . .'

The voice droned on, at one moment pausing to cough harshly, at another to sniff; there was the sound of a piece of paper being turned over. The voice spoke of the conspirators, of the need for all military authorities to ignore any orders that might come from the conspirators; it said anyone issuing illegal orders must be arrested, shot on sight . . .

'I am convinced that with the uncovering of this tiny clique of traitors and saboteurs there has at long last been created in the rear that atmosphere which the fighting front needs . . .'

Dietrich glared fiercely round at them all; Klinger touched nervously, and as if indicating an identifying badge, the stitched wound on his forehead.

The next morning, through an open window across the courtyard, Klinger heard Dietrich screaming at Major Preidel. The major went away a few hours later in a car with two SD men. Dietrich called what was left of the unit together that afternoon and told them, with a satisfied, predatory smile, that arrests were taking place in Paris and all other headquarters. That Preidel was a traitor – his name was not to be spoken again.

In the days that followed, Dietrich assembled them to announce fresh triumphs and initiatives. The Hitler salute was declared for the first time to be obligatory; it must replace the standard military salute at all times. Political officers were being assigned to each regiment – perhaps if this had been done earlier, said Dietrich, these terrible events would not have occurred and the traitors unmasked before they began. Added to Dietrich was a constant stream of encouragement and threat from the radio. The army had been treacherous and would be punished; the army would be victorious and rewarded. On the first of August the Americans broke through the front at Avranches. That day Dietrich informed them that Wahl had been invalided home, presumably to get over his grief and madness at the loss of his book – the rest of the garrison was ordered to prepare to retreat to the fortress at Brest.

'In the meantime,' said Dietrich, 'we have a duty to perform for our murdered comrade, Lieutenant List – and you, Klinger, as his friend, will have the pleasure of recording that duty.'

'What do you mean?'

'Hostages, my good sir. Ten for one. That's the regulation. These people have been warned. Back of the harbour, in the dock sheds tomorrow morning, seven o'clock sharp. Bring your camera for some good pictures.'

'They've caught the men who killed your friend?' said Julia.

'No – I told you. These are hostages. Old men – boys – we keep a floating population of eligible candidates in the old fort behind the dock.'

'But you said you were leaving tomorrow – all of you.'

'As Dietrich said, the law is the law – "Why should ten men live to enjoy our absence."'

'But the war's never come here . . .'

It was perfectly true. The harbour was on a spur of land that curved into the sea. All roads were to the south. And those roads were packed with trucks and cars and horsedrawn carts loaded with wounded, and exhausted soldiers pulling away to the south and west. But none of them came here. Why should they come here? And in the morning – it was early evening now – the garrison would be gone too and the only real evidence of the war would be ten dead bodies in a shed that stank of fish and cordite.

All afternoon there had been confusion and movement in the barracks, papers being burned, wagons loaded; Dietrich vainly shouting down a phone, trying to contact regional HQ on a line that had been cut. It had been easy for Klinger to slip away after he had packed the rest of his stuff.

Why had he kept Otto's terrible photographs; his translations? The presence of them in his case. Why did one perform actions which went against one's feelings? He could rationalise – there was little time, nowhere that he could dispose of the photographs in his room; Dietrich was supervising the burning of papers – he did not want to face him.

He lay in bed with Julia all of that last evening, and they made love gently for a long time. Afterwards he fell asleep – when she woke him, the sun had gone down. There was a sound of glass breaking in the street. He got up and peeked round the curtain. A group of soldiers were pushing their way through the door of the café across the way. They stayed in the café for a few minutes and then came reeling out, clutching bottles in their hands and under their arms.

'The same thing happened when we came into the country,' he said. 'Now it's for a different reason.'

'What are you going to do?' she asked.

'I don't know.'

'You can't surely see those men killed.'

'You mean stop them being killed?'

'Can't you do that?'

'No.'

He could see them lying dead already. He didn't even need his camera. That was the mark of the true artist, he thought bitterly, that he no longer needs his material, nor the means of expression, but can simply imagine and dismiss it from his mind when he has finished with it.

'When your people leave, I'll go back to the farmhouse,' said Julia.

'Why?'

'You won't go that way, will you? And I shan't be too popular with the locals here. Not after entertaining a German officer in a hotel room. The place is practically a brothel anyway.'

'Don't say that.'

'Come with me. To the farm. You'll be safe. We'll be safe. You said that it's over.'

She sat up in bed, in the growing dark of the room, her arms clasped hard round her knees.

'I couldn't do that,' he said. 'My comrades . . .'

'What of them? You told me one was blown up – your commanding officer arrested. It's all over. It's a circus, for God's sake.'

He said nothing. He looked at his watch. 'I must go.' He got out of bed and began to dress.

'The Americans will be here soon.' Her voice was low, almost begging, he thought. Perhaps she truly did love him. 'If you go with your people you'll be killed, won't you.'

'It's not all lost.' He pulled on his boots.

'You will be.'

'How will you get back to the farm?' he asked.

'I'll walk. It's only a few miles.'

'When would you go?'

'In the morning – when the rest of you do. You must come with me, Walther. There's nothing else for you.'

'If,' he said hesitantly, 'if I should see you tomorrow . . .'

How the hell was he to get away? He returned to barracks late. Dietrich wasn't about. He went to his room and lay down on the bed. Turning away from the window, he half expected to see the shape of Otto under the blankets on the bed across the room, to hear his slow, childish sigh as he turned in his sleep. The night darkened outside. There was no call to duty. No proper sleep; he dozed fitfully on the margins of sleep, afraid to lose consciousness, yet accompanied by one of those nightmarish narratives that trouble restless half-sleep. Then he lay fully awake. He resolved his escape in his head. It still seemed like something out of a boy's book – adventure, escape; juvenile action set against bogey-man villains and cardboard castles and papier-mâché dragons. Go before dawn. He couldn't travel at night for fear of getting lost in strange country. But he knew the cliffs in daylight.

He would get up now – it was almost three o'clock – but he couldn't lie there any longer, in that particular slough of shame and decision. And he needed a full hour before the sun began to rise.

11

Now she reads to him in the oil lamp's light a beautiful book he does not fully understand – the events in it seem so far away, and her slow musical accent is so strange in this place.

'On the pleasant shore of the French Riviera, about half-way between Marseilles and the Italian border, stands a large, proud rose-coloured hotel . . .'

'I want to make this night so splendid,' she'd said, like a character out of the book. 'They've all gone away.' She had made stew from the tinned meat in the larder and vegetables from the garden. There was plenty of wine, she said. Plenty of wine.

It had been a long day. The early morning inhabited his head. The sea mist had clung to the rocks and weathered bent-back trees of the cliffs as he came along the coast paths. He hadn't gone through the main gate of the billet. He knew the sentry; he could have made up any excuse for letting himself out at that time, but then they'd know for certain how he had gone. In the end, he didn't even have to excuse himself from the army. A narrow gully led up between the yard wall and the tower; the orderlies used it to throw barrack slops and waste down into the sea – Klinger had seen the streaked cliff from the launch. You could make your way to the top of the gully, and from there on to the narrow concrete ledge between the tower and the cliff-top. He picked his way up carefully, case in hand, like a tourist slipping from a hotel without paying. There were voices from inside the tower and a low yellow light glowed softly in the embrasure from which a heavy machine gun pointed. The pompom anti-aircraft gun placed on top of the tower wasn't manned; its barrel leaned idly up into the sky that tumbled with alternately muddy and silver-bellied clouds. The port was in darkness, shabby and formless without the morning light to define and make it live. He had to get about six kilometres away in the dark. The air was cold; there was some rain in it off the sea. Further up the coast there were knocking noises as if giant skittles were being scattered and put up again and scattered again. He hurried away from the tower, bending down in case anyone should glance out of the side slits. After what seemed a long travel along the cliff, the tower at last began to diminish and a sudden dip in the ground hid him altogether and he knew there was no further look-out post to bother him until the next big bay.

He hurried on. The ground rose; now that he could see it again, the tower was satisfyingly distant, picturesque, dark against the sky. For a good half hour he walked the wandering edge of the cliff-top. Had he misjudged where he should be? He searched up and down a hundred-metre stretch, then, beginning to panic a little, saw the dark cleft in the bushes that showed a path. He started down carefully, disappearing like a man going into a cellar.

Here he would sit, on a boulder on the sandy, deeply cut path, until the dawn came and then six and then seven o'clock; until he knew they were too busy preparing to go, too busy to look for him, and then he would come out and go on along the cliff.

Now that the clouds had cleared, the moon inland cast him in shadow. The point of coast from which he had walked, its inlet and the port lay east. Behind him, up on the cliff, in one of the trees a single bird began to chatter loudly. He sat on, hunched in his greatcoat.

At last the topmost height of the sky started to change and grow light, turning through plum-blue to lilac then dove-grey, until the first pure gleam of white-silver cloud was lit up very high in the sky. He watched for half an hour. The gulls began to fight and make a racket over the bay. The sea lightened slowly to a sight like a great besieging army laid bare by the dawn, its tents and murmurings and slight distant movements glistening as it gathered strength and tipped towards him in a brightening sword blade. Then, like the rays of a giant cinema projector, the sun took the whole sky and the land behind him.

Time for him to go. He stood and undid his case. He took out the civilian suit and laid it on the sandy path. Then he undressed and stood naked, a thin white shape against the huge cliff. It was tempting to walk down to the water. To enjoy the feeling of the very much colder touch of the sea on his nakedness, to swim out there. He pulled on the trousers. The white shirt. The coat. The same service boots. He clumped back up the path.

The light had intensified; a print developing, the features of the land came into place, slowly and then very rapidly, the nearest – the stones in front of him, tufts of grass, the faint turning of the grass that indicated a path – all of these defining themselves suddenly, the farther inland lighting up, the sea becoming at once the sea.

He began to make his way, getting whatever cover he could, along the edge of the coast.

She wasn't there when he got to the farm. It was locked up. He went into the orchard and sat against a tree, keeping the house in view, but able to hide himself quickly if need be.

The morning wore on, birds talked amicably among the trees, the warm air circulated like perfume through the wood. At about eleven, exhausted, he fell into a doze.

Julia woke him, just after noon.

'You looked very young asleep. I didn't want to wake you. I didn't think you'd come.' She smiled down at him.

There was the sound of thunder coming from the south. 'Listen.' He stood still, holding her hands.

'Is that the Americans?' she asked.

'No – they couldn't be. Not this early.'

Could he see across the country from the top of the house? Right across? he asked urgently. He must see something, confirm something before they could be happy and have any peace of mind. Yes, she said, go right to the top, past the room you have, there is a step-ladder leading to the attic, in the roof a skylight, in the side facing south. He kissed her, squeezed her hands and ran up through the house.

The road ahead of the house was empty, but he could see straight across the flat, unwooded land. From where he guessed was the road his comrades would have taken, the road that led down to Brest, about eight or ten kilometres off, he saw drifting clouds of smoke, stretched back in a line of purple and dark brown ribbons. He couldn't see the planes but heard a fresh distant series of detonations. They were bombing the convoys on the road. By this time his own convoy should have been long gone, unless it had been delayed.

Soon the explosions ceased. He watched a few minutes more, then stepped down from the skylight. He squared his shoulders in his jacket. Guilt? Shame? It was nothing any more to do with him. But it drew him back up for most of the afternoon. Julia said nothing, but he could tell she thought he was being foolish; there was nothing he could do after all. And there had been no further sounds from the south; the smoke now hung in a thin brown lace curtain high in the sky, dissipating slowly.

An idyll?

They had three days, almost; two nights. The house was provided with a few tins of salted pork. There was wine in the cellar, water from the hand pump in the kitchen, fed from the well below the house. They had candles and oil lamps. Enough to last the week. Klinger told Julia that the Americans would be here in only a few days, the country was largely undefended between here and the bases on the western coast. He would be made a prisoner then, he supposed. God knows when they would see each other again. 'Meanwhile be quiet. Let's shut the world out,' she said, folding his hands around hers. 'Let's pretend that we have been here for many years, that there has been no war. That what will happen will be only for a while – and then we shall be together again.'

So they agreed to pretend.

The house was not silent that first night; small creaks and whispers; the clock ticking in the hallway, their voices, the click of knives and forks, clink of glass; a parody, after the noise of war, of a peaceful, domestic summer night.

They sat on the sofa in the living room, in the soft yellow glow of the lamp.

They talked about what they would do after the war . . .

When I come out of whatever camp, I shall come back here and take you to America, he said. I can see the pictures I'll take without even seeing what I will take. Europe is exhausted. The only pictures an artist can take, the only images I or a writer or a painter of any sort can use from this continent now are of exhaustion; of age; of decay . . . we'll escape from all that. These were the words in his head. What he said was, 'Read me that American book.'

So, she'd started to read from *Tender is the Night*.

'It begins like a fairy story,' he said.

'It's not as sweet all the way through. It tells of terrible things.'

'Oh, Julia – you don't know what terrible things are.'

'They are what they are for everybody.'

'Neither of us knows,' he said, relenting. How could he tell her of something really terrible? There would be no way. He could show her pictures, but they would mean nothing more than tiny images of tiny people in tiny, dirtied places, crawling over each like mounds of insects, standing guard like solitary insects.

'Let's go to bed. Now. Please,' he said.

The next day, the war still kept away. He would work, he said. Freely – the first full day's work since – oh, since, he couldn't remember when. This was the first day of his liberation. Whatever happened now, he was irrevocably free. 'All that.' He waved his hand to the world outside. 'All that is nothing to do with us any more. This is our world today.'

The warm sun came between the leaves of the apple trees. Klinger took many photographs of Julia, of the orchards, the house; every single thing in the world was his subject; and every single thing was contained in this house, this garden. The photographs he knew were going to be wonderful. How could they be anything else? They were imbued with love and freedom, those mysterious qualities that become visible in great works of art and in the few, tender commonplace acts of life.

That second evening he developed the day's pictures, up in the room where he had stored his things. He covered the window with a blanket and a torch with some red crêpe paper Julia found in the bottom of a drawer. He hung the prints to dry in a closet. He could hardly bear to look at the work of this day.

Full of it, of himself, of his love for Julia, the world, his art, he ate with her again in the kitchen, taking in every joyful gleam and shadow of the copper pots on the wall, the great black presence of the cooking range, its caged fire that made the room too warm, the plaited bundles of bronze-skinned onions hanging from the middle oak beam under the white-washed ceiling. He looked at her steadily. She smiled back, a little puzzled at the intensity of his gaze, then smiled again when he said, 'Tell me about Ireland. Tell me about your lovely island.'

He was upstairs when he heard the motors coming along the track. He went to the gable window and looked down. It wasn't the Americans. Two sedan cars, with white Lorraine crosses painted on their roofs, the doors opening as they drew to a halt. The figures that sprang out from the first car, in white shirts, sleeves rolled, hands clutching rifles, trousers baggy and dirty, were unmistakeably French. From the second car, another figure was helped out. It was old Thérèse. She stood by the car, smoothing her black dress. She pointed to the house, up at the window where he stood. He stepped back. It was the end, then. He composed himself, breathing deeply in and out. He smiled at the room.

The floor was covered with yesterday's images of Julia. He hadn't time to pick them up. She would come up and find them later. A pleasant surprise. She was very much more beautiful the way he had taken her in these pictures. He smiled at his vanity and at the same time felt proud of these pictures and of himself.

He picked up his civilian jacket and put it on. He felt in the pocket and found his officer's pass book. It was over. He heard Julia saying something downstairs, then footsteps rushing roughly up the stairs. It was astonishing how quickly the man had come from the car to stand in the doorway with the rifle pointing at Klinger's stomach. Klinger had his hands raised in readiness.

'No need to shoot, my friend. I surrender. May I – my case?'

He picked the case up as casually as he could, but feeling all the time as if the man might shoot him. The man's companion appeared at the head of the stairs.

'Is it the German?'

'Yes, it is.'

The men were in their thirties, farm or market garden workers, working-class, tough-looking, ready to shoot.

They took him downstairs. Thérèse was in the hallway.

'That's him, that's the German,' she shouted.

'We have established that fact,' said Klinger good-naturedly. One of the rifle muzzles poked him in the back, pushing him into the living room.

Julia was seated on the edge of the armchair, smoking, casual and cool. She smiled at him.

There was another man in the room, tall, thin, bespectacled and very young, a revolver dangling from one thin-wristed hand.

'You are a deserter?' the young man asked politely.

'Yes.' And Klinger felt ashamed of himself.

'You will have to come with us. You will be handed over as a prisoner.'

'They say I can't come with you,' said Julia. 'I have to travel separately with the other gentlemen. I'll be in touch.'

'You'll be here?'

'No – I shan't be here. I'm going home. I'm told I'm going home.'

How strange were these stilted exchanges with their brittle attempt at humour. It was like a play – only in a play or film he should have embraced her passionately; the guards would have turned their eyes compassionately away. Instead, he felt nothing inside. Her eyes were unhappy, but he could not guess what she was thinking.

'We must be on our way,' said the young man with the revolver.

Klinger got into the back of the car. The young man sat beside him. The two other men were in front, one as driver.

They weren't unfriendly. He presented no threat to them. It was over. They were enemies; rather, they had been enemies. Now he was no longer a part of it all.

They started down the track, followed by the other car. He turned to see if Julia was in it, but then the track twisted too and he could not see.

'Keep still,' said the young man, in the same calm, neutral tone. Then he asked, 'Where is your uniform?'

Klinger began to tell how he had disposed of it. The young man interrupted him.

'What is in the case?'

'Personal effects.'

The young man gestured with his revolver. Klinger slid the case from his to the other man's lap.

'What were you before the war?' The young man snapped the locks open and began to carefully lift the edges of the few folded shirts and underwear, the papers, the manuscripts of himself, of Otto . . .

'I was a photographer.'

'What are these?'

'Literary works – of a sort,' said Klinger smiling in a self-deprecatory way.

'I'll have to hand them over. You'll get them back if they're innocent.'

'Oh, perfectly.'

With the case lid up, Klinger couldn't see what the man was examining now, but he suddenly looked up and glared at Klinger. 'Pull up, pull up,' he commanded the driver.

The car slowed and bumped on to the grass verge. The car behind had slowed too, and the young man said, 'Wave them on.' As they went past, Klinger saw Julia stare out of the side window at them, at him, then twist and look out of the oval back glass as her car sped away.

'Photographer, eh?' The young man closed the lid of the case and spread Otto's Russian photographs on it. Then he said coldly, 'Here's another one.' The men in the front seat craned round.

'Those aren't mine,' said Klinger. 'They're a friend's . . .'

'Get out of the car.'

'A friend's. Another officer's.'

Klinger's cajoling voice falls away in his own ears, a terrible diminishing echo. Now, for the first time in his life, Klinger feels fear. He is required to stand outside the car. The day seems to stand still, burning coldly round him. He wants to run away but his legs won't move. All the men are out of the car – the sky is suddenly closing round them – they might as well be angels or ghosts walking in the midday around him.

'Stand by the roadside. On the verge. Kneel down. Look down.'

There are freckles of white dried mud spattered in a particular constellation on the man's left boot. Klinger lifts his head slowly. The trousers are thick, ribbed brown corduroy with wear at the knees. He is looking at the end of the revolver muzzle, a black hole, ringed with blue metal, oil gleaming on the first spiral rifling in the barrel. The black hole beckons him, seems to draw him inside itself. This circle holds the whole of creation. He lifts his head. 'They are not my pictures. They are not,' he beseeches. 'I was never in Russia. Check my record. You just have to check my record.' He sees the young man's eyes shut in a blink behind the spectacles as his finger whitens on the stiff trigger.

The gun is lifted away . . . This landscape vanishes away . . .

Klinger does not desert. He says goodbye to Julia in the hotel room that night, and deceives her, knowing she will be safer at the farm, and saying that he will join her. He goes back to his unit. He drinks too much, along with everyone else. He is woken early the next morning – early, but after it is light, and in the long morning shadows he follows Captain Dietrich and a platoon of men across the town to the dockyard shed. The hostages are waiting. Klinger takes pictures of their execution.

From one of the boys shot the brains spurt against the wall. An old man fouls himself. There is a melancholy silence following the echoing away of the last shots, the coups de grâce, from the officers' pistols. Klinger has hidden in his lens and feels that this is the end of the world; shed, fish smell, the light on the dock outside the door. The fact that they turn away and leave these people here, sprawled, and he cannot help comparing their bodies, the overlapping of their limbs, their emptied faces to shots he saw and admired from the New York tabloids of murder victims. So, they troop, their footsteps echoing, out of the fish-market shed.

A little later they board lorries and cars and carts. No one is in the street to watch them go; no one, it seems, looks out of a window, but they know they are watched. And so they pull out and turn south and then bear west. At the junction just outside town, where one road goes along the coast, and leads to Julia's farm, and the other forks south-west towards the fortress, he feels, of course, a terrible pang of pain and lost love.

But he still can think and imagine. And he imagines, and codifies in his head in words and images, that this army, an army in retreat, resembles a wounded dragon, pulling itself from history to myth. He is riding in the convoy when it is bombed, when its walking, shambling remnants are overtaken by the Americans.

He is a prisoner for months, in a wire-caged compound from which no one has the slightest wish to escape. The war ends. A few weeks later he is interrogated, released, dressed in a dead man's suit a size too small, with a travel warrant to a town of his choice in Germany – not Berlin. Berlin has gone. He travels to Cologne. It takes him months to recover his nerve, but then he finds himself excited by the daily moonscape of the bombed city and begins to photograph it.

He is one of the '47 generation, for it is not until that year that any real form of cultural life springs back, then the first books are published, mostly by the young; the old are still reticent.

He obtains a job as, once again, a press photographer, and through the late forties and early fifties his reputation for his own original work grows, particularly for his studies of the terrible damage done by the Allied bombing in his book *Favilla*

– Latin for the still-glowing ashes of the dead – and he holds his first exhibition in Bonn in 1958. He marries and divorces. He goes to England several times to visit his mother. The English are polite to an ex-enemy. He visits America; he marries. Not Julia – he has never tried to contact Julia. He returns to Europe, tires of Europe, of his wife, and, after much travel – the family investments having proved remarkably durable – he settles for three years in the French colony of Niger, in the sub-Sahara. From this stay flowers his great book of photographs, *African Dance*. This and subsequent works cement his reputation as one of the great photographers of the age. He completes his autobiography – having carried the manuscript all this way with him – and like most of his contemporaries he makes scant, regretful reference to the war.

He dies in London in 1997. His obituary is carried in all the broadsheet newspapers. He enters history. And is forgotten.

So, he has been spared, not in some fashionably imagined alternative universe, but by an intercession of mercy, a pardon. The gun barrel is lifted away. The Frenchman is a philosophy student, an educated man; he cannot do such a thing; he has seen that there may be some cause for doubt. He lifts away the revolver, disgusted with himself, with all of it. He says, 'Get back into the car.'

Klinger prepares for another future. His car follows Julia's. In the sheer relief at still living the blood sweeps through his body and he cannot think of anything but the sheer wondrous beauty of the world seen through the windscreen of a car, between the heads of two ugly Frenchmen, at his side another, an educated man nursing a feeling of cowardice perhaps. Of humanity, says Klinger exultantly.

There is no pardon.

The next day, a GI perched on top of a tank, in a line of tanks come to a temporary halt, sees the body sprawled in the ditch, a dark hole in the centre of the forehead. 'Poor bastard,' he says, thinking, because of the civilian clothes, the body is that of a Frenchman murdered in the enemy's retreat. 'Poor bastard,' he says aloud, and raises his camera and takes a picture.